BORROWING TIME:

A LATINO SEXUAL ODYSSEY

CARLOS T. MOCK, MD

ANDREA ALESSANDRA CABELLO, EDITOR
UNIVERSITY OF CALIFORNIA, BERKELEY

Floricanto Press

Floricanto Press
650 Castro Street, Suite 120-331
Mountain View, California 94041-2055

(415) 552 1879 Fax: (702) 995 1410

www.floricantopress.com

BORROWING TIME

INTRODUCTION

Borrowing Time: a Latino Sexual Odyssey, is a book that is hard to put down once you start reading it. It's ALIVE; it takes you to the depths of the soul and to the extremes of erotic fantasies. It's a mixture of many themes: spirituality, searching for love, family values and dealing with life as it is. Juan Subirá-Rexach searches in his soul, shares it with the reader, as he tries to make sense of it all and to find meaning to his life. There is a philosophical stream running through the book. The sense of time, past and present, the dreams and reality and the meaning of love are all weaved into the story.

Although the theme of homosexuality pervades, reading the book can easily be experienced as a spiritual adventure, as Juan becomes a seeker that moves from doubter to believer, confronting his traditional Catholic upbringing and seeking answers to life's riddles. Love, loyalty, friendship, pleasure and, above all, the shame and guilt associated with the homoerotic attraction.

Even though the book does not include scientific research or statistics regarding the gay lifestyle—other fine books have dealt with this—it allows us to see the complex process of discovering one's sexual orientation and the coming out process. *Borrowing Time: a Latino Sexual Odyssey* allows you to enter into the internal process of someone who grows up in a heterosexually biased society and finally makes peace with his reality. We get a glimpse of how uncovering the "secret" impacts the relationship with family, friends and working companions. One becomes aware of the prejudices, the ignorance, the hypocrisy and the fear that pervades our society when we deal with homosexuality.

To speak about homosexuality has become possible only in recent years. With the emergence of AIDS (Acquired Immune Deficiency Syndrome) in the early 80's, over twenty years ago, homosexuality came "out of the closet". It was openly discussed in the press, in talk shows and in scholarly debates about prevention programs and the use of condoms. During those first years, the words "gay" and aids were used almost interchangeably. The homophobia that had been latent became more obvious and a sense of self-righteousness manifested itself by the belief of many: *"This is a punishment from God. Homosexuals deserve it for their evil ways"*.

In *Borrowing Time: a Latino Sexual Odyssey* we get a glimpse of the different manifestations of AIDS: the fear, the shame, the regrets and the final victory. The "AIDS" crisis has been an opportunity for the homosexual community for growth, for strengthening ties, for reclaiming rights from the government, and, above all, for reflection. The AIDS epidemic can be seen by many as a curse, and for others, as the opportunity to bring out the best in you.

My work as a sex therapist over 23 years with couples and individuals—many of whom are gays, lesbians, and bisexuals—has put me in touch with an issue that inevitably comes up: feelings of self-hatred and shame that many homosexuals internalize. The lack of tolerance for sexual diversity and the myopic vision of many fundamentalist religious groups have contributed to the prejudices. Books like *Borrowing Time: a Latino Sexual Odyssey* can be antidotes for this lack of understanding and acceptance. It can also be a useful tool for any homosexual or lesbian to understand and accept him or herself, without judgments. It takes the reader, gay or straight, into the mind, heart and dreams of Juan Subirá Rexach with great candor, honesty and humor. I feel enormous gratitude to Carlos for giving both the gay community and heterosexuals a glimpse of this very complex process.

Dra. Gloria Mock,
Sexologist and author
San Juan, PR, June 15, 2003

Acknowledgements

I have a confession to make, and it has nothing to do with my sexuality. I cannot type. I have to thank my life partner, Bill Rattan, who so patiently typed for me and encouraged me to finish. I know I would have never been able to finish this work without his support. Thanks also to my sister, Gloria, for her encouragement and her kind words in the Introduction and to my friend Art for his help with this manuscript. Finally, to Roberto Cabello and Floricanto Press for believing in me and *Borrowing Time: a Latino Sexual Odyssey*

Realismo Mágico (Magical Realism) is a phrase chiseled in history by the Colombian Gabriel García – Márquez. In *One Hundred Years of Solitude*, The Nobel Laureate defined new terms for reality. He taught us how to bend, reshape and redefine it to fit our means in trying to tell a story.

This is a work of fiction. Fiction is a marvelous thing. Some places in the book really do exist; I have used them only to help the story move along. As it is based on some of my experiences growing up, I have taken many liberties to change the plot to fit my story: the events are told from my magical and imaginary world. References to anyone living or dead are coincidental. All names have been changed to protect the guilty. Innocence, of course, needs no protection...

Brief History
of
Puerto Rico

Puerto Rico is the smallest and easternmost of the Greater Antilles; discovered by Christopher Columbus in 1493 and claimed by Spain until 1898. We became a United States colony as part of the loot of the Spanish-American war of 1898.

Our cities are built in the traditional Spanish Colonization style with a Church and City Hall in the central square and the rest of town radiating out from that. The main focus of the town was the church; the main focus of the Spanish was the christianization of the barbarians.

• On April 12, the Foraker Law (Organic Act of 1900) was approved, establishing civil government and free commerce between the Island and the US. Puerto Rico thus became the first US unincorporated territory.

• On March 2, 1917, President Woodrow Wilson signed the Jones Act and Puerto Rico became a territory of the United States – "organized but unincorporated." A bill of rights was created which, among other things, established a locally elected Senate and House of Representatives elected by the Puerto Rican citizenry with elections held every four years. In addition, it granted Puerto Ricans U.S. statutory citizenship, which means that we were granted citizenship by act of Congress, not by the Constitution and citizenship is therefore not guaranteed by it. As citizens, they were allowed to join the army; only 300 rejected the citizenship and many others refused to join the army. During World War I, over 18,000 Puerto Ricans served in the US armed forces.

• On July 4, 1951, the "600 Law" was passed, giving Puerto Rico the right to establish a government with a proper constitution.

•   On March 3, 1952, the flag of the Commonwealth of Puerto Rico was officially adopted—based on a flag designed by a group of patriots in the year 1895.

•   On July 25, 1952 (Puerto Rican voters in a referendum approved the New Constitution in March), Puerto Rico was proclaimed as the freely associated Commonwealth of Puerto Rico. (*Estado Libre Asociado*)

•   On November 4, 1952, Luis Muñoz Marín was re-elected governor to his second 4-year term, with 64.9% of the vote.

•   1953 The largest migration of Puerto Ricans to the United States mainland occurred, with 69,124 emigrating (mostly to New York, New Jersey and Florida).

•   Law Number 1 of 1993 declares both English and Spanish as the official languages of Puerto Rico.

Politics & Culture

Politics is a sport. The last election saw a 92% turnout and that is normal for the island. Of the population, 47% favor statehood, 48% favor commonwealth (status quo) & 5% favor independence. Every family can claim at least one member of each of the three ideologies and thus politics is seldom discussed at family gatherings. We do not vote in the presidential elections and have only non-voting representation in the congress; however we do not pay federal income taxes because of that whole "taxation without representation" thing.

We speak Spanish at home but commence bilingual (English) education as soon as we go to school. We think in Spanish and then translate to English. Prepositions cannot be translated; we are always using the wrong one.

The population is 95% Catholic. The Church is strong with a fundamental Christian base to the morals of the culture. In

1964, the Catholic Bishops formed a political party and threatened excommunication for anyone who didn't join their party. Abortion was illegal (until Roe v. Wade) and homosexuality was illegal until the Supreme Court Lawrence decision. Machismo is the norm —women are secondary and subservient to males. Gay men are well below women in the social structure, where homosexuality is generally equated only with drag queens and effeminate men.

Race is a very quiet, but hot, issue. The original Indian population, the "Tainos", was almost wiped out by the Spanish. The Spanish then introduced slaves in the 16th century to work in the sugarcane plantations as the Indian work force died off. The white masters mixed with the black slaves thus we have a large mulatto population. Everyone has some African mixture, but the more you have, the more you seem to deny.

Puerto Ricans are like any other Latin American race—very nationalistic. For example, it might be an insult to call a Puerto Rican either Dominican or Cuban and vice-versa. To help explain: Cubans took many jobs from Puerto Ricans with the mass exodus in 1959 when they were fleeing Castro. Dominicans are currently entering the country illegally and are usually employed in the service industry taking more jobs away from the locals in a tough economy. In a normal economy, and it's worse when things are bad, much of Puerto Rican business is "under the table." So, the issue of valid citizenship in employment is easily circumvented. It is said: "when the US sneezes, Puerto Rico gets pneumonia". Meaning, when the economy turns sour, the island gets kicked in the ass. Everything is magnified so that Puerto Rico is very much controlled by the whims of the larger US market. Which explains some of the love/hate relationship that exists with the US. Of course, economics isn't the only reason that you have to be careful with nationality. It goes much deeper than that in a way that is completely unexplainable. Latinos/as are very proud of our culture and we each have a unique and beautiful heritage. To lazily lump everyone into a generic "Hispanic" label is to disregard that we are unique human beings.

"La vida no es la que uno vivió, sino la que uno recuerda y como la recuerda para contarla."

("Life is not the one you lived, but the one you remember, and how you remember it when you tell it.")

Vivir para contarla, (Live to tell) Gabriel García–Márquez

PART ONE

Time it was, time it is.
And what a time it is.
A time of innocence,
Shattered confidence.

Long ago, it must be
Before that bad disease
A time for Peace and Love
A time finding your soul.

Not long ago, it must be
Under the tyranny of the clock
Between just waking up
And my first coffee cup.

From ashes to ashes, so it is
I comfort myself with the thought.
Tomorrow will be a better day
Is this the guiding light ahead?

Family and friends, so it is
Turn our lives around
A time of renaissance
A time of providence.

The prophets of our time, so it is.
Create a hypnotic delusion,
All I can do is dream,
I'm a critic at best.

Juan Subirá-Rexach

CHAPTER 1

Remember when you were a kid and weeks took forever to happen? Life was eternal, but our lives were short. I love the temporal, the physical. I remember going from the first grade to the second seemed to take a lifetime. Now I look back at that time and it all seems to be a blur. My partner Bill says that it is because when you are six years old, a year of your life is one sixth of your lifetime, but when you are forty, it is only one fortieth.

That could be why since I found out I was HIV positive it seems only like it was yesterday, even though it is now going on 5 years. That is why, perhaps why since I was admitted to the hospital three days ago I can't remember where the days have gone.

When I first found out I was positive, I was afraid to look at people. I watched others wondering if they could guess, then avoided them and their eyes as well. I feared it would show in my face. I hated myself for it. I was filled with guilt, my soul shaken, open in remorse. Circumstances had led me there, but circumstances were no excuse. I should have known better; I should have prevented it. Why hadn't I stopped it?

Now, I find myself at St. Joseph Hospital in Chicago. All fight and anger have gone out of me. I remember Bill brought me up to the emergency room. I wait numb with grief, an empty feeling so deep that I could not even feel the passage of time. The nurses wanting to know what my insurance was, even though all I want is something for the pain. I answer questions about my allergies, about my condition, and all the medications I am tak-ing. They draw blood and as blurred as time is, I remember a

young emergency room doctor inform me that I had drug induced pancreatitis due to DDI, one of the meds used for keeping the HIV virus under control.

Being a doctor myself, although I had decided to go on disability since I found out I was positive for HIV, I am aware of
the severity of the disease. I am thankful to that nice nurse that
gives me a shot of morphine and wish I could remember her
name. I did catch her face: the same dirty blonde hair common
in the Midwest, growing low on her brow and straight and thick
out of her skull. The same small gray-blue eyes wincing with
empathy that would be the object of my desire when a nice young
man's face would look at me innocently with them. The same
full lips, though with worn out lipstick from a long shift, which
keeps reassuring me that everything will be all right. The same
rangy, slender body stiffly maneuvered, as though manipulated
by the long sticks of a shadow puppeteer that so efficiently goes
about her business and gently undress me, changes me into a
hospital gown, and skillfully starts my intravenous fluids which
are to become the only source of nutrition until today.

Next thing I know, these four walls surround me giving me
a view of downtown Chicago. I was in another room before this
one, but I was in a daze when they moved me. I was told I
needed some X-rays and then I was placed in the intensive care
ward. Even though now I am in the isolation room; everyone
who comes to the room reassures me that I am not a menace to
anyone around me. They each repeat that it is the only room
available and perhaps they can find me another room sometime
later.

I think I can picture that very frightened intern who came to
do my required hospital history and physical exam. His charm
is oblique, his humor professionally understated and his looks
are appealing only to the innocent. He wears contact lenses, or
so I think, because he keeps squinting his eyes. He wears the

routine blue surgical scrubs with a white lab coat over it. Noticing his apprehension of dealing with a Board Certified OB-GYN, as my chart read in bold letters in front, I do my best to dictate my story:

"45 y/o white male with a five-year history of HIV on Viracept, DDI, and Epivir admitted with a one-hour history of acute right upper quadrant pain, rebound tenderness and multiple episodes of emesis. Labs were suggestive of acute pancreatitis...."

Even though I can't remember the name printed on his nametag, I will never forget the look of relief when I ease him into his task. I ask him not to move me much, for even though the morphine had started its analgesic effects, I am still extremely sore to the touch. I help him lift my back so he can listen to both my heart and lungs. Due to my acute pain, he defers the rest of the exam until later. I keep looking at my intravenous fluids as I am overcome by thirst, for I know I am extremely dehydrated. As soon as he leaves the room I open the IV to run as fast as I think it will run.

My regular doctor, Dr. Ross, finally shows up. I can't estimate how much later because time is irrelevant when you are high on morphine. He takes one look at me and opens the IV even further. He looks worried. Ever since he had shaved his thick black moustache, his black straight hair accentuates his youthful face. What might give his age is his thin mouth and the smudges under his round small black eyes, as though he has been drinking too much coffee and sleeping too little, the sort of dark circles you associate with worrying too much, and not enough appreciation.

He tells me what I think I will hear: my pancreas is damaged from the DDI and the only treatment for it is to give the pancreas a rest. I need a break from my HIV therapy. I am to have a naso-gastric tube to pump all my gastric fluids out of my stomach and nothing to eat until my pancreas has healed. I will receive nutrition through my IV. He suggests I get a Foley catheter to empty my bladder since I am not mobile enough to move around and relieve myself. I think the only thing I ask him is if I am going to die. Funny how a brush with death will bring about your mortality. He is as reassuring as he can be under the circumstances. Amazingly, to this day, one look from his sweet face, one word from his soft lips, one of his innocent embraces (he still routinely hugs everyone of his patients at each visit), and you are immediately filled with hope. If healing could be considered an art, he is the master.

Reassured, I fall into a dreamless sleep. It is as if morphine has closed the cellar door that lets dreams into the head. Sleep is my friend. Dreams are my unwelcome guests. One of the advantages of narcotics is that time just disappears. I can manage any kind of problem, since, in my mind, they do not exist. I do not dream, I do not remember, I just fade away. I can easily ignore reality. When I come back, I have to start from the beginning...

Chapter 2

I was six and I liked to play with dolls. My brother Manny always made fun of me. He was older; he was my idol; yet I was afraid of him.

My little sister Elena let me borrow her dolls; she liked to play with me. We would hide from Manny in our dollhouse. *Papi* was so proud when my sister Elena was born, that he moved the family to a very nice suburb of San Juan. He built the wooden dollhouse in our back yard, so large that it would fit all of us inside.

He had it painted pink, with a small *balcón* outside. Its *veranda* was in the old mahogany style from the Spanish times and gave the balcony a colonial flare. It was almost ten-feet tall, about two feet above ground with eight-foot ceilings. As you walked in, a small kitchen would greet you with life size appliances. Then you could see a small living room with a green taffeta sofa and two mahogany rockers. The *sillones* had belonged to our *abuela* when she was a little girl growing up. They had been in her old wooden house in Ponce, on the south side of the island.

The back of the dollhouse had the only bedroom. There was a four-poster bed; complete with a small lace covered footstool to help us get up onto it. The room had no closets or bathrooms, but then again, *papi* had joked that most of the population in the island had needed to use an outhouse. He was always teasing my mother as to where he would dig the hole for the *letrina*.

Mami would always get furious. She was very proud of her garden. She had made all of us go to the small rivers in the island to search for rocks to give her tropical paradise garden a border. She had planted bamboo, mango, guava, grapefruit, lime and banana trees and surrounded them with gingers, birds of paradise, ferns, *mundo japónico*, orchids, and palm trees. She had the grass removed and then filled the ground with the small river rocks, using the larger ones to create a border. There were round construction grade stones, about three feet in diameter that would serve as paths. There was a path from the terrace to the dollhouse.

We had two dogs, *Ginger* and *Pitusa*. Being Doberman Pinchers, I was very afraid of them (more afraid than I was of my older brother). *Ginger* was the classical color: all black. *Pitusa* was her daughter and she was brown. They were always fighting; only being nice to *mami*. She was the only one who could come near them. They were free in the yard and would always bark at us. Even Manny was afraid of them.

Elena and I would wait until *mami* was feeding the dogs and then we'd take the stone path and stay at the dollhouse all day, thus avoiding the dogs.

We would play for hours. *Mami* would come and get us when dinner was ready. Elena would pretend to be the mother and wife, and I would pretend to be the father and husband. Her dolls were our children. I would help her dress them. I loved creating new outfits for the dolls. I wanted to learn to sow; I wanted to design clothes for them.

Manny never played with us. He was the second child from *papi's* first marriage so we were barely related. He had come to live with us because he had gotten into trouble with the law. He preferred to go hang out with his friends playing soldier and war. It was the time of the Vietnam War and it was all kids their age would talk about. He could not wait to be old enough to go to war. I hated playing with them, because they would always capture me. I was the enemy and I would be tortured. I was terrified. I really preferred to stay with Elena and play house.

Chapter 3

I awake in time and consciousness, as if after a blow to the head I find myself in this strange hospital bed. It is daylight; I lay in a hospital room in my own bed, the mattress soaked in my sweat. I wake up to the face of two very shy nurses. They are coming with a naso-gastric tube in their hands and once again they are very scared of the fact that I am a physician. They are the nursing equivalent of Penn and Teller. They are in full protective gear: face mask, hat, protective eyewear, full gown, and gloves. They attempt a smile, a big comic smile that is discordant with their outfits, as though they are wearing a Greek mask from a classical play. Their mouths are covered but their noses seem big and hooked, either from the effects of my painkillers, or from the effects of their silly outfits. They attempt a noise, trying their best to communicate to me what they need to do. Realizing what their intentions are, I call them over and ask them if I can be of help. I explain to them that I will insert the tube myself. Amazed in disbelief, but afraid to contradict a doctor, they reluctantly hand me the tube. Having passed many of these tubes in my career, I shock these two poor souls by doing the deed all by myself. They hurry up and connect the tube to a pumping machine (called intermittent GOMCO, but why should I bother you with that detail?) It slowly and intermittently pumps all the contents out of my stomach. For my pancreas to get a real rest, I must not have any of the gastric juices produced in the lining of my stomach go to my intestines and call the pancreas to action. Starving is not enough.

When they are done, they call around to show their colleagues what I have accomplished. My response, of course, is that with the help of morphine, and enough knowledge of the task, I am the best qualified person to do the procedure, since I can control the speed of the tube as it fights with my throat's reflexive gagging. I would think that I would eventually be able to control my gag reflex!

I sleep again, or so it seems. I open my mind to sleep. Nights and days blend and pass as in an icy cave. The noise of the world is deafening and formless. I have medicated myself with my patient-controlled analgesia.

I forgot to tell you, somewhere between the shy intern and Dr. Ross visits, another angelic nurse came with a very smart device: my very own PCA. PCA stands for patient controlled analgesia. About ten years ago, and after extensive medical research, it was discovered that if you allowed patients to medicate themselves after surgery or in cases of extreme pain, as in my present situation; patients invariably used less pain medication and achieved better pain control. So the PCA was developed and now by pressing a magical button pinned to my hospital gown, I am allowed to self-administer a small dose of painkiller. The action is accompanied by a bell sound, and has a time lock of a few minutes to avoid an overdose.

The nurses forget to mention this lock mechanism and I have managed to press the button seven hundred and fifty two times in a four-hour period, which they tell me is a hospital record. Even though I am only medicating myself every ten minutes, the sound of the bell is creating a false high for me (talk about Pavlov!) I manage to laugh at the image and come back to reality to awake to yet another frightened girl.

I think it's a girl...she's hiding herself under another hospital gown, full with facemask, gloves, hat. She has a very high-pitched voice, not like a girl, more like a choirboy. Although I guess she can't be more that twenty-six or so, she has a frightened look of someone very old, someone who had lived through the great bubonic plague.

"Dr. Subirá, I am Ms. Smith and I am from registration. I need your signature for billing purposes. Would you be kind enough to sign this form?" And she made a timid attempt to come forward.

"I will do so when you remove that silly costume and bring it to me. You, above all should know that I pose no risk to your health."

"It is hospital policy, Dr.," I do not recall signing the paper. With the echo from her statement I go back to my oblivious dreamless state.

I hear music. I feel a rhythm. I am floating…

Chapter 4

I was wearing a dress. I was dancing.

My family had two maids: *Tita* and *Tina*—sisters. They did not look much alike; later I found out they had different fathers. *Tita* was a good-looking *mulata.* She was a little on the short side, with broad hips. She was conspicuously broad. She gleamed; she was perfect; her jaw-line was heroic. Her gaze was crystalline, her mouth an unusual combination of the sensual and the severe. Her particular beauty had suited the taste of the times, dressed in an immaculate white uniform, which made poetry of her buttocks. I remember telling her that I wanted to use chlorine bleach to make her skin whiter. That way she would be able to go out with me everywhere...

Tina had been somewhat pretty once, but she had not aged well. Her face was a mess. Her eyes were large and luminous black. Their brightness was enhanced by the darkness of her skin and the thickness of her lashes. Her African nose was flat; neither her nose nor her mouth was delicate. Her lips were full and thick; her chin was robust, almost masculine. Her hair was black and very curly. I had heard my brother call it *pasú,* a term of which *mami* disapproved. She looked like she had been attacked, punched repeatedly. At the time I did not know this was the result of poorly controlled acne. She was raw in places, pale and powdery in others. She had the appearance of a woman that had suffered intensely, and kept suffering inside. Her white uniform gave her a familiar appearance. Without it I would have never guessed they were sisters.

Mami had rescued these two at ages seventeen and nineteen, respectively. Their family was unable to feed them so it was decided they would come and work for us. They were offered room and board and a salary that was mostly sent back home to help their family of fifteen kids. They had been with us since my birth. I was supposed to feel guilty because their house was smaller than our dollhouse. *Mami* was constantly using this when we were misbehaving. We were always reminded of how lucky we were...

Tina dressed me up in her hand-me-down clothes. *Mami* had given her this black velvet dress; shiny as *Ginger's* coat. It had a long skirt that in my short stature would come down to the floor. I remember that I had to keep twirling to prevent the bottom of the skirt to reach the floor. Tina kept playing *mami's* phonograph and encouraged me to keep moving.

The music was the Spanish *copla: Los Nardos (Spikenard).*

> *Por la calle de Alcalá*
> *Con la falda almidoná*
> *Y los brazos apoyaos en la cadera*
> *La florista viene y va*
> *Y sonríe descará.*
> *Por la acera de la calle de Alcalá.*

> *Juega un mozo que la vé*
> *Va y le dice venga usted*
> *A ponerse en la solapa lo que quiera*
> *Que la flor que me usted me dá*
> *Con envidia la verá*
> *Todo el mundo por la calle de Alcalá*

> *At Alcalá's Street*
> *With her starched skirt*
> *And her arms poised on her hips*

The flower girl comes and goes
Laughing without fear
Through the sidewalks of Alcalá Street.

There's a man that sees her
And he is called to her
Please pick something for your lapel
Because the flower that you pick
Will be the look of envy
From everyone on Alcalá Street.

I felt like a beautiful flower girl with my long pretty skirt. I was the envy of all the men in Madrid. They all wanted my flowers. I placed my hands on my hips and started rotating. I would not get dizzy. My beautiful skirt was high up in the air.

As I was in the middle of the chorus, I noticed Tina had stop singing. The record was abruptly stopped complete with the scratch the needle makes when being suddenly raised to stop the music…

There he was. *Papi* was home early from work. This was undoubtedly the stupidest thing I had ever done. (I knew I was doing something wrong, but I had no idea what). If I was having fun, (and I was), *papi's* face told me otherwise. A strong feeling of shame invaded me. There was no going back on it. Life, like a movie, only goes in one direction. There was nothing to do but go with the flow and hope there would be a happy ending waiting for me in the last reel…

Papi was home early because *mami* was having a miscarriage.
Funny how I can't recall if I was punished or beaten. Had I caused *mami's* miscarriage? All I know is that to this day, every

time I hear *Los Nardos* I feel like I have to vomit.

I guess I was not able to understand the why of things at the time. *Mami* had German measles…

Chapter 5

The warm comfort from the bleached white bed sheets around my body is forming a barrier that excuses my brain from the activity of thought. I don't move, I simply adjust my body to the bed as best I can. It's as if I believe that by assuming a critical point of view and acknowledging the absurdity of the situation I can forestall anyone's attention, forever being left alone.

The center of inactivity makes any thought process rebound from any chance of being created, keeping me anchored to my hospital bed. On the one hand, the fear begs me to try to escape, to run away from the present situation, which seems to be the after life, yet before death. On the other, the analgesic effects of the drug induced high makes me deaf, blind and thoughtless to any stimuli.

It is like nothing has ever existed. Ghostly figures from a bad dream, nothing more. In the dark of the room, only the monitors that surround me break the silence. I try to hear my heartbeat, as if this is the clue to my freedom. But the fear of the nothingness around me is much stronger and I dream of myself as an inanimate cadaver. I dream of nothingness and the terrible fear of not being able to wake.

I wait. I continue to wait. It is as if I am waiting for all my bodily functions to cease. It's too boring to be alive, as if I am waiting for the real rest from my existence. It is as if the cycle of life is coming to an end, as if skies are closing on me.

It seems endless, like a dog chasing its tale, a closed circle outside of time. It's as if I am a ghost, a spirit without end.

My name is Juan Subirá-Rexach.   I need to find a *voice* to tell my story. Sometimes I feel like I have performed a ventriloquist act of homage to literary figures whose style I adored, and inevitably perverted.

In early 1993, I met my present lover. Guess what! Bill (so often pronounced "Beal" by my Puerto Rican friends that to this day I can't hear it in any other way). A local business owner, (he owned a hair salon) and we met on New Year's Day in a bar in Kansas City. We were immediately attracted to each other. He had a thin reddish goatee, curiously matching his full red hair, intelligent blue eyes, a languid manner and studied smile. Everything about him was studied, as if he was advertising that he had been friendless and unloved. It was as if he had the zeal of a good student, one who is trying to master all social skills, but cannot hide his insecurities. I was very good at that game. I had played it all my life, though I suspected I had started my lessons at an earlier age. (I also was seven years older than he). He was lordly and intended to be inaccessible. As he extended his hand for an introduction, his facial expressions alternated complacence with a nervous critique of everything going on around him.

What else was I supposed to do? I was smitten by his charm and lack of self-esteem. It was as if I was looking at a mirror image of myself. I felt that I had found my soul mate. No matter how far we are from Earth's gravity center, invariably we are attracted to its gravity field. There is an invisible current that will pull you towards the earth. Like water droplets, like the compass to the North Pole, like blood-to-blood, like desire to desire. It was as if Bill was the negative charge and I was the positive charge (although sometimes it was the reverse). Our bodies would work like two poles in a battery, as if when we were together, we would be in a series that would create the spark to light the fire. Our lovemaking would become a very strong electric current, like a battery that never gives (that stupid Eveready bunny does come to mind: still going and going...)

Bill was born with an immense capacity to make everyone around him happy. While most gays are relentless in their pursuit of sex, drugs and good looks, Bill had discovered the great power that communication has to either bring together or separate people. One look at his face, and you could tell whether he was happy, or sad, worried or having a good time. It was as if his thoughts were distinct entities and at the time he was thinking them they would become energy that would travel through space in a form of wavelength and my mind had the capability to receive those transmissions. We started a monogamous relationship and, as the rules of the time were, we waited six months of serious monogamy and got tested to be able to have sex without those darned condoms. There is nothing more important in a relationship than trust. With gay relationships, trust takes a new dimension. One lapse, one night of weakness, too much alcohol; and you can bring into your relationship a deadly disease. (God, it has been so long since I have had sex without condoms!!)

Unfortunately, we both tested positive, so we had a short period of denial, tested ourselves again, and then realized we would have to deal with the problem. Being in the medical profession, and after a brief meeting with my lawyer, Paul, a wonderful and completely beautiful soul, it was decided that rather than deal with the possibility of a presumptuous HIV transmission to any of my patients, I would just quit. My disability payments would be enough to support both of us, and there was no reason to put up with patient fears or misconceptions and the fear of a lawsuit. We both decided to go on disability. Bill sold his business and all was well until the night before my hospital admission.

I was completely controlled on my present medication regimen, my viral load was undetectable and I had a decent T cell count (over 600 cells). I had achieved a dumb state of perfect peace and harmony. Then this severe pain in my right upper quadrant started. I can tell you the exact time it started: 10:20 PM on that infamous Thursday night. I can tell you that there was a very light snow in one of our mildest winters to date. It was as if time had frozen—I managed to glance at the clock and then it never was to move again unless I stopped looking at it. Bill was peacefully asleep next to me, so I tiptoed to the medicine cabinet.

I am prone to kidney stones, so after having passed a few of them, I always carried some hydrocodone (that wonderful pain killer). I took one pill and large quantities of water, the treatment I always used for a kidney stone. At 10:25, the pain was still so severe that I repeated the water and the dose. At 10:55 I woke Bill up and gave him the bad news:

"Honey, something is wrong, I think you are going to have to drive me to the hospital."

"What is going on?"

"I believe I have a bad kidney stone. The pain is awful! I am on the third pill and it has not touched the pain at all. I am afraid I may have another renal colic like in 1997." I was barely able to finish that statement when I rushed to the bathroom to puke (my first of several emeses on my way to the hospital).

Scared by the vomiting, and looking at my distress, Bill was in his clothes in three minutes (which is saying quite a lot since he's such a clothes horse—it takes him half an hour to pick an outfit usually) and we were off to the St. Joseph Emergency Room. We did not need to talk; our thoughts were connected by our usual synch. We knew what was going on and he was able to feel my pain, just as if it was his.

Love is a verb; you show it with your actions. You may

show it with kisses, hugs, acts of generosity. One look from him and I knew that I was loved, that he was there for me, and without a single word, he was my knight in shining armor, he gave me strength.

For the first time in my life I learned the silence that is required to really talk to a loved one. As strong as the whisper of your beloved smile, the waves breaking in a romantic getaway on the beach, the dry leaves that are carried by the first winds of autumn, the music that came out of his body when he was happy, I was being told that I was very much loved. It was so loud, that for a while I was unable to hear him when he said:

"Juan, we're here. I'll help you out of the car."

Chapter 6

Manny is twelve years older than I. Somehow I had blocked everything about him until many years later when I happened to bump into him; he was married with two kids and living in Maryland. He had white hair in close ringlets that seemed incongruously excessive above his sullen blue eyes. Like my father, he had grayed prematurely and the tight fitting corduroy jeans with a suggestion of bell at the bottom seemed to place him back in another time. Soft soiled sandals covered his manly feet.

But, any memory of what he looked like back then was blocked from my mind. I was only six! I was too afraid of him to remember!

Manny had built a tree house in our mango tree in the back yard. The mango tree always was full of blooms; so there were always neighborhood kids trying to get close to steal some of the delicious treats. He would go out there and smoke with his friends—it was very cool. I had found his cigarettes once and had tried to light them. I inhaled…I got sick. I was coughing so bad that *Tina* heard me and thought I had swallowed a mango pit; she came to my rescue. She found me with the cigarette still in my mouth.

That night *papi* was given a full report. Although he was a five-pack-a-day smoker, I was severely punished. Manny got in trouble, too. He was grounded and was not allowed to go out with his friends. That meant he would be home to torture me.

That night I lay in bed unable to sleep.

Ever since Manny moved in with us, I had to share my room

with him. *Papi* had gone to J. C. Penney at *Plaza Las Americas* and ordered a set of bunk beds. I was given the top bed and Manny took the bottom. Since he was old enough to drive, and his curfew was midnight, I never saw him. I would be asleep long before he came home. However, tonight he was there.

When he got up to turn the light off, I pretended to be asleep. Not only would I avoid his abuse, but also being a school night, I would get some rest.

Suddenly I heard a mysterious groaning. Manny's breathing had accelerated. I checked to see if my vision was used to the dark and I swear I almost gasped when I saw what Manny was up to.

He was playing with his *pipi*. *Pipi, poto, bicho, salchicha, salchichón ,falo, fálico, gusano, pene, órgano, pinga, pingón, guanajo, matraca,* all of these terms did not prepare me for how big it was. It was just so big! It was just so big!

He was grimacing and concentrating so hard that he did not realize I was mesmerized by what he was doing.

As his breathing got heavier he let out a sigh and I noticed a stream of thick fluid coming straight up toward me. The ejaculate left his organ, traveled to the bottom of my bed and made a "splat" sound, like when you use a fly swatter to kill a fly. In my mind the noise was so loud, that it almost froze me and I was unable to return to my bed, before Manny came back from wherever his mind was.

Even though I am unable to remember what Manny looked like at this period of my life, I can describe to you to the minutest of details the shape of his beautiful cock. It was at least eleven inches (twenty four centimeters) and it rose straight into the sky until the large glans started. There, it had a slight curvature forward. It was circumcised although I would have been unable to tell you this at the time.

What really impressed me the most was that I wanted to play with it. I wanted to kiss and lick his organ and help him satisfy himself. It was obvious that Manny had enjoyed these actions. As much as I was never good enough for him, I was sure I would be able to please him in this fashion. Perhaps he might be able to like me a little if I helped him out a little.

Manny finished high school and joined the army. He went to Vietnam like he wanted. *Papi* was very proud of his soldier son and next time I saw Manny, it would be in Maryland on my way to college.

I never had a chance to tell him how much I wanted to help him masturbate. I never got a chance to please him…

Chapter 7

I am an American Airlines girl: a Platinum Advantage member. I got Bill hooked right away.

Upon our arrival at Charles de Gaulle Airport, we danced our way to the Admiral's Club in Paris, where we showered and changed underwear and shirt. We then took the Metro from the airport to the Les Halles station where we walked with our suitcases to our hotel: Hotel de La Bretonnerie, where USD$150 will buy you a large suite that can sleep up to three persons in the middle of the Marais where most of the action is.

We checked in, knowing very well that our room would not be ready by 10:00am, so we just dropped our bags and started our sightseeing. We yielded to the spell of the city immediately. I had warned Bill about three things: Parisians do smoke, just get used to it and do not complain. Do not ask for ice in your drink, (it will be served cold) which is something that only ugly Americans do in France, and be careful what you say at dinner. Of course, Bill always reminds me that the only warning that I really needed to give was that talking at dinner—he may not have traveled, but he watched a lot of it on the Travel Channel and knew that Parisians smoke like chimneys and you don't get ice. The local spots where I liked to dine were without tourists, but they paid rent by compressing all the tables together so you would be rubbing elbows with your neighbors at dinner. They would involve a prix fixe menu and some of the best house reds in the world, probably made by some sweaty boys in their own kitchen and bottled that evening (no cork required). I had mentioned in passing that they were not as rude as they used to be, but that we would definitely see some of that behavior. I just told him to yell back. Parisians always rose to the occasion and understanding their French I knew perfectly well how they treated each other. It has always amazed me how they will insult each other with words I know damn well are not dinner conversation, carry on a shouting match and when they are done, they just go to the next bar for a good glass of their best red for appeasement where they will fight over the right to buy you a drink.

The rudeness did not wait long to materialize. As soon as we arrived and went to the Metro station in town to buy a seven-day pass for our stay, I was involved in a very heated yelling match with the public attendant for not knowing what I wanted. I had the nerve to ask for a suggestion on which package deal was the best and after being ignored by the attendant, she was clearly upset because I gave her a very large bank note; the only French money I owned, courtesy of the friendly ATM machine at the airport.

Amazingly, we were unable to find another rude Parisian in our seven days, except perhaps for a taxi driver that refused to take us to our hotel because we had not taken the first in line waiting at the taxi stand. But we did find nice ones. On our way to the Baccarat store and museum at 30 *bis*, *rue de Paradis* on the 10th *arrondissement* we were temporarily lost and a man saw us struggling with a map and asked us in a French accented English if we needed help and was helpful enough to point us to the store. We bought a decanter that matched our pattern.

By day, we did all the touristy things. I was up to the very top of the Tour Eiffel, the only time in my many visits to Paris that I waited in line to go up to the third level. (Luckily it was a rainy day in December and the lines were short). We even found the Paris Catacombs, something Bill had read about in his guide and was proud enough to introduce me to. (That year we used a picture of us in front of the catacomb's bones to announce that we were "dying" to hear from our friends and incorporated the picture in to our change of address to let everyone know we were moving together).

At night, our little suite in the *Marais* was home to some of the best sex in the world. We went on and on at dinner one night, commenting on how many times we had achieved orgasm the night before when the straight couple next to our table (and almost rubbing elbows with us) said:

"Are you on your honeymoon?" asked the woman.

Bill turned three different shades of red and answered: "You could say that."

"We are from Amsterdam and are very liberal." The man reassured us.

Gerard and Marguerite had driven in for the weekend from Amsterdam and were on a second honeymoon. They looked very alike. They had similar dirty blond hair and gray-blue eyes. The same full lips, though hers were covered by an orange shade of red lipstick. They were both in their twenties. Gerard gave us a vigorous, pumping handshake, while Marguerite's was fragile. Gerard was already turning gray at the temples, his aged masked by an unabashed plum body, with forearms round and hairless. He had a huge smile under a wispy blond moustache. Marguerite was very well put together, with a charming white dress that accentuated her figure, matching pearl earrings and necklace. We ended up discussing our lives, shared a few drinks, smoked bad French cigarettes together, and talked until very late in the night.

We were unable to go inside the *Louvre*—it was closed by a museum employee strike the first day we tried to see it—and we ended up going on our second day and entered through the Metro to avoid the long lines. We had thought ahead to buy a museum pass.

I also hold dearly the smaller museums with smaller collections, thus we saw the *Rodin*, *Picasso*, and *Jacquemart-Andre* museums. I know we cemented the relationship after our first trip to Paris together; Bill told me over *café au lait* in a small coffee house overlooking the Seine:

"I always judge relationships by the way people travel together. We will do very well."

Bill's previous relationship didn't end well.

Bob was 33 when he was diagnosed. His dark brown hair used to fall in his face, like the ones we see on the Abercrombie and Fitch commercials. Or perhaps it is the Polo man. I can never get them right. His eyes were close to each other, and they were also dark brown. He would wear a goatee that had the fierceness of showing off the only premature gray on his body. He was definitively a very handsome man.

His disease progressed very fast. This was in the days before the famous "cocktails" were available. And, his unreasonable fear of doctors kept him from finding out he was positive in time to do anything about it. He suffered many complications and ended up having a bowel obstruction, which resulted in a colostomy.

It was as if he lost all his desire to live. No matter what the doctor tried, He continued to lose weight and vanished to 80 pounds. After several back-to-back bouts of pneumonia, Bill finally said "enough." He decided not to treat the last recurrence just so that Bob could have some peace. We are reduced to things: matter that waits the moment to integrate to the place where there is no time or pain. By avoiding the fight he thought he would avoid the pain and defeat.

"Juan, Juan; wake up! You are having a bad dream!" Bill's face brings me back to the real world. Even though I am unable to respond, I am able to see and hear him.

I am very afraid of what this world has in store for me. How would my life be if I had met Bill before the plague? How would it be if we both had started our relationship before either one of us had been infected?

Would we still be negative? Would we have survived the daily temptations of the gay world?

I dream of a world where AIDS has never existed. I dream of a world where our worst fear is trying to stay away from herpes or crabs, or perhaps go back to the good old days of a bad case of the clap.

Perhaps this is never possible. Perhaps this is nothing more than a delusion born out of my brush with death to tempt me to blame my present seropositive-status: to tempt me to forget about my present happiness with Bill. To try to forget the immediate and tangible danger by distracting myself with questions that can't be answered.

Perhaps our sin is that we never repented for our actions. We have all that wonderful sex with as much pleasure as we can muster. In as much as I do not believe in hell, hell is what I saw many of my friends endure as they fought the gay plague, heaven would have been someone finding a pill to make all the pain and suffering disappear. It is probably as close to my understanding of the concept as I will ever get.

Within a few years, I saw many of my friends disappear; their individual consciousness that clearly delineated them from the other human beings (what some may wish to consider their souls) vanish and be lost with a whole generation of brothers.

Their loss, what we long for keeps us alive now. Their souls are the essence that we will call life.

Death puts anger in the past tense. I recognize the depth of my fury even as I let go of them. The dead are so much easier to forgive than the living.

Chapter 8

Titi Elisa was dying. I remember like it was yesterday. I was in the second grade and Elena and I were pulled out of school. Manny was already fighting in Vietnam.

Titi Elisa was *mamita's* sister. *Mamita* was my grandmother on my mother's side. They lived together in a house in Ponce on the other side of the island. At the time, there was no expressway to go to Ponce, so the trip would take three and a half hours, (these days it is only an hour and a half) assuming that *papi* would not take one of his famous *"short cuts"* in which case you would never know how long. The worst case that I could remember was a seven-hour trip door to door.

The road to Ponce was carved into the slope over two mountain ranges making it very dangerous and curvy. *Tita* and *Tina* would need to take anti-nausea medicine, otherwise they would inevitably get sick on the trip. That would be another reason for us to take longer. If either of them would forget their medications, we would be forced to stop until they would get better. Sometimes we would have to stop just to let them puke.

Because of the severity of the situation, and because we had no idea how long we would be in Ponce, it was decided to make the trip with just the four of us: *Mami, Papi,* Elena and I. Papi was forbidden to use any of the shortcuts. *Mami* was visibly upset. More than one time, we were told not to talk.

On our trips to Ponce, Papi would play *Veo Veo* (I see, I see). It would go as follows:

Papi: Veo Veo (I see, I See)

Mami, Elena, and I: ¿Qué Ves? (What do you see?)
Papi: Una cosita (A little thing)
Us: ¿Con qué letrecita? (Starting with what little letter?)
Papi: La letrecita (The little letter)

Then we would guess what he was seeing and whoever guessed would be *it*.

Other times we would sing. In the days before computer games and video recorders, we were forced to come up with our own forms of entertainment. We would do the things that would never be done at home, and they were done as a family. We were forced to be together for a long time, in an enclosed place, so it was hard to get out of it. At our destination, we might part our ways, but here and now we were forced to put on a perfect face without going crazy. In the car, nobody was perfect, yet nobody cared.

Today, we did not sing, we did not play games. It was a very long three and a half hour trip. All I was thinking of was that my great aunt was going to die. It was a curious term for me. I thought that she was going to go somewhere where we would not see her again. I was unable to understand why. Why would she leave *mamita* all alone?

Suddenly, a curious calm came into my soul; a kind of dreamy indifference to my situation. Had I been able to understand more of what was going on, I would have concluded that I was not afraid because none of this could possibly be real. Of course I did not reason this out. I was too young to reason at this moment. I was here to *witness* death, I was here to become a living instrument: a flesh-and-blood camera, recording this event.

Mamita's house finally came into our visual field. The house was a small Spanish style house in the subdivision of Santa María in Ponce: the stucco was washed out pink; the roof was red-tile.

There was a great deal of elaborate tile work at the front steps with an ironwork enclosed balcony with the tiles themselves surrounding the area where windows had been removed to open the balcony to the outside breeze. The tiles were bright blue, turquoise, and white: with complex patterns lending a touch of beauty to the façade. I had posed for pictures at that ironwork when I was a little baby, with *mamita* and *Titi Elisa* behind me. The front door looked as though it was meant to keep all-evil from the house. How had death found its way in was beyond my comprehension?

We were rushed inside to *Titi Elisa*'s bed. The rest of the family was already there. I saw cousins that I had no name for, people that would only come together when someone got married, or, like in this case, when someone died (or was about to die).

Mami's sister, her husband and three kids were there. They had already paid their respects and were lined up in the living room awaiting the inevitable. *Mamita's* sister, *Merche*, her husband and three kids were there. They were also waiting.

As we were being prepared to say our final goodbye, *mamita's* brother arrived with his wife and daughter. There were people there that I had no idea who they were. They were crying; crying aloud. They were holding rosaries, and hitting their chests. (Funny how they were always the same at all the funerals I had been to. I always wondered if they were servants, or were they just paid to add flare to the event...)

The family doctor (also a relative) came out and gave *mami* an update. *Titi Elisa*'s kidneys had completely shut down. Her blood was unable to filter the impurities her body was making. I overheard the word *uremia* (Uremia). Apparently back in those times, we had not perfected dialysis, so all there was to do was wait for *Titi Elisa* to fall in an uremic coma; followed by death.

My turn to go inside. Mami asked me to be on my best behavior and kiss *Titi Elisa.* As I walked inside the room I saw *mamita.* I ran over to her and kissed her. She was crying. There were more of those ladies inside. They were from the groups that were always crying at funerals. *Mamita* guided me to Elisa. She told me to be a good boy and say goodbye.

It was strange to hear it put that way, but she knew what I was supposed to do. Who was I to question her? It wasn't easy, if I had let my attention drop for a moment, I would have wanted to ask so many questions, but I knew that was not proper. I wanted to be myself, but I was also supposed to follow instructions.

Titi Elisa looked very gray. That was the only way I could describe her. She was dressed in a beautiful blue lace nightgown and had the biggest crucifix I had ever seen on her bosom. Her hair was carefully combed and held together by a lace diadem that matched her bedclothes. Her face had been beautifully made, as if she was going somewhere special.

It was when I noticed the Christ on the cross that I felt the presence of father Eduardo. He was a Jesuit priest from our parish in San Juan who had come for the event. I was told to kiss her quickly, because they were going to give her the holy sacrament of *extremaunción* (the last rites).

Elena was rushed in, with *mami* and *papi,* so that the holy servant of God could do his work.

We then began the process of waiting. There were many servants around. The people that were crying had stopped their mourning duties to go help in the kitchen. A big pot of *asopao de pollo (chicken rice soup)* was being prepared.

Dinnertime came and one by one, the large multitude of people ate until they were satisfied. Just before dessert, there was a foul cry from the room. *Titi Elisa* was dead. One by one, we went into the bedroom where she lay.

She looked happy. I would be unable to describe my recollection in any other way. She looked at peace. I had trouble understanding why everyone was crying.

It felt to me like this was a game. Nothing seemed real. Everyone in the room was playing a part, and *Titi Elisa's* part was to lay still. It all felt like it was an illusion. On Monday morning, everything would go back to normal. I would go to school and everything would be the same. All I had to do was not spoil these people's dreams. They wanted me to play a part in this sham so I had to go along. They wanted me to believe that *Titi Elisa* was dead, so I was to act accordingly. I was to put on a perfect face (sad) and not go crazy like they were. In the end, my life would become the same daily routine.

PART TWO

Once a young boy had a dream.
He dreamed he felt a self.
A self that meant to live
A life that wished to be expressed.

And so, he dreamed, this boy of mine,
That his dreams did soon transcend,
The lines that shape reality,
For the dream became the self.

In trying to express his dream,
He wrote a story.
And the lines he wrote,
Eternalized his dream.

Juan Subirá-Rexach

Chapter 9

I was in room 2202 in the medical ward before I was transferred here to the ICU. Ross ordered some X-rays, mostly routine, and decided that it would be best to transfer me at that time.

My very angry husband has been going on and on telling me how miserable he's been. Between my periods of semi-consciousness I hear Bill complain about how scared he was when I did not return after the X-rays. He called the nurse supervising the floor to request information on my condition and ask about my whereabouts.

"May I ask what is your relationship to the patient?"

"He is my partner."

"Sorry, we are only allowed to release information to the next of kin."

"I _am_ his next of kin!!! He is my boyfriend."

"I am afraid you will have to take this up with my supervisor, in the meantime you will not be allowed any information on Dr. Subirá."

First thought in Bill's mind was that I had died and they did not want to tell anyone but my mother. Next, in his mind was that dreaded call to my mother. Mrs. Zulema Rexach de Subirá, (widowed now for 10 years) and Bill barely tolerated each other. He was dreading the bad news of the pancreatitis, but a death! He could not deal with that right now.

It was in that moment that he remembered that Paul had made us sign powers of attorney to each other and he had in his bag that wonderful legal piece of paper that gave him power to ask about me.

Armed with a fierce courage that he was still displaying here in front of my semi-conscious state, he stormed to the nursing supervisor's office where he slammed the power of attorney down on the desk and threatened them with a lawsuit if he was not lead immediately to my bedside. They apologized for the inconvenience, stressing the rights of the hospital patients to privacy (blah, blah, blah), and reassuringly lead him to my new room in the ICU.

That probably explained why he had embraced me to the point that it literally hurt. I mean; pancreatitis pain can be compared to appendicitis, kidney stones and birthing pains all combined at the same time. Having had the first two before, and having delivered over 5,000 babies I felt I owned the analogy.

"What do you mean, you are having a baby?"

"Sorry, it just hurts that much. So please don't hug me right now." As relief washes over me with the ringing sound made by the self-administered morphine going straight to my blood, courtesy of my very own PCA. Love my PCA (Patient Controlled Analgesia)! Have I mentioned that?

A dream is a true experience of sorts, but so is the result of a narcotic high. But an experience is never enough; a hard cold wisdom that requires your self-awareness is necessary to dream. That might be perhaps why even if you were to dream while heavily sedated, you probably will not be able to remember any of it. That may be why time and words lose their relevance. You are not self-conscious at any given time and your mind has trouble grasping reality, much less the passage of hours or days or the meaning of words.

There is the issue of language. English is my second language. I grew up on an island where Spanish is spoken at home and English is learned in school, starting as early as our first brush with our educational system. English, to me, seems the largest of human tongues, with several times the vocabulary of Spanish, my reasoning for preferring to think in English these days. I think it is the richest and most flexible of the three languages I can communicate in (the third being French). It's very variety, subtlety and utterly irrational, idiomatic complexity makes it possible for me to say things in English that I can't communicate in any other language. It almost drove me crazy, until I finally learned to think in English. I felt that I was given the gift of words. It was when I stopped translating from my Spanish thoughts and began to think in the Queen's language, that I was able to differentiate between I like you, I have feelings for you, I lust you, I want you, I need you, or I love you. I still can't tell the difference between in, on or about!

"I love you Bill" and my mind was off wondering again in that never-land drug-induced pleasure. I think Bill said:

"I love you too...."

I believe that being trilingual is a hindrance when you are this "high." Words begin to lose their meaning because you can't remember which language has been spoken. I need to hear from Bill that he loves me. Right this minute it's the only emotion that will anchor a concept to its verbal expression. I want to hear words more than anything. And I want to hear English. I am thinking in English and trying to avoid Spanish or French. His "I love you too" has given me the awareness to anchor my mind in a language mode. Otherwise all I can conceive is the abstraction of ideas. I need something as powerful as our feelings for each other to give me back my ability to communicate. I myself can seldom find the right words. Now, more than anything, I want to listen.

Sometimes the only order in life and the universe is injustice and chaos. That would explain why madness is the only way to become integral with reality. I wish for madness to help me cope with my fear of death and extinction. I know this is not real; but whatever it is, it is the way I feel right now, so it is very real for me.

For the first time in my life I feel defenseless: not life nor faith, nor any of the structures that surround me, nothing...nothing more than fear.

What other experiences are left? Death, nothing else.

I can't think of anything else. And with death comes a feeling of terror because in spite of all the philosophical theories, any of life's satisfactions, and any religious belief, they all seem false right now. They just seem like lies to soften the panic of extinction.

Is it morbid?

No, I try not to think about it.   I try whistling in the darkness.

Should I buy a religious faith just like I had bought my last pair of Calvin Klein's?

I would give my right arm for a stronger faith. It would make things more bearable. The truth is that religion just makes me laugh. It feels as if they are nothing but disguises of our self-preservation instinct, a way to cope with the fear of not existing anymore. A way to enlarge, but failing miserably, our lives that are so horribly transient.

Do not be afraid, do not believe in extinction.

Death feels like a dream, like a game. I am going to play to die and then I will go shopping for another life: a longer and much more entertaining life.

I try whistling in the darkness again. I hear my own sound. It reassures me that I am still here and now.

Chapter 10

Today I have my first communion.

I have been going to catechism school for the last three weeks getting ready for this day. *Mami* was so concerned that we were in a private school that she had us sign up for religious education. I was to learn in three weeks all the dogma as preached by the Catholic Church.

I had to learn about the original sin, and the Immaculate Conception. Did you know that according to Catholic dogma the Virgin was conceived without original sin (the sin traced back to Adam and Eve for eating the "apple") so that she could become the Mother of our Lord? For the longest I thought that it dealt with the way Jesus was conceived. And, don't even try to get an explanation of how she was conceived without original sin or even what that means! No one has an answer for that one. One of the reasons Catholicism (as well as most religions) thrives is its inherent vagaries.

I was amazed as to how much guilt they can pack into three weeks. We not only were taught the Ten Commandments, but also were taught how to feel guilty ten different ways if you sinned.

I suppose it would have been too much to ask to stress how loving our father is. Instead we stressed eternal damnation. By the end of the three weeks, Purgatory* was sounding like a good alternative.

"Please, Jesus, let me be good enough for purgatory." Knowing, by the end of the three weeks, that I was nowhere near good enough for heaven.

We then learned how to be worthy of the Holy Communion.

First, you must go to confession. No one is free of sin. To say that you are free of sin would be an act of vanity, a cardinal sin in itself. (Funny how later on, lust would be my biggest problem). They have everything designed to catch you. Isn't that handy?

To confess you must correctly do an examination of your conscience. Find out what sins you have committed by either action or omission. That needs to be followed by a good act of contrition. You must feel very sorry and promise never to do it again (yeah right...).

Then you must go and confess your sins to the priest. (I was too young to see the connection, but after all the sex scandals in the church, the confessional became a metaphor for the glory hole. It still reminds me of nothing but a sexual act. While talking to the priest, I always felt an ecstasy run through my body like I had just come).

Finally, after the priest absolves your sins, you must do the penance. It usually involved praying a few "Hail Mary's" or "Our Father's."

Now that your soul is in the state of "grace", you must do a sacrifice of fasting (the amount of fasting has changed throughout the years).

Then we were taught how to eat the "cookie" without chewing, to show respect for the body of our Lord Jesus Christ.

We Catholics call it Jesus or the "holy" Eucharist. We eat our Jesus. But before we eat him, we have to bow down in front of the gold thing that holds our Jesus and worship him. The gold thing is called a *monstrance (monstrance: strange how that is so similar monstrosity).* The Eucharist has been referred to as the Catholic "wafer god." I think that is an appropriate name for it. Without eating our Jesus, the Eucharist, we Catholics believe we can't go to heaven. Our Jesus, the Eucharist, is also called "The Sacrifice" and "The Victim." You see, we don't believe that the work of Jesus Christ was finished on the cross—He is supposed to be a perpetual victim always being sacrificed over and over again. Dying over and over and over…

• Purgatory—**pur·ga·to·ry** (pûr?g?-tôr??, -t?r??)—A state or place of purification after death; according to the Roman Catholic creed, a place, or a state believed to exist after death, in which the souls of persons are purified by expiating such offenses committed in this life as do not merit eternal damnation, or in which they fully satisfy the justice of God for sins that have been forgiven. After this purgation from the impurities of sin, the souls are believed to be received into heaven.

Chapter 11

Summer. School was finally over! I finally had time to worry about my problem. You see; I had never been in this position before. The last time I felt this much fear was when our two Dobermans, Pitusa and Ginger, had fought to their deaths. I had always been very afraid of those two. They were only friendly to Mami, and they were ferocious towards everyone else. And, I was even more scared of what would happen when they had a fight. After I hadn't seem them one day, Papi had told me that they had such a fierce fight that when it was over, they had eaten each other completely to the point that only the tips of their tails remained. Whatever, I never saw them alive again. Actually, they did have a fight and had injured each other to such a degree that they died. Papi took them away so that I wouldn't see and instead gave me a much more entertaining version of reality. That's my father's sense of humor.

I had noticed it just before the final exam in my math class when I went to relieve myself. It started like a shadow, then it progressed, and soon there were hairs on my crotch. I was ashamed and guilt-ridden, as only kids can be when they think they've done something horribly wrong. I thought it was because I had started to play with myself. My best friend at school, Tito, teased me saying that if you played with yourself you would get pimples. I also had started to sprout pimples.

My upbringing was what you could call middle class. I went to a Jesuit prep school that went from grades 7 to 12. I had always felt safe at home, because it was a place where I knew my parents would always protect me. Trouble might arise, but usually my parents would take care of me. My tragedy lay in the fact that this was the first time I could not go to them for a solution. There was no one who could help me with this one.

What was I going to say? "Mami, Papi, I have played with myself and I now have hair and pimples. What can you do to fix it?"

I had thought of pulling them, perhaps borrowing my father's razor to shave them. But of course, everyone knows that pulling hairs only makes them grow back thicker! Either way, I was just too afraid to undress in front of my classmates in gym class. Summer vacation had postponed the problem until next year. I would figure out what to do by then. Meanwhile there they were. Looking at them for some reason aroused me in a way that ended up in jacking off (a practice, I learned much later in life, that was used by most men most of the time they couldn't get anyone else to help out – at the time, I thought I was the only one who knew about this fabulous feeling). I just could not help myself. What had started as a curiosity of exploring something new, looking around for new growth, had developed into a very pleasurable sensation, an erection, and eventual spanking the monkey until release; something my friends in school referred to as "*jalarse una puñeta.*"

Around this time, our local television (PR TV was way behind the mainland) had started airing a new series called *The Rin Tin Tin Show*. It told of the adventures of a troop in the conquest of the American west. There was a very handsome lieutenant who had found an orphan, Rusty, abandoned after an Indian massacre and the troop had adopted him. Every episode I would yearn for the young, handsome lieutenant. I wanted to be Rusty, the orphan recruit, adopted by the troop and surrounded by the manly soldiers. I wanted to be held by the handsome lieutenant. I wanted to have adventures with the troop. I wanted to have a dog like *Rin Tin Tin* that would do tricks and be my best friend (unlike the terrible Pitusa and Ginger). Funny thing is, I can't remember the lieutenant's name. But, I remember every detail of his face! He had a big mole on the right side of his chin....

The Jesuit priests at school had told me that if you loved

someone very much, you could give them your seed and nine months later, you would get a baby. (This, and only this, was what sufficed as sex education in the Catholic Schools). In those days, my limited knowledge of the subject could not prepare me for the fact that one night, while hugging my pillows and watching my lieutenant on the television show; I started to hump my pillows (an action that came very naturally to me) and did not stop until I felt something wet on the pillow which had evidently come out of me! I was shocked and tremendously scared! I was afraid I got my pillow pregnant! How do you explain to your parents that you got your pillow pregnant? How do you explain to your parents that you are dreaming about making love to a grown up man? Next year, in ninth grade biology, I would learn the reproductive physiology and what was involved. Right now, I was very worried. How do you marry a pillow? Of course, abortion was out of the question (I was a good catholic)—even if I had known what that was.

It was about this time that I had my very first wet dream. It involved Puchi, Mami's handsome cousin, who had visited us that year. I was thinking how beautiful he was and how wonderful it would be to hold him in a long embrace – what twelve year old boys think of love and sex until they learn otherwise. He had a beautiful mop of dirty blond hair that was always attractively unkempt. He had a long, elegant nose, with a pronounced chin. He wore round tortoiseshell glasses. He looked classically beautiful in a studied way. He had come to visit us in San Juan from St. Louis, where he had a successful dental practice. While we were showing him around, we were invited to my uncle's yacht in Ponce on the south side of the island. I had spied on him by pretending I was sleeping while he changed into his bathing suit. I got a mysterious thrill from peeping at him, unknown, naked. Later, I dreamt he was holding me; it felt very good. I felt a surge of pleasure and when I came, I noticed my cousin Puchi was loosing his four limbs. One by one, they would fall off as I shot a big wad all over the place. The sperm was filling the small cabin to the point of overflowing. I woke with a sense of drowning and feeling both satisfied and guilty about causing him to loose his arms and legs.

I had until Sunday to worry about it. I was going to confession and I would have to tell the priest. Fortunately, Father Roberto would be on confessional duty; he was the nicest man. Everyone knew that when you needed a truly decent, devoted priest, you could count on Father Roberto. He was as tall as he was round, with a full set of dark short hair. He had the sweetest, most gentle eyes that always made you feel safe. Always kind with a good word, and loved teaching Religion class. I had learned from my classmates that all you had to tell the good Father was that you had had impure thoughts and could not control your actions. He always let you off with three Hail Mary's and three Our Father's. Then I looked at the bright side. It was only Monday! Now I was free to play with myself all week and the punishment would be the same.

It was not a good thing if I waited until Saturday to play with myself. That meant that I only had one day to enjoy my impure acts and not feel guilty. After all, I would go to hell just the same, but it sure was fun not to feel guilty for a few days. I would then jerk off as much as I wanted until my next confession. First, I would use one hand, and then I would try the other. It was as if by changing hands I was trying something new. Then I would get creative: the hole of the toilet paper would be just right size for me. I had learned that by using my mother's talcum powder it would not chafe as I introduced my *pipi* (as all young boys, mine was named *"Pepe")* to the perfectly sized hole. I had also discovered the pillows. One below, one above, and you would have a perfect lover. I had decided that to avoid the mess, I would get the plastic wrapper from my lunch and wrap *Pepe.* That way I would just throw it away when I was done and I would not get the pillows pregnant (my idea of condoms on a budget). By next year, and more knowledgeable I would not even worry about that. I had learned that my seed was water-soluble and would easily go away with a little soap and water. Life was suddenly very good.

Chapter 12

"**C**an Juan come out to play?" I heard Tito's voice. Tito was my alpha, the leader. He and his brother Willie were my closest friends. Tito was a year older at 14, two years ahead in school and tall for his age. His blue eyes set him apart from the local crowd; his wavy bangs gave away his northern gene pool. He had a high forehead, long nose and a confident face. Although not buff, his figure asserted his authority. He was the oldest in our group with a reserved, almost formal manner until he smiled, and then his eyes nearly shut, his skin stretched as thin as parchment across his face, and something Romanesque appeared. His voice was thin and faint, contrasting with his muscular, thick necked, powerful body. He was completely masculine. Willie, one year my junior, at 12 was the perfect balance for us. Always cheerful, always enthusiastic, he complemented the strong brother with the feeble me. Willie was as slender and as smooth as I was. He had large blue eyes; a long face and he exuded sweetness, a quality that I found irresistible. He was shy, and always trying to please his brother, another reason why I identified with him: we both were always trying to please Tito.

I had not seen them since way before exams. I was wary of sharing my new secret, yet, I always thought of Tito as the wise one, and the energy generated from my anticipation of the summer ahead was an easy introduction to the theme.

Tito was quite sympathetic. He told me that there was nothing wrong with me and that I should be proud of my developments. Tito, while he already had the changes that came with puberty, was still unable to achieve orgasm. He was very proud as he showed me all the hair in his crotch.

We lived in Santa Maria, a middle class development in the outskirts of San Juan. Back in the late 60's there had been a surge in construction and most of the lots were already being built on. In hurricane country, and since there aren't enough trees left on the island, houses are built with as much concrete as possible (concrete is actually considered a status symbol). It was not unusual for the work to start and then the concrete shell would be left unfinished until more financing became available. When Papi bought property in the new sub-division, my grandfather made fun of him for moving into the country and out of the city (San Juan). That subdivision is now in the center of the city and the country is many miles away.

Tito led us to an abandoned lot. The past school year had seen a huge rush in construction. Somehow, this lot, which was parallel to my house four blocks east, was unfinished. It had the skeletal four walls and no roof.

As soon as we were inside with all the privacy provided by the four walls, Tito wanted proof of my newfound talent. He was as helpful as he was curious. As soon as all three of us had our pants down to our knees, Tito insisted on helping me. I screamed like a young girl when he touched me (my voice was still changing).

Tito tried to soothe me by informing me that he and Willie were always doing this. It was as normal as changing your underwear and I should be learning to enjoy it. Weary at first, I discovered the pleasure of my friend's hands. Somehow, it was a lot better than when I did it on my own; either with my left or, my much preferred right hand. While all three of us were able to get erections, I was the only one who was able to ejaculate. The warm fluid that shot out of me amazed both Tito and Willie. They were immediately jealous. It was as if somehow, by beating them to this rite of passage, I had inherited the power of the most powerful army. I was suddenly the new general and these were my loyal soldiers.

The empty lot was soon christened "*el fuerte*" (the fort) and these meetings became as much a part of this hot summer as the smell of chlorine left over from the pool had been the last year. Tito, as alpha, would call meetings to the fort and we boys were soon to follow. Trying to get both Willie and Tito to ejaculate, I soon learned to reciprocate in the manual activities: with both hands.

Around this time, I named my hands, Rosie and Louie. I would have Rosie days and then I would have Louie days. It was as if I was dating two separate people. I even had the courage to introduce them to my friends. I would either give them Rosie jobs or Louie jobs. Tito had a love affair with Rosie, while Willie was head over heels over Louie. This was the extent of our little family for a good while....

Tito and Willie, bragging of my prowess, were soon to introduce another fellow to the club. Tabito was already fifteen and in Tito's class. He was what you might call a sex maniac, but he was an amusing and generous one. He was like a lovable, mischievous cartoon character; a giant anvil might fall on him, but he would just pop right back up, dust himself off, and go on to find more trouble. He was never repentant for his actions because he never saw any of them as bad. Because he was a year older, he was always boasting about his ability to ejaculate.

The first time that Tabito was invited to the fort, he was not only eager to drop his pants, but forceful in trying to engage in closer physical contact. It was the second time that I looked at a fully developed organ (first time being my brother Manny) and was both impressed and scared of its size. While Tito calmed Willie and me by saying we would have ours grow that big some day, I had my reservations. Tabito's eagerness drove Tito to such a state of excitement, that he joined that day in the exclusive club of those boys that had become men. (Gay Latinos, latent or otherwise, maintain aggression as a way of life strictly due to a society that sees aggression as a normal way of dealing with the world around them. Indulging in pain – seeking it for itself or afflicting on others can become quite erotic. As he breaks away from the adolescent sex games where it's easy to have "sex" with other boys without much societal restraint, the Latin male has to fundamentally become a top. As long as he is the active one, he does not have to think of himself as gay. He may even have a wife and kids. As if by being very aggressive, he can hide his homosexuality and survive). All three of us were taken aback, as Tito ejaculated, and the rules of engagement were formalized. Since Tito now possessed the gift, he was soon to become the true alpha-male of the group again.

Somehow, rumors spread of the club's activities and other members joined. Since Tito was ahead in school, he was the one who brought new pledges to our fraternity. Soon we were six or seven boys: the contests were organized in a circle, and were determined by the speed of the deed, the size of the member, and the number of times the deed was achieved (ties were decided by distance shot). One argument was resolved by convening at a later time to bring a ruler to measure organ size and it could not be resolved because Tito was unsure as to whether width or length was more important. It didn't matter that I thought the shorter, yet much wider one was very cute.

As summer vacation ended, the fort was lost to the returning construction crew and the club dissolved due to lack of meeting facilities.

I was transformed by this summer. Soon the frequent dreams of arousal had a recurring male theme, and my lieutenant pillow/lover was replaced by memories of classmates. One boy in particular would come back to haunt me next year at school.

Confessions at church were also transformed. Now I was shamed by the fact that I had done sexual activities in the company of strangers. Unable to justify them with my usual confessional jargon of impure thoughts only, and taken aback by the transfer of good Father Roberto to another parochial district, I was soon to endure this Sunday purification ritual with a new priest.

Having fasted the usual hour before communion, and after a very good thought-out act of contrition, I was presented with the task of choosing a new partner in sanctification. I read the names of all the priests on duty at the confessional, and mysteriously I was drawn to Father Eduardo.

Father Eduardo was new last year and had come to my Religion class. He was clad in black pants and his black robe. When the weather would cool (in PR "cold" means below 75 degrees), he would wear a smartly tailored matching black jacket. He knew how to wear his Jesuit collar with style – if there had been a way to accessorize a priest's collar, he would have found it. His hair was neatly styled in silky short waves and he wore large Ray Ban gold-trimmed sunglasses as he assessed us from the doorway, as if reluctant to enter or leave the room. He was very sensitive and all the students felt they could trust him with their problems. He had a unique technique in didactics, where he used church teachings only as they applied to regular people's lives. I had felt very at ease in Religion class, and not being bored like the year before, thought Father Eduardo might bring me back to my lost state of "Grace." It helped a lot that he was nice to look at.

"Forgive me father for I have sinned" I began. "It has been one week since my last confession," I continued. "My sins are: I lied to my friend Tito, I forgot to return my friend Willie's GI Joe rifle and then I lost it. I had impure thoughts and could not contain myself and acted on them."

"Were you alone at the time?" interrupted Father Eduardo.

"I don't know where I was."

"You don't know where you were?"

"Yeah, I lost his rifle sometime, but if I knew where I was, I probably could find it."

A pause. Then, "No. When you acted on your impure thoughts."

Long silence. Astounded by the interruption of my ritual and not knowing what to say I added, "No, I had company"

"Who was with you at the time?" Father Eduardo inquired.

"My friends Willie and Tito" was all I could get out. Barely, at that.

Miraculously, things got easier very quickly. Not only was Father Eduardo inquisitive of, or shall we say probing into, all the details of the fort activities, but also he showed so much interest and enthusiasm that I almost missed Holy Communion. Father Eduardo kept me for almost forty-five minutes, almost throughout the entire length of all the Holy Mass, and amazingly, was very lenient in the Penance. Instead of Hail Marys and Our Fathers, I was told that my sins were forgiven and, I didn't understand why but, with a subtle increase in his breathing, he requested full reports every week of my activities. And, as his breathing started to return to normal, Father also encouraged me to have my friends Willie and Tito come to him for confession. That was the beginning of a bond that would be present for the next four years of High School.

Chapter 13

Number 40 Geranium Street was the only address I had ever known. Years later, Mami (Zulema Rexach-Subirá) told me this was not the case. When I was one year old, and Mami was pregnant with Elena, Papi (José Antonio Subirá) had moved the furniture and me to our present house. Thus, Elena, my baby sister had been brought home from the hospital to the exclusive suburb of Santa Maria in burgeoning San Juan, Puerto Rico.

At first, there were many empty lots and fresh memories of cows grazing and the morning's rooster serenade. But soon the empty lots disappeared and construction crews came and filled them with the most exclusive and architecturally significant houses that Puerto Rican society could conceive. My grandfather's prediction that no one would move so far away from the city had proven wrong. Papi had made a great invest-ment and proven Grandpa John wrong. This was still a sore subject between them, since Grandpa John had missed out on the opportunity to invest in the subdivision. Fearing indepen-dence for Puerto Rico would make real estate prices bottom out; he had passed on an excellent opportunity to own large portions of the neighborhood.

Concrete houses and the latest-model cars soon replaced the cows and the roosters. As middle class goes, my parent's house was not a bad one. It was a concrete ranch style built in an "L" shape: with three comfortable bedrooms and two-bathrooms on one side, and the living room, dining room and kitchen on the other. In the southwestern corner of the house there was another room, about fifteen feet by fifteen feet, which held the laundry room. Behind it, further southwest, there were the servant quar-ters: a one bedroom, one bath freestanding structure. Our lot was 1200 square meters, which for our standards, was a big one.

My bedroom was the middle one; a good place to be in the tropics, it was dark and cool. Lying down on the soft, cool bed felt wonderful. I had managed to decorate my room with fluorescent "peace and love" posters, complete with a black fluorescent light. My room was the first in the house to get wall-to-wall carpet, shag of course, and the first to get an air conditioner. I was, after all, the oldest son in a Latin family.

Papi was an admirable man. He was five feet five inches tall, but just as wide (average height & width for straight Puerto Rican men). Papi enjoyed eating anything that Mami would put on the table. Very masculine, with a bull neck and Roman nose, which was the perfect setting for his clear blue eyes.

Papi had the best sense of humor, but sometimes his jokes came at the expense of his family.

"*Papi, ¿puedo ir al baño? Tengo que hacer caca.*" (Can I go to the bathroom? I have to poop. Which translates literally as "I have to make poop.")

"*¿Por que no la compras hecha?*" (Why don't you go to the store to get some?)

Then we would run, mad as hell, to the bathroom to flee from the laughter of his friends.

Papi had a very close friend who had graduated with him from Central High School in San Juan who was African and quite dark. Any time his friend would come to visit, Papi would say to my sister: "*Saluda a tu papi.*" (Say hello to your father). This would invariably get Elena quite upset, again to the laughter of everyone in the room. (Racial jokes are still acceptable in PR. The term Politically Correct is barely understood as some kind of foreign concept. No beating around the bush. Fat is fat, not weight challenged. Black is black, not African American. A fag is a fag, not anything as positive sounding as gay).

Papi had worked very hard to attain everything we had. He had lost an executive position with the local Pepsi–Cola bottling plant when Grandpa John had decided to sell the company rather than let his son take it over. This was still another sore point between them. Papi had been let go with a lump sum of money that he had invested in his own consulting firm and was doing well.

Mami was his second wife. She was a petite five-foot woman who was 10 years younger than *papi* but looked much younger. She wore her hair short and wavy, and would only allow the salon to do her color to keep her hair brunette. (She felt that coloring your own hair was beneath her— something the Dominicans would do!) Mami loved to accentuate the blue in her eyes with different shades of blue eye shadow, but always tried to be conservative on her make-up. It had been a shock to hear my classmates say she was very good looking, because I only knew her as Mami. She was tired of my father's repetitive jokes, but somehow managed to laugh at them after all the years. Not always…

It is a well-known story that one time Papi kept Mami waiting to go out to dinner because he was getting drunk with friends. Driving very fast through a hospital zone, he was stopped by a policeman and tried to joke his way out of the ticket. Mami told the officer, "Yes, he was speeding and he is also drunk and was late for our date. Please ticket him." The officer took one look at my furious mother, another look at my father and decided that she was all the punishment that was needed that night.

My sister was two years younger than I. She was always on my tail and would be angry when we excluded her from any escapades. She was a few inches shorter, but had inherited blue eyes and light brown hair from my American grandfather. She could actually be blonde by the end of summer after soaking up all the summer sun.

Last summer Elena (whose asthma got worse and her doctor prescribed swimming as therapy) had drawn everyone in our family to the swimming pool. When my high school was recruiting young swimmers for a new swimming team Elena had turned out to be a natural. She won every race she ever entered. Suddenly Papi was talking only of his daughter. It was as if I, the oldest son, was suddenly invisible.

I started swimming this year, but I was not as successful as my sister. At the last swim meet, Papi had teased me that I had come in fifth in my race because there were only four people in it and the first swimmer to end the following race had finished before I had.

Willie and Tito, still my closest friends, lived in a bigger house, with an in ground swimming pool. Their father, Don Ramon Ferrer, was a well-known engineer and, much to my dismay, made a lot more money than my father did so I considered my friends to be the right kind of people (I was thirteen, I didn't know any better). Willie and Tito were also on the swimming team, and since they also were not as successful as Elena was, it helped us get even closer.

Regional trials were coming up to qualify to compete for Puerto Rico at a swim meet in Miami, Florida. I had never left the island and I was looking forward to my first airplane ride. Training had started early in the summer and now that the "fort activities" were over, I had time to concentrate on the swim of my life. Elena, who was now 11, had qualified first in the butterfly in the 11 – 12 year old category. She had done so by breaking the Puerto Rican national record. All I needed was to come in fourth in the freestyle to qualify for the relay. That meant I needed to beat my friend Tito. Even though Tito was 14, I was forced to swim against him in the 13–14 year old category.

It was a gorgeous sunny day in July. The meet was held at the old Casino de Puerto Rico swimming pool in Condado. The pool was 25 meters long and 6 lanes wide. There was a short spectators arena; probably a few hundred people could watch a race at any given time. Our weather has always been somewhere in the 80's all year round, but this summer was very hot; it was a very unusual 95 and very humid.

Because the pool was shorter than the usual Olympic sized 50 meters, it was of utter importance I work on my turns. The 100-meter race was to have three instead of one—I needed to concentrate on these if I was to make the cut.

"Swimmers on your marks..." and then the gun. The race of my life was under way. I was seeded fifth, but needed to finish fourth. I was in lane one, which meant I needed to beat my friend Tito, the swimmer in lane five, to go to Miami. I always start strong, so I was not surprised to be ahead of everyone at the first turn in the 25 meters mark. I almost missed my turn, but I was still ahead. Here I knew I would start losing my strength, and I could only allow three swimmers to pass me. I had trained very hard, and it worked out great. I made a perfect flip turn at the fifty-meter mark. I was still third. I knew that the third lap was my worst one, so I put all my remaining effort into it. I only breathed once through the last lap and was still third when I came out of the 75-meter turn. I had another great turn and went with renewed confidence to the finish mark.

I had to struggle but was able to come in fourth. I managed to squeeze into the national team and was as proud as I was when I had achieved the deed in front of all my friends. In qualifying, not only had I beaten my friend Tito to the team (thus rising in my clan status), but also I had stunned Papi, who had not even bothered to comprehend that his son was also going to need a ticket to Miami.

Papi, upon realizing that both of his children had made the team, decided it best to fly the whole family to Miami and finally, after Mami's reminders about 7 years of promises, take the kids to Disney World. Mami also told him that we would have to go to J. C. Penney's at Plaza Las Americas to properly outfit the family. I was aware of the monetary strain this deed had caused my father, and for the first time in as long as I could remember, I was pleased.

Chapter 14

Preparations for the trip to Miami were as exciting as I had anticipated. I had to leave behind my home team, ten minutes away from my house, to train with the national swimming team. Where as Elena was used to the arrangement (she being a two year veteran of the team and all), I had trouble adjusting. Where as Elena knew everyone on the team, I was foreign to all the procedures and a stranger to all the kids.

Alberto, who swam for a rival school, and who had placed third in front of me in the freestyle event was the only person to talk to me that first official training session as a unified team. He was my age and had started developing nicely. A small boned, delicate boy, tall for his age (almost five feet seven at thirteen) had the sensitive face of a young Jesuit student. He had a small mouth, an aquiline nose, and heavy lidded clear blue eyes . Neither his arms nor his legs were unusual; it was just his chest—like the armor of a Roman general—his pectoral muscles made him unusual. There was a strange dichotomy between his body and his personality.

Alberto had addressed me as "*oye tu*" ("hey you"). He wanted to know my name and who I was. Inexplicably, the sound of his voice had sent chills through my spine. A bulge had formed in my swim trunks, and I fought the uncontrollable urge between my legs. Fortunately, the pool water was very cold, and exercise always sent the blood flowing to other parts of my body.

That night I had an incredible dream about my new best friend Alberto. I dreamt that we were alone on an island and I was thirsty and there was no water to drink. Alberto had learned in survival school that you could drink your own urine in emergencies to stay alive and was so thirsty that he stripped whatever clothing was left on my body and started drinking from me like a water fountain. Astoundingly, not only was this the logical solution to our problems, but also it felt very good. I was aroused in a way I could not explain; the pleasure generated by Alberto's mouth was unbearable, and I was reaching climax. At that point, I realized that I was dreaming and this could not be possible. I was shocked awake to a sticky pillow. The dream had suddenly become true. My pillow was dirty and I had no clue how I was going to explain this one in confession on Sunday!

I had done nothing to arouse myself, I really had not done anything to achieve orgasm, and somehow, I could not erase a feeling of guilt that was budding like the morning sun that was intensifying over the horizon. I knew, as sure as the sun would be warm that day that I was in trouble, yet I could not come up with a resolution to my ordeal (at least, one that would sync with the Church's teachings).

Alberto was cheery the next day in practice and wanted to invite me to his house for a sleepover. Elena had done the same with her female teammates, so I was eager and pleasantly surprised when my mother agreed to drive me over to his house that evening.

The important thing was to make sure that I had all the right clothes to wear. I started out packing clothes to wear at the beach, clothes to wear around the house, swimsuits and accessories for a week, and finally enough outfits to wear for a lifetime together with my new found friend. It would entail packing three suitcases, but somehow I decided to narrow it down to the essentials and just stuffed my workout bag with the bare minimum.

Alberto lived in a middle class suburban house in Hato Rey. It was a white, two-story colonial, probably built in the forties. It had the traditional terracotta red roof tiles of the period and tall palm trees in the front yard, probably as old as the house. White columns promised a majesty the interior somehow failed to deliver. The front door opened onto a dark, narrow hallway bisecting the living space: family room, living room, dining room and kitchen. There was a majestic staircase leading to the up-stairs' bedrooms. Alberto was an only child, so the house sufficed with the three bedrooms; one for Alberto's parents, one for Alberto, and a guest room that Alberto's mother used as a sewing room. Alberto's room was right there off the staircase.

We had a simple dinner with both of his parents: Mireya and Alberto Senior. The dinner consisted of traditional *"arroz con pollo y habichuelas"* (rice and chicken covered with red kidney beans) and *"amarillo dulce"* (ripe plantain. As you may know, Puerto Ricans consider plantains to be a food group). Mireya was a good cook, so I was not lying when I complemented her dinner. As she turned away to clear the table, exposing her profile, I realized she had been a real beauty in her youth. Although she was probably as old as my mother (around 40), there was no single or precise thing that brought her beauty to focus. Her face was oval under a cap of hair the color of polished bronze. Her brown eyes were set wide. Her nose was small, mouth wide and generous. Her figure was good but scant: tall and with curves gone to slimness.

Don Alberto Senior talked very little and mostly to his wife. He had dark sequins of almond eyes and angled cheeks. He had a butter complexion and stringy moustache hanging like a curved frame around purpled lips and narrow chin. The creases on his cheeks and forehead were as much lines of sorrow as of age. I was happy that he did not address me personally, for somehow he inspired fear in me.

Alberto was very pleased with my choices for clothing. He was very approving that I had decided to leave most of my other clothes behind. After the lights went out I started to confide in Alberto my dream from the prior night. Alberto listened carefully to my fantasy, was quite sympathetic that evening, but curiously was more distant at practice the next day. I never got invited back to Alberto's house and the other swimming teammates started pointing, whispering, and laughing when I would arrive at practice. It took me many years to figure out what they already knew.

Chapter 15

The day was finally here! First to Orlando to have some fun, then on to Miami to swim!

The anticipation of my first plane ride had been insurmountable. The night before the trip, I dreamt that there was an emergency landing in the Atlantic Ocean and I had taken my friend Alberto to safety by swimming him in the shark-infested waters to Miami. It was a miraculous feat. I had single handedly carried him almost forty miles to safety. Then I had given him mouth-to-mouth resuscitation (which lasted an undue amount of time) to the amazement of the rescue workers, and still had helped them locate the survivors of the plane by guiding the helicopter driven rescue to the crash site. Alberto had decided that I was his best friend and could not get enough of me. I was then honored in a ticker tape parade through the streets of Old San Juan and given the medal of honor by the Governor: Don Luis Ferré. I was a hero…

"Wake up Juan." I heard Mami interrupt my deserved honoring festivities, "we are going to be late for the airport."

We had spent the night before packing. We needed to be at the airport by eight in the morning, so the bright morning sun awakened me as it came into by bedroom. The Subirá family was ready for their first family excursion. No expense had been spared; every detail had been attended. We had matching Samsonite suitcases, the latest model that the J. C. Penney catalogue showcased on page 134. We had matching outfits for travel: Mami insisted that both Papi and I had to go to the Velasco men's store and get navy blue, Italian, three piece suits for the trip. Mami and Elena were in their new matching gowns from Nono Maldonado who was dressing *"everyone"* that summer.

The car ride to the airport was dreadful. Papi kept drilling my mother about: "did you turn out the lights? Is the garage light on? Who is going to water the garden while we are gone?" As always Mami would have the right answer to it all and, except for the near collision at the light just before getting on the expressway, we had an uneventful ride to the airport.

The airport was filled with thousands of people. It is a Puerto Rican tradition to have as many relatives as you can scrounge up at the airport to send you away to the United States. No decent person would show up at the airport with less than twenty relatives. This day it was no exception. The official delegation was around one-hundred people, but by the sight at the airport, you would think the whole island was emigrating with the team. Chaos was fighting and winning with the busy chaperones, whose sole job it was to make sure they would not lose their kids. I believe that is why the Luis Muñoz Marín San Juan International Airport was the first in the nation to allow only ticket holders beyond the security zones.

We finally boarded, pulled away from the terminal and were ready to take off, when we were forced to go back and retrieve José Rodríguez, the ten-year old sensation who had locked himself in the cafeteria rest room and whom his mother, who was too busy chaperoning the ten-and-under kids, had forgotten to account for. Years later I would relive Mrs. Rodriguez' screams when in "Home alone" Catherine O'Hara the mother of that silly and obnoxious Kevin, realized she had forgotten her son. Luckily, we were just a few feet from the gate and not yet on the tarmac and the captain was very sympathetic (he had no choice, there was not enough Valium on the plane to calm down an hysterical mother, much less a hysterical Puerto Rican mother) and easily returned to the gate, where the security officers were holding a teary eyed José. After a round of applause and cheers from the crew, we resumed our trip to Orlando.

The plane ride was bumpy and long. It took almost two hours to make it to Orlando from San Juan. We were all seated in the back half of the plane. There were four seats in row thirty-two and my family managed to sit together. The food on the plane was quite good; I had never tasted a better sandwich wrap, and was thrilled to drink three cokes, all of them, free of charge. As the plane landed, I was glad to join my teammates and family in applause of approval. Elena, the expert in foreign travel, told me that everyone in the team always did this. It seems it is another Puerto Rican tradition. To this day, upon returning to San Juan, this tradition continues as some of my fellow country-men applaud as the plane lands in San Juan.

Orlando turned out to be a mixed blessing; Disney World was not what I had thought. Growing up with Tito and Willie, I had grown to believe Disney was "It's a small, small world after all" and "Pirates of the Caribbean." I had watched "The Wonderful World of Disney" with my two friends. Puerto Rico would get the show dubbed in Spanish a few years later, so I was not knowledgeable of the latest trends.

The team had practice in the morning and was free to go to the theme park in the afternoon. While my teammates kept talking about Space Mountain, I was stuck in line at It's a Small World After All. In my fury to see my perceived "cool rides" I had forgone the newer section of Disney World, not realizing what I had missed.

The hotel was inside the Disney resorts, which turned out to be a blessing since we only had three days to explore Disney World. We were fast approaching the meet: our reason to be here. As we were getting ready for the bus ride to Miami Springs, I had the best dream of my life. I dreamt that I could walk on water and while everyone else had to actually swim the race, I could run over the water. Everyone knows that running is much faster than swimming, but since no one was able to see me run over the water (this is a dream so I don't have to explain that part) everyone assumed that I was, in fact, swimming. In their eyes, I was swimming like everyone else, so I turned out to be a world record-breaking swimmer. The first Puerto Rican to do so! I was about to be inducted into the Swimming Hall of Fame, when all of a sudden Elena realizes that I had been running over the water and tries to disqualify me. Before I could strangle my sister, Papi woke me to get on the bus for Miami.

The bus ride was four and a half hours. I joined everyone else on the bus with an occasional "are we there yet?" Growing up on an island one hundred by thirty-three miles long, there had never been a reason to ride a bus for that long. Our tour guide said that we would be passing an oil refinery and Papi turned around to tell everyone around him that he was waiting for the smell of the refinery to help him camouflage a fart that he felt was coming. He was quite upset when the refinery never materialized, since that forced him to hold it until Miami. (When he wasn't abusing his family with his "humor" he was being plain gross).

The swimming meet was quite exciting. The Miami Spring Invitational is held every year at their 50 meter, eight-lane Olympic pool. It gathers local teams from the Miami area and international teams from the Caribbean and Central and South America. It runs two days, with relays at the end of each day.

My sister Elena had managed to win the one-hundred meters butterfly while setting a meet record on the first day. Papi carried Elena on his shoulders celebrating her triumph to receive her first place trophy, which was beautiful! Puerto Rico was first among the International teams. I had managed a measly third place finish in the four by one hundred relay the first day.

I had only one chance to validate myself. We had qualified first on the shorter relay, the four by fifty meters; finals were that evening on the last day. The local team was the competition and my three teammates and coach had decided to change strategy. Normally the best swimmer goes last. My teammates (and somehow I suspected Alberto was behind this) had talked to our coach with the idea of making me go last. That way they would build a huge lead and hope that Miami's best man would not catch me. By creating an early lead, we were trying to psych out the other team and make them think they could never catch us.

The first three men had swum. I was given a ten-meter lead with fifty meters to go. The tall Miami swimmer jumped in the water and started closing in. The local crowd was on their feet yelling. I knew the other swimmer was much faster that I was, but I was determined not to be caught. I took a deep breath and swam the last ten meters without breathing. What my teammates had forgotten to mention was the fact that this swimmer had broken the record in the one-hundred meter freestyle the day before, and our lead swimmer was afraid to swim against him because he did not like to lose. Had I been any wiser, I would have never agreed to this charade – it was all designed so that I would lose the race for the team and would take all the shame home with me. However, since we were supposed to lose to them because their times were faster than ours (we had all swum the event and we could all add our respective four times together) I felt I had nothing else to lose. I was also stronger in the first half of the race, compared to the second half, which would help our cause, since we were only swimming fifty meters, not one hundred. We had come in third place on the four by one-hundred meter relay, but we wanted to do better in the shorter race.

I touched the finish pad one tenth of a second faster than the local team, and in doing so we broke the meet record. My teammates were so excited that they carried me on their shoulders. I felt like I belonged for the first time in my life!

That evening, while packing to return to San Juan, Papi told me that I was lucky that the pool was not a foot longer. Otherwise, I would have disgraced the Puerto Rican delegation.

That was the end of my triumph.

Chapter 16

Thunder woke me and I was too nervous to go back to sleep—school was going to start today. I had not been this excited since I discovered I had a gift between my legs. I was going to show off my other trophy at school.

"*Buenos días m'hijito*" I heard Mami, as she drove my daydreaming away. The night's storm had given way to a clear and diaphanous sunshine. The dawn's light had a white wine color. The morning dew in the grass was silencing the "*coquis*" (tiny noisy frogs that infest the island).

"What would you like for breakfast?" My mother interrupted my thoughts again. "The usual, Mami" blurting my automatic response. The "usual" consisted of French toast and bacon with fresh squeezed orange juice. We would always end it with a big cup of "*café con leche*" (milk and coffee). (To this day, I must have a cup of strong espresso coffee with as much milk and sugar as I can squeeze into the cup. The saying goes that "no coffee bean died to make my coffee." I was unable to teach myself to drink that colored water the *norteamericanos* call coffee). Even though the Subirá–Rexach's had two live-in maids (something that was not uncommon for middle class families at the time), my mother took pride and joy in getting her kids off to school by herself.

As we sat at the breakfast table, Mami, Papi, Elena and I, I was deep in anticipation of my show and tell day in school. I certainly had a great tale from this summer! A tale that I could actually tell this time. Papi read the San Juan Star and barely talked through breakfast. It was Mami's day to carpool and soon, Tito and Willie were at our door to get a ride to school.

Ready to go, I took my books and grabbed my trophy for show and tell. It was tradition for the homeroom teacher at San Ignacio High School to ask what the students had done that summer. I was certainly ready this year. I had a gleaming trophy to go along with my tale.

As usual, Mr. Fernandez asked everyone who had something to share with the class to stand up and come to the front of the room. It was our first period of the first day back to school. Mr. Fernandez was our Spanish Literature teacher and had come directly from Spain where he grew up. His family had run away from Franco and he always had tales of the Republican struggle against the "*caudillo*." He liked to engage us in activities and show and tell was his favorite way to ease us back into the school year.

I was very eager this year and could not contain my anticipation. There were six other students up front, each with a tale and a gizmo to show and share with their friends.

Abraham had spent his vacation in the Holy Land and was describing his pilgrimage with his family. He stood first and had brought back pictures and dust from the Holy Land. He was the only Jewish student we had ever met, and he was always reminding us about his faith. Raised in a country where 95% of its citizens were officially Catholics, and going to a Jesuit prep school, he got very little understanding from the rest of us.

As I was thinking what a better tale I had to tell, an urge arose in me. I had been there before, I had bragged about my ability to pass gas, but somehow I did not feel that this would be the right time or place. I tried to distract my thoughts, as if by not thinking about it I would forget about the pressing need. To my dismay all I could think of was the tune that my father would sing on the way to visit our relatives in Ponce, at the other end of the island. To pass time while we were driving, Papi used to

sing to his two kids: (vaguely to the tune of "The Beverly Hill-
billies" theme song).

> *"Nació en la montaña de San Antón.*
> *Comía mucha pana y tiraba mucho follón.*
> *Un día una avispa en el culo lo picó;*
> *Y Pancho, Pancho López de un peo la mató."*
> "He was born in the mountains of San Anton.
> He ate a lot of breadfruit and he farted a lot.
> One day, a wasp, bit him on the ass,
> And Pancho, Pancho Lopez killed it with a fart."

Mr. Fernandez interrupted my silent tune to ask me what I
had done for the summer. I presented my trophy and told the
class how I had been the hero of the relay and how I had helped
the Puerto Rican National team set a record at the Miami Springs
Swimming invitational. Gradually, I became aware of the fact
that I could not contain my urge to relieve the pressure. But this
was my moment of triumph—I was not going to let this opportunity slip away from me—I would get through this and tell my
story. However, I was now praying that I might get away with a
silent one. Seconds turned slowly; I was lost in the words that I
was saying but nothing had any meaning. I could not fight the
urge. I mentally started counting from five hundred. 500, 499,
498, 497, 496, 495, 494, 493, 492, 491, 490, 489, 488, 487, 486,
485, 484, 483, 482, 481, 480, 479, 478, 477, 476, 475, 474, 473,
472, 471, 470, 469, 468, 467, 466, 465, 464, 463, 462, 461, 460,
459, 458, 457, 456, 455, 454, 453, 452, 451, 450, 449, 448, 447,
446, 445, 444, 443, 442, 441, 440, 439, 438, 437, 436, 435, 434,
433, 432, 431, 430, 429, 428, 427, 426, 425, 423, 422, 421, 420,
419, 418, 417, 416, 415, 414, 413, 412, 411, 410, 409, 408, 407,
406, 405, 404, 403, 402, 401.

It was working: I was losing myself in the procedure and
had lost track of the impending sphincter relaxation event. Four
hundred, 399, 398, 397, 396, 395, 394, 393, 392, 391, 390, 389,

388, 387, 386, 385, 384, 383, 382, 381, 380, 379, 378, 377, 376, 375, 374, 373, 372, 371, 370, 369, 368, 367, 366, 365, 364, 363, 362, 361, 360, 359, 358, 357, 356, 355, 354, 353, 352, 351, 350, 349, 348, 347, 346, 345, 344, 343, 342, 341, 340, 339, 338, 337, 336, 335, 334, 333, 332, 331, 330, 329, 328, 327, 326, 325, 323, 322, 321, 320, 319, 318, 317, 316, 314, 313, 312, 311, 310, 309, 308, 307, 306, 305, 304, 303, 302, 301.

My countdown was briefly interrupted by a childhood rhyme that went:

> *"Caminando por la vía del ferrocarril,*
> *Siento que una churra se me va a salir.*
> *Me meo, me cago, me tiro un buen peo...*
> *Eso es felicidad."*

"Walking down the railroad tracks,
I feel the runs as they escape my ass.
I pee; I shit, I cut a great fart...
That is happiness"

As I fought the urge, I continued with my mental countdown. Three hundred, 299, 298, 297, 296, 295, 294, 293, 292, 291, 290, 289, 288, 287, 286, 285, 284, 283, 282, 281, 280, 279, 278, 277, 276, 275, 274, 273, 272, 271, 270, 269, 268, 267, 266, 265, 264, 263, 262, 261, 260, 259, 258, 257, 256, 255, 254, 253, 252, 251, 250, 249, 248, 247, 246, 245, 244, 243, 242, 241, 240, 239, 238, 237, 236, 235, 234, 233, 232, 231, 230, 229, 228, 227, 226, 225, 224, 223, 222, 221, 220, 219, 218, 217, 216, 215, 214, 213, 212, 211, 210, 209, 208, 207, 206, 205, 204, 203, 202, 201.

I was pretty sure that I was winning the battle. I was still hoping it would be a silent one. Last year in the seventh grade, I had gained a reputation for making silent and deadly gas (something I obviously inherited from Papi. What a ridiculous thing to have passed down through something so complex and important as genetics). It was a well-known fact that if you smelled that cloacae aroma that I used to call affectionately *"eau de peu"*, either the sewers had over flown, or I had produced a new one. (Our school was infamous for having a bad sewer system). But I was infamous for not making a noise, so it was almost impossible for me to get the blame. Two hundred, 199, 198, 197, 196, 195, 194, 193, 192, 191, 190, 189, 188, 187, 186, 185. 184, 183, 182, 181, 180, 179, 178, 177, 176, 175, 174, 173, 172, 171, 170, 169, 168, 167, 166, 165, 164, 163, 162, 161, 160, 159, 158, 157, 156, 155, 154, 153, 152, 151, 150, 149, 148, 147, 146, 145, 144, 143, 142, 141, 140, 139, 138, 137, 136, 135, 134, 133, 132, 131, 130, 129, 128, 127, 126, 125, 124, 123, 122, 121, 120, 119, 118, 117, 116, 115, 114, 113, 112, 111, 110, 109, 108, 107, 106, 104, 103, 102, 101, 100, 99, 98, 97, 96, 95, 94, 93, 92, 91, 90, 89, 88, 87, 86, 85, 84, 83, 82, 81, 80, 79, 78, 77, 76, 75, 74, 73, 72, 71, 70, 69, 68, 67, 66, 65, 64, 63, 62, 61, 60, 59...

It was the loudest fart in San Ignacio's 24-year history. It was louder than the thunder that woke me that morning. From this day on it would be known as *el peo del siglo* (the fart of the century). The walls shuddered. Classmates were screaming thinking it was an earthquake—remembering tales of "the big one" in the 20's (a title whose meaning was forever changed). The noise was heard all the way to the principal's office. The fire alarm was activated due to "vibrations of unexplained nature" and because the new prefect of discipline was inexperienced in kids' bodily functions. Students were evacuated in an orderly fashion and every one of them wanted to know where the noise had come from. Word spread as, one student at a time; my name was passed along as my class joined the others in the school gardens. I was about to become a legend.

In the chaos and confusion, no one seemed to notice the brown stain running down the inside of the leg of my pants.

Part three

Today, for the first time in my life,
I don't feel as lonely as I could.
For today, returning to my daily strife,
The sun shined as hard as it should.

It wasn't the warmth of its rays
That lightly appeased my broken soul.
For it was the remembrance of a yesterday
When a friend used to knock at my door.

The remembrance that when I awoke,
And I saw the sun unprovoked;
My friend would always be there,
And we would have our hopes to share.

Juan Subirá-Rexach

Chapter 17

Bill and I have an overwhelming desire to be loved, so we take our relationship very seriously. Much more seriously than getting married. Neither one of us feels we need that piece of paper to validate what we feel for each other. Besides, the straight world, in spite of their piece of paper, can only boast a 50% success rate for their relationships. We had both been in relationships before, and we had just decided to commit, never to lie to each other. We had decided never to deceive each other, to stick by each other come what may, so when we both found out about each other's HIV status, we simply got closer. It is, then, just a natural role for him to be seated next to my bed, ready to comfort me as needed. As far as we are concerned, it is part of the deal.

"Hi sexy – waking up to your pretty face is giving me a fluffy"

"Honey, if you ever write about this day you should remember that a true confession story should never be tarnished by any taint of the truth. Let me then say that I find you and your tubes to be as sexually appealing as you find facial hair."

I believe you may have never encountered complete honesty between two people; I know I hadn't until I met Bill. Bill is innocence; I know what makes him tick. It is as if he has never tasted from the fruit of Good and Evil. When we met, he had the shadow of a goatee. I really hate facial hair. The porn ideal of the sweaty, unshaven handy man does very little for me. (The joke is: "have him shower and shave before you send him to my room.") I know the goatee looks good on him, but I know I like him a lot more when he shaves. Between our first and second dates, he had shaved his facial hair to please me. He guessed correctly that I would like that better. Bill has never forgotten the incident and loves to remind me at any opportunity.

At the moment, I am not a pretty picture. I have an EKG machine connected to my heart with the traditional three leads coming to life above my head, in a monitor, just like in the hospital shows. I have a pulsimetry on my right index finger. That little machine measures the amount of oxygen saturation in my blood and would tell the nurses if I need more oxygen. The stress of the pain has made my heart beat very fast and the doctors are administering oxygen through a tube under my nose to try to slow it down. Another tube comes out of my nose and empties my stomach of any fluids that are there. That goes to a bottle that is filled with the green colored stuff being suctioned off my stomach. Then there is the regular IV, where the doctors are attempting to hydrate and feed me (and do not forget my friend the PCA). Finally, there is a Foley catheter coming from my bladder, to empty the urine as it collects. It is obviously difficult for me to move around with all these tubes, so a trip to the bathroom is the last thing I need. Had Bill said anything but that statement, I would have felt very disappointed. I am not a pretty sight. Bill knows how to flatter me into a blushing silence.

Now in my forties, aberrations have developed in my birthday suit, my elbows have worn thin; my complexion is no longer smooth and unblemished. My ass is collapsing, there are dimples on my thighs, hair is growing from my ears and nostrils, my eyes and mouth are surrounded by the deep crevices of laugh lines and my lipodystrophy has given me a barrel shaped torso and a typical *Cushinoid* belly that I can't control, no matter how conscientiously I diet.

This is the first time in as long as I could remember that none of that matters.

Sex is an appetite that must be fed everyday. Thousands of previous meals will not nourish your body tomorrow. Like the vampire that craves for his next drink of blood, we crave for our next victim. We may want to be in love for it to be meaningful. We might only enjoy it if it is with someone new every time as if by each new conquest a reaffirmation to our lack of self-esteem is made.

It may be with someone older, younger, our own sex or the opposite. It can be acted, staged, or spontaneous; oral, anal, vaginal, or mechanical (toys). It can be sensual, auditory (phone sex), or visual (porn— live or film). It can be by yourself, with someone else, or in a group. The tragedy of sex is that one can never know what this most intimate act of communication has actually said to the other people involved. You may not even be able to tell if the message, if received at all, is welcome.

Interestingly, there is a rift between my political correctness as an enlightened gay man (who can't believe that gay sex is wrong), and my reactionary libido. In as much as I recreate guilt and shame with every blow job and butt-fuck (needing a lynching for being a pervert who needs to be punished) I enjoy the shame that is integral to my desire; a fact that may appall the politically correct who insists that gay sex is a well adjusted and life-affirming expression of commitment.

The libido has an ancient memory and has not caught up with modern times. No matter how much we think of ourselves as "liberated", we exist in an artificial realm that bears no relation to the real world. Sex is, and will always be, a drama that will only exist in the theater of the bedroom. (Until the invention of the Internet, sex was confined to the bedroom. Now this labyrinth has created new paths as we explore the chat rooms of AOL, reducing sex to either the cyber space, or a quick anonymous visit. The mouse has turned into the new age bathhouse).

That is why when I met Bill (in the middle of this madness

and after feeling like a loser because, at age 39, I am unable to stay in a meaningful relationship) he fulfilled my sexual appetite. It is as if all of the above mentioned hungers are satisfied by his clever way of communicating his attraction to me.

One might say that I love Bill like a brother, even though brothers love each other either indifferently or grudgingly. My love is friendlier, more tentative and respectful. It is like a stream that seems as still as glass, until you impede it with your hand and it suddenly swells and sputters around your fingers. The impediments can make it visible.

That is why no shame or blame was attached to our sero-conversion. They are Aphrodite's spoils. There comes a time for every human when he must decide to risk his life, his fortune: short of grabbing the bull by the horns, nothing would do. For us, this is such a time. To fail this challenge would have made us nothing more than overgrown children, never amounting to anything. The only fear we feel is the realization that one day we may be faced with what is happening today – the realization that one of us would get sick before the other, and would be faced with a tragic loss. Our only regret is that with the advances in HIV therapy, we should not be here right now, facing this hospital admission and having to deal with our sense of mortality. Just as "the pill" had freed women to do with their bodies what they wanted, we feel antiretrovirals (those famous cocktails) make us invulnerable to the puritanical menace of this disease.

I cannot erase my past, just like I can't really save it.

Chapter 18

Jimmy was his name. He was five feet seven with classic, even features. Jimmy had corn blonde hair worn in a short haircut and shaved neckline, as if he had just walked out of the barbershop, and the talcum powder was still on his skin. He had a faint flush of sunburn that turned apple red instead of the shades of coffee I tanned. His family owned a sailboat and he was constantly out in the sun. He had ruddy cheeks with small and bright clear blue eyes that made me foolish with desire. It must have been the blue eyes: as I recalled that all of my friends had that trait, I realized that both Willie and Tito had blue eyes. It seemed that I was inevitably drawn to blue eyes, pale white skin and blonde or strawberry hair.

Jimmy was of North American descent, and spoke fluent English. I loved that because I wanted to practice my English and that gave me the perfect excuse to be near him. I always wanted to end up in the United States; I wanted to go to university there. I had placed high on my SAT scores and wanted the whole American cultural experience. It was as if by hanging out with Jimmy, I was living the American way of life. Jimmy was my American Dream.

Jimmy was very withdrawn. Some people have a wall around them, but it is usually because there is nothing inside the wall, and they don't wish to be found out. In Jimmy's case I sensed paradoxically the presence of enormous tenderness, a love of life and people just waiting to be awakened, so I was immediately drawn to him. He sat right in front of me in math class; he was forced to talk to me by chance of seat assignments. The beginning is the time for taking the most delicate care that the balances are correct. I needed to be careful in approaching him; I wanted to be accepted by him. When I finally managed to talk to him, I did not reveal my desire and attraction for him, but I managed to get an invitation to his sailboat. I had some experience with boating. Tito and Willie's family owned a motorboat (as did my cousins) and I was invited all the time to go out on the water with them. I had two good sea legs. It was quite easy to get invited when Jimmy was complaining of the fact that his family was short by a pair of hands for the next sailboat race. I saw the perfect opportunity and I immediately offered my services as a master sailor.

As Sunday arrived, I met Jimmy's family and they were very pleased with me. We had to travel to Fajardo, on the east coast, where they kept their boat at the marina. The trip consisted of the drive east from San Juan to Fajardo, a sailboat race from Fajardo to Icacos and the return drive. I was ecstatic; somewhere this day had passed a decision nexus in the deep unknown. I knew the time area surrounding them, but the here and now existed as a place of mystery. It was as though I had seen myself from a distance. I rose into the sky and looked down at all of us inside the car.

I could see that Jimmy's parents, the Jones, both medical doctors, were a great couple. Dr. Jones had come from Virginia to start a practice in Obstetrics and Gynecology twenty-five years before and was now settled and semi-retired as a professor in the Medical School at the University of Puerto Rico. He was in his early sixties and kept himself in good shape. The rheumy shine of his blue eyes, the cracked cheeks burned by the tropical sun, the rounded curve of his shoulders, and the thin set of his lips with the cranberry-colored stain of wine, gave his age.

His wife, *doctora* Jones, had a part time pediatric practice and was also a professor at the Medical School. She was a few years younger than her husband. There was a familiarity to her face, as if features out of endless dreams comforted me to tranquility. Dark shiny hair, carefully tailored by a headband, brown eyes that were gracefully placed in a full face as if someone had placed equally measured pearls in a strand. Her nose was covered with sun block; her lips had the perfect tone of ruby red lipstick; which was the only sign of make up. She was enjoyable and forthcoming, yet not inquisitive.

David, Jimmy's older brother, was a one-year-older copy of his brother and quite extroverted. You could see the family resemblance in the overhanging eyebrows and the rock planes of cheeks and bones.

After several rounds of exchange, details were exposed about the family. It turns out that Jimmy had gone to counseling because of his bashfulness, and his family was thrilled that Jimmy was making friends in school. All of them wanted to know about me and wanted to make me feel part of the clan. I gained some advantage in all this exchange of knowledge.

The weather was excellent for the race. The wind was strong and constant and the sea was calm. Not a cloud in the sky, and a pleasant eighty-five degrees. The marina was on a narrow road in Fajardo. It was just a quay with lots of boats and as you went out it was protected from the roughness of the Atlantic Ocean by a huge wave breaker. The Jones owned a 35-foot sailboat and they were entered in the 35 and under sailboat race. Icacos is a very narrow, long island about five miles east of Fajardo. It was a destination by itself. On any given weekend, you would see tons of boats anchored on its pristine, clear beaches with bathers enjoying the tropical weather. There would be the water skiers, the scuba divers and then the ones who just wanted to have a picnic at the beach, or enjoy the sun.

There were forty sailboats entered in the race and we were all lined up in front of the marina. As the sails were raised, I felt a sense of belonging with the sea. The easterly winds soon gave us a push and we were on our way. The thing about sailing is the tranquility. As soon as the wind carries the boat, the engines are shut off. Peace and quiet reign. To achieve sailing from point A to point B, the wind either needs to be at your back, or you must sail in a zigzag fashion and you must go back and forth. Being used to motorboats, that just go in a straight line, I was fascinated by the mastery of sailing and the constant change of direction. I learned to keep my head away from the tilting mast, and soon enjoyed the slant as the wind raised the boat to achieve speed.

As we approached Icacos, I was informed that there were judges posted to make sure we turned around a large buoy that was placed on the eastern side of the island. Turning counterclockwise would disqualify the boat. I was concerned that we were somewhere in the middle of the pack, but I was reassured by Dr. Jones that most of the boats ahead of us were larger boats that were not in our category and we were doing just fine. The sail back to Fajardo was as peaceful and enjoyable as the sail out. We all enjoyed beers or sodas and were pleasantly surprised to learn that we managed to finish second. The best they had ever placed was fourth! I had enjoyed myself so much; I would not have cared if we finished last. It was obvious I got part of the credit for the achievement. I was skilled with the ropes and proved myself useful in navigation. I suppose they would have been just as happy as long as I did not fall overboard or get seasick. The truth is that they were so pleased with the way the day went, that I got asked to sleep over with them and come back again another day.

The drive back to San Juan was enjoyable. To the east, the night was growing a glitter of incandescent colors. There was a beautiful show of lights in the dimmed sky. I was struck for words to describe the shattered red horizon as it gave in to the dark. The tropical sunset had touched life into our family day trip and was guiding us to the Jones's family stronghold.

The Jones had a two-story house in the Villamar sub-division near Carolina. Their four-bedroom house came complete with a pool table and in ground swimming pool on the first floor. Dr. Jones's study and the carport with room for their two cars completed the first floor. Lush tropical vegetation landscaped the garden. The second story contained the bedrooms, the kitchen, family room, living room, dining room, and a small library. I was fascinated by their house and would find any excuse to visit regularly. Even though I did not confide my attraction for Jimmy, our friendship grew. I started telling him stories about my family and school.

Not surprisingly, Jimmy started reciprocating. He became more extroverted and this pleased his family even more. I finally had the guts to tell him about my true feelings for him, and Jimmy just shrugged his shoulder and let me know that he had known from the first day but that it did not bother him in the least. He made a pact with me that we would sort this thing out together. He promised me that if he ever decided to satisfy any homosexual curiosity, I would be the first to know. He even went as far as to tell me I would be the only one with a chance to enjoy him. At the same time, he told me we would be each other's best men at each other's wedding when, and if, they happened.

As friendship with Jimmy blossomed, friendship with Tito and Willie wilted. Their family sold their house with swimming pool and all, and moved to another development. At school, I barely saw Tito or the "fort" friends. Since he was a year ahead, Tito was now heavily into dating girls, going out dancing at the school mixers, and trying out for swimming and other varsity sports. Luckily, at swimming we still shared our stories. I would become part of the "cool" crowd when I managed to place first in the tenth grade intramurals in the freestyle and backstroke events. I was finally becoming the jock I had always wanted to be.

Chapter 19

Our high school, San Ignacio, was holding our first intramural competition. The tenth grade was separated into the four homerooms: A, B, C, and D. Jimmy and I belonged to homeroom A. Homerooms entered participants into swimming and track and field events. I entered the 100-meter freestyle and 50-meter backstroke events. No one gave us a chance, since we were in the "smart" homeroom. San Ignacio was no exception when it came to stereotypes: they all assumed that smart kids were just no good at sports. In my case, they were right. Out of the water, I was unable to do much else.

The day of the intramurals we were experiencing typical tropical weather: hot and humid—the poolside thermometer read ninety degrees. We had a rain the night before and you could feel it evaporating just enough to get all that moisture up into the air and then to hang there. The heat from the sun would burn even those of us who were used to tanning. Everyone was wearing baseball caps, some had brought their sun block; the sun and heat are something you are always ready for in the tropics. As warm as it was, it was great for swimming: not a trace of wind to slow you down.

San Ignacio's Olympic pool was six lanes wide and twenty-five meters long. Since this was our first competition, no one knew the caliber of the swimmers. No one but me. There were no age brackets here today, so I swam only against people in my grade. Since I knew the best swimmers on the island and I knew the all kids in the tenth grade, I knew I could win my races.

I swam in the middle of the pool, lane three. As I looked to my right, I saw the only swimmer that could give me trouble. His name was José Esparza. He swam for a rival team: the

Caparra Country Club. He was a few inches taller, but I had
beaten him at all the meets we had swam this past year. There
were girls from the neighboring Academia María Reina at the
poolside. María Reina was our sister high school, and just as
San Ignacio was a young men's school and run by Jesuits, María
Reina was a young women's school and taught by nuns. It was
located at the other end of a huge city block and it was possible
to go from one school to the other along dirt paths through the
undeveloped land. The girls were on their free period and had
heard of the intramurals and came to see the events. The pool
had an atmosphere of celebration, so of course the Jesuits were
busy monitoring the socializing. All through the events I noticed Jimmy was talking to some girls. I recognized two in particular: the Rodríguez sisters.

    Jimmy was cheering at the sidelines when I jumped into the
water. I had a very easy swim, and not only did I win the race,
but also managed to break the minute for the one-hundred meters
freestyle, a feat I had never done before. It was a much easier
win than when I had placed fourth and qualified to go to Miami.
It did make a great difference that the other good swimmers went
to other schools. I repeated a win in the fifty meters backstroke.
Jimmy was there to cheer me again. He showed an unusual
enthusiasm to the point of leading the wave of cheers for our
grade. My show and tell experience had overshadowed any athletic ability I could ever be capable of; I just caught most of my
classmates by surprise. As unexpected as my wins were to my
classmates, I was more perplexed by Jimmy's first words after
my win.

    "I got us dates for the School dance," Jimmy blurted out to
me as I went into the locker room to change. "Lula Rodriguez
and her sister Beba. They have agreed to come to the dance with
us."
    I went to the locker room and changed out of my swimming
trunks. My field of vision full of naked boys distracted me from

Jimmy's announcement. I was having a hard time trying to ignore the kid to my left. He had a huge pecker and I was seriously trying not to stare, and failing. As I thought I would get excited, I turned my concentration to the school dance. I knew there was a dance coming up; I knew that we could invite girls if we wanted. That certainly calmed my excitement and my erection. I just did not know anything about girls.

When I met Jimmy back outside, I pretended to be excited. As much as I was afraid to damage my relationship with Jimmy, I was terrified of asking any girl. The Rodríguez sisters were older. I wanted to go to the school dance but I would have been happier to go without a date. I would have preferred just to go with Jimmy and meet girls there.

"That's great!" I heard the words come out of my mouth of their own volition as my thoughts were on what lay ahead. At least Jimmy had taken care of the asking.

"I will be at your house at nine on Friday then we will meet the girls at the dance" as we walked to the track. "I will need to spend the night at your place. There is no need for my mother to have to drive back and forth the same night. See if you can have your mother drive me home the next day."

"I will take care of it, consider it a done deal; what will you wear?"

"Jeans and a Polo–shirt, do you think that will be all right?" We had to repeat our answers as we were overpowered by the crowd's roar. One of our own classmates had surprised everyone by winning the one-hundred-meter dash.

Having never gone to a dance, I had no idea what to wear but I agreed with Jimmy as if I was an authority.

"Cool. I'll see you Friday."

The intramurals were over and we had placed second out of

four. I had also gotten an invitation to my first dance; and gotten my first date. I was unsure as to who my date was. I tried to sort these things out, but as usual, I was confused. In the end, I thought it was a good day: I had won my races, I was going on a double date with my best friend and, best of all, he was spending the night in my room.

That night I had a fantastic dream. I dreamt I was in a glass house. Every room was made out of glass: glass windows, glass doors, glass walls, glass ceiling, glass roof, and glass floor. The furniture was transparent; I could see through it all: sofas, chairs, beds, tables, lamps, appliances, stereos, T.V., refrigerator, stove, oven, microwave.... I was very concerned because there was no privacy. I could see straight into the bathroom. I kept thinking that at least someone should have thought of putting some curtains there. I made a mental note so I could tell the owner.

I went three steps into a room, dropped my backpack onto the floor. I heard a door close behind me and studied the place some more. This room ran about eight feet before it hit another glass wall. There were small paintings hanging to my left about six feet away, so I assumed there was another wall there. A low desk with a glass of milk full of bubbles occupied the center of the room. Four chairs, all translucent, ringed what seemed to be a table. A faint anomaly in the room's air current told me there was another exit to my right, behind clear filing cabinets.

Then I saw Jimmy. He was there with the Rodríguez sisters. I tried to say hello, but it was clear he was busy and unable to hear me through the walls. I could see Jimmy through the glass as he was making out with Beba. I was getting so excited watching my friend go about his business that I did not notice that there was Lula going down on me. They were all able to see me too. The Rodríguez sisters were not virgins and they wanted to completely enjoy Jimmy and me. I saw my friend undress and immediately got excited. Lula thought it was because of her. I tried asking Jimmy for help, but I did not want to interrupt his fun. Besides, I knew he could not hear me. Jimmy was having a good time, but I had no idea what to do with Lula. I could see him through the transparency of the walls and, suddenly, panic evolved into erotic pleasure. There were mixed emotions of guilt; guilt from exposure and lack of privacy, and shame; shame from the acting out of my sexual fantasy, shame from acting it out with the wrong party. I awoke to a wet pillow not knowing if people were able to see through my glass dream.

I could not help but to feel that in my past, every experience before this night had become like sand curling in an hourglass. Piling up on the bottom of the glass bit by bit until there was a mound of sand – not a solid mass, but a mass of pieces indistinguishable from the whole.

Chapter 20

"**I** am so glad that we are doing this outside of confession, Father." I said, as I was working up the courage to tell father Eduardo the developments with my new friend. He had agreed to meet in an empty classroom on one of my free periods to hear my confession.

Father Eduardo sat across from me and threw back his hood to reveal his neatly styled hair in their silky short waves and his large Ray-Ban gold sunglasses. Why he was not in his smartly tailored black jacket was beyond me. His hair was combed straight back from a high, narrow forehead. He had mysterious brown eyes, and rubbed a scar beside his nose. He was tall and slender, but something about him emanated maternal warmth of an atypical character. I had never before seen him in this hood and once again, he had assessed me from the doorway before joining me, as if reluctant to enter or leave the room.

"It has been eight weeks since we last talked." I continued. "I have not acted on my impure thoughts but there is someone new in my life."

"Have you met someone new?" He was inquisitive.

"Yes, Father"

"Here in school?"

"Yes, Father."

"Tell me about him."

I proceeded to inform Father Eduardo of my new friend, Jimmy, of our new friendship and I shared my feelings.

"Do you have fantasies about Jimmy?"

"Yes, Father."

"Go on."

"Well, it is not like the usual fantasies like a few years ago. I really care for Jimmy. I think I love him"

"Do you want to get physical with him?"

"No, I don't think so. With Jimmy, I feel like he fulfills me in many other ways. I feel like I can tell him anything and he would still like me."

"Have you had erotic dreams about him?"

"Yes, but it is different." I was unable to contain my emotions as I told the good father about last night's dream in the glass house.

"I dreamt I was in a glass house. Every room was made out of glass. The furniture was transparent; you could see through it all. I could see straight into the bathroom. I kept thinking that at least someone should have privacy there." I continued to tell the good father my dream.

"Have you told Jimmy about this?"

"Yes, Father."

"What was his reaction?"

"I may as well have given him the baseball scores, or the weather report. He had no reaction."

"How did that make you feel?"

"Fine, I guess. He still likes being my friend. He wants to go to the school dance with me."

"As your date?"

"I don't think so."

"Would you like him to desire you sexually?"

"I don't know, Father." I was lost for words. "I don't know how to react to him"

"Would you like it to be different?"

"Different how?"

"Would you like it if your feelings for Jimmy were not considered wrong? Would you like it if you did not feel guilty about it?"

"I don't know how to feel guilty anymore. This should not

be wrong, should it?"

"I do not make the rules. Do you feel guilty?"

" I don't know anymore."

Silence. After a moment of ecstatic stillness, Father Eduardo's melodic voice interrupted my thoughts:

"All I see around me is a desire for love, the hope of love, the assumption that it exists. I actually see very little love. Perhaps between parents and children, perhaps at the onset of infatuation, like between you and Jimmy. Most of the time, people go out looking for love and end up with sex instead. Sometimes, like you, they cannot even get sex. People want sex, dream about sex, and look for sex far more than they can have it. I think people looking for Love should be grateful for a reliable supply of sex, because even that is hard to find. Do an act of contrition and go to communion."

"Thanks, Father"

"By the power vested in me by the Holy Spirit I absolve you of all your sins in the name of the Father, the Son, and the Holy Ghost, Amen. See you next week. Why don't you have Jimmy talk to me too? It might help."

"Yes, Father."

Math class was a series of theorems and theories that I preferred to ignore. I had to deal with the fact that my best friend and I were going on a double date. My dream of having Jimmy all to myself was shattered, but I was trying to be reasonable and cover my losses. I knew the Rodríguez sisters. They were a year ahead of us at María Reina. They lived in the neighborhood and their parents knew my parents. They had seen my swimming and knew I had won two events. Who knows, perhaps I had something to offer to the evening.

Besides, and this was the best part of it all, Jimmy would have to spend the night at my house and I would be the one to sleep with him that evening.

Chapter 21

Friday had arrived after Thursday, right on schedule. It was the night of the dance and two hours before I was supposed to meet Jimmy, I caught myself trying on another outfit. My room was full of clothes thrown everywhere. There were three pair of jeans on the desk, there were twelve shirts, including my favorite t-shirts and polo shirts, (you know, the ones with the alligator), all spread along my bed. Then there were the three pairs of shoes, two pairs of tennis shoes and one pair of topsiders, the ones that made me look so good when I went sailing with Jimmy. It is amazing how that works: pants, shirt, shoes—the possible permutations of combinations is 108. (3 x 3 x 12— those being the articles I had narrowed it down to wear). I had only run through about half of my possibilities and was still not satisfied. My biggest concern was that I would not have time to try all of my wardrobe options.

I heard voices; Jimmy's mother was visiting Mami. Jimmy had arrived and would soon be in my bedroom and I had yet to pick an outfit. I looked at what I was wearing, this particular blue jean and white Lacoste polo shirt was on me for the third time. To top it off, I was also wearing my lucky topsiders, the ones from our big sailing day. I took it as a sign from the gods and settled on them.

Since neither of the parties involved in the dance tonight drove, Jimmy and I had agreed to meet at my house. Jimmy's mother would drop him here and we would walk to the dance, since my house was just down from the party. Because we would be leaving the party after midnight, it was agreed that Jimmy would spend the night with me and Mami would drive him home the next day. We were to meet our dates at the dance – their dad would drive them. That gave me the extra time alone with my friend Jimmy.

It was a beautiful clear night. For Puerto Rican standards, it was on the cool side, perhaps in the low 70's. It was perfect for the short walk up to the dance with Jimmy. It was just after nine in the evening, and the sky looked black and cold. I immediately contrasted this sky with the brightness on the sand and the golden sun on the blue clear water of the Atlantic, as when I last had been out with Jimmy.

Jimmy had opted for a very confident casualness. He wore the standard blue jeans, with a light orange Lacoste shirt. He seemed to float on his brand new pair of sneakers as he addressed me about the evening.

"Are you as excited as I am? We're going out with girls together. We will not even need to worry about the chaperones."

Ah, the chaperones! The Puerto Rican custom of chaperoning had been fulfilled since each sister was chaperoning the other. Lula was the younger of the Rodríguez sisters. Although her beauty was a bit ethnic (for my taste), most would agree that she was very good looking. She was thirteen, one year younger than her sister. She came in a very attractive white dress, and was very simply made up: artificially blue eyes and a black mane of hair, elaborately feathered. She was short, but just how short was not really determined until her high heels were off at the end of the evening. These added a few inches to her height, which made her the perfect height for me, just to my shoulder. Beba was an older copy of her sister, and they were dressed and made up in a similar way. I was completely truthful as I met Mr. Rodriguez and promised that I would be a perfect gentleman with his daughter. We had arrived at the dance at the same time. It was a good thing, since Mr. Rodríguez refused to leave until he checked out the space and met the two young gentlemen that were courting his family treasures. He was reluctant to leave until he had met both Jimmy and me. After deciding on curfew, he left the party making sure he had intimidated us with a mean glare.

Lula was quite inquisitive and wanted to know all about my swimming adventures. She was awed by the relay story in Miami and was probing about my plans to go to college in the United States. She was also thinking of doing so, and had her mind set on Boston College.

The dance had started at nine in the evening. When our foursome arrived at nine-thirty, fashionably late of course, the music could already be heard from outside the house. Couples were at the dance floor; "*salsa*" and "*merengue*" beats were competing with the slow paced "*bolero*" for takers. While the faster beats were popular with the girls, the slower music was the big draw for the boys because it gave them a chance to get close. Then there were the vigilant eyes of the party chaperones that every so often would separate the wild lovers when they were dancing unacceptably close to each other.

The decorations were redundant. Jorge's house, where the dance was held, was beyond reproach. Further north on Geranium street, it was what every child dreamt about. It had a beautiful terrace where the jukebox was placed and enough room for fifty or sixty people to dance. It had an Olympic sized swimming pool, left from the days Jorge was a swimming champion. (He had retired at age thirteen after winning all the freestyle events). There was a basketball court, a tennis court and manicured gardens with surrounding benches, marble and granite on the floors, a bathroom in the pool cabana, a bathroom in the terrace and three more bathrooms inside the house. The girls appropriated the inside bathrooms and a chaperone was set inside to guard all activity in them.

There were alcoholic beverages, but like at my own home, I noticed that there were adults supervising the serving. No one was served if they were considered drunk. Jimmy was careful with his alcohol consumption, so I followed his lead. I knew that the only time excessive alcohol was tolerated was on the student drinking escapades or "*bebelatas*" which were traditionally single-sexed. Puerto Ricans are the number one consumers of hard liquor (mostly rum) in the world and we start our drinking early. Unlike the "*norteamericanos*", not only is it socially accepted, but also it is encouraged and supervised. My parents have been stressing the importance of responsible drinking for as long as I can remember.

I found out that Jimmy was a good dancer. Even more important, I found out that I was also a good dancer. Once Jimmy and the girls lured me to the dance floor, I found out I had moves that I did not know I was capable of. I actually was enjoying myself so much that I didn't notice the passage of time. The girls had a midnight curfew and Jimmy informed us that it was almost time to leave. It was eleven thirty and I had not bothered to look at my watch—not even once!!

Jimmy immediately took Beba to a bench in the back gardens. I followed suit and sat Lula on the bench across. Jimmy placed his arm around Beba, and subsequently I did the same around Lula. I held it there for what seemed an eternity and when we left, I had lost all sensation in my arm. I also noticed when we stood up that Jimmy had a bulge in his pants. I didn't understand why he would get a bulge for Beba and not for me, but I was so happy to be around Jimmy that I was a willing participant when it got to be time for the goodnight kiss. Mr. Rodriguez was back at the door, just in time for Jimmy to recover from the excitement of the rendezvous and for the girls to have rearranged their hair and make up.

Jimmy and I were about to start the walk to my house. We were just discussing what a magnificent evening it had been for everyone. Just as we were outside the Garcia's door, this student by the name of José Esparza (the swimmer I had beaten at the tenth grade intramurals) who had probably consumed a few drinks too many and I supposed wanted to have some fun before going home was yelling:

"Hey, *Maricones* (faggots)! Are you going home to sleep together?"

I was finally able to react and grabbed Esparza's hand closest to me and said: "No one fights with my friend without hitting me first."

Jimmy was quick and grabbed the other hand and repeated the same words:

"No one fights with my friend without hitting me first."

Someone else was leaving so, distracted from the events at hand, we all took a step back and Jimmy and I continued on our way home after tucking our shirts back into our pants. About three steps down, we both gave each other a high five and joked about it all the way to my house.

It did occur to me that the only way Mr. Esparza could have read my mind was that he had thought about it himself, but I was too inexperienced in these matters at the time to make any sense of it all.

We were in my room; Mami had arranged a spare mattress on the floor where Jimmy was to sleep. The excitement of the evening had drained both of us, and I, as disappointed as I was that I did not get to have a nice talk with Jimmy, was relieved by the sweet sensation brought by a deep sleep.

That night I had a happy dream. I dreamt that I was married and that I had a nice house in Santa Maria filled with children. I had a nice terrace and a swimming pool with a cabana. Funny thing, Jimmy was there and there were no children. There was no wife for that matter. It was just Jimmy and I. We were in bed together as man and wife and I woke up excited and with a huge erection. Jimmy was silently sleeping on the floor next to my bed and my commotion woke him.

"Perhaps this dating business is not as hard as I thought," I said as I moved around and tried to regain sleep.

All I got back was Jimmy complaining that his arm was asleep because the floor was too hard. I noticed he did not have an erection as he turned around and next thing I knew it was morning.

Chapter 22

"Father, Father we need to talk!" I could hardly contain my excitement.

"Sure, meet me after class, as usual"

I felt I had to tell my mentor of all that was going on. I was beginning to convince myself of some sort of normality; perhaps even a life with girls was not as bad as I had thought.

"I was here last Thursday and you asked me to come back after the dance on Friday" I began.

"So how was the dance?"

"It was better than I expected. This business with girls is very easy. Especially with Jimmy's help."

"How did Jimmy help?"

"I found out that I could dance almost as good as Jimmy. The girls had a midnight curfew and Jimmy informed us that it was almost time to leave. I had not checked the time at all! At eleven thirty, not even once…!"

"How were your feelings toward your date?"

"When Jimmy took Beba to a bench in the back gardens, I followed suit and sat with Lula on the bench across. Jimmy placed his arm around Beba and I did the same around Lula. I also noticed when we stood up that Jimmy had a bulge in his pants. I didn't quite understand that, but I was so happy to be around him that I did not care."

"Did you have any impure thoughts about your date?"

"No, I could never do that. I think I could marry her. She was so nice, I feel she could be the mother of my children."

"You want children?"

"I have to have children. The family name dies with me unless I do. So I figure I need to have at least three or four sons."

"How about Jimmy? Where do you see him?"

"He will always be there. He is my best friend and I think I could do anything as long as he was there. So, after the dance, Jimmy and I were about to start the walk to my house – he spent the night instead of going all the way home. We were just talking about what a great night it had been for everyone. Just as we were outside the Garcia's door, this guy José, who was drunk and I guess wanted to have some fun before going home was yelling:

'Hey *maricones*! Are you going home to sleep together?'"

"So how did that make you feel?"

"I felt exposed."

I told him all about the dream, then "I woke up excited and with an erection. Jimmy was silently sleeping on the floor next to my bed and I accidentally woke him up."

"What did he say when he saw you excited?"

"All he said was that his arm was asleep because the floor was too hard. I noticed he didn't have an erection anymore as he turned around and next thing I knew I was waking up the next morning."

"Do you think you two will continue being friends through college? Have you thought about where you are going to college?"

"No. Jimmy wants to be a doctor like his father, but I am so good in Math that I thought I should be an engineer."

"Does that mean that you two will not be going to college together?"

"I hadn't given it any thought. I guess I should talk this over with him soon."

"You do that. Let me know if I can be of help."

"Thanks. Father."

"I will see you soon. I feel a kind of elation. I believe you have crossed a barrier into an unknown territory. It feels as if I can sense darkness ahead, yet nothing is revealed to the inner eye. The next step you will take will plunge you into a well…or into the trough of a wave where the future is invisible. Your life landscape has undergone a profound shifting. We will need to talk again soon."

"See you, and thanks again" as I left, as confused as when I started the conversation.

Chapter 23

As I approached my sixteen candles, I had asked Jimmy to coach me for my driver's permit. We had become inseparable. Jimmy was very supportive and took me to the driving course in Isla Verde. Mami's old Toyota station wagon was the setting for innumerable driving lessons. We started at my house in Santa Maria, and worked our way onto the road, then the trip to Jimmy's house and finally the actual test course. On my birthday plus one (my birthday had fallen on Sunday that year) I became the proud owner of a driver's license. And I had passed the test with the exact score Jimmy had predicted.

With my newfound self-confidence and Jimmy's coaching, I finally started noticing girls. I was particularly fond of Rosa. We both swam for the local swim team, and we could talk about anything.

Rosa was a year older than I, she was almost as tall, but she also had those sky blue eyes that I so admired in all my past dreams. Her light brown, long hair covered her square face like a hat would cover mine. Rosa was a breaststroker and she was good enough to make the Puerto Rican National team. We shared lots of time together at swim practice, and she had noticed me on our trip to Miami Springs (she was part of that team).

I started talking progressively more with her, and even got Rosa to agree to go to the movies with me. She lived in Santa Maria. I longed for walks with this woman. We would drive out to Old San Juan and talk until the hours of the evening abruptly collided with Rosa's curfew.

Old San Juan was the local hangout for teenagers. Near Calle del Cristo there was a bar called Tia Maria, where we were never carded and were able to drink as long as we were able to pay. There were also dining spots. In front of plaza San José, where Juan Ponce de Leon's statue was erected, there was a little dive called Amadeus. A pair of brothers whom everyone knew as Cheo and Daniel owned it, and it served the best Puerto Rican food (yes, there actually is such a thing as Puerto Rican food) in the area. I loved taking Rosa to these spots, and for dessert we would go down to El Convento Hotel, near the Plaza de la Rogativa to get frozen, fruit ice. We would then climb the old walls at the Rogativa plaza and watch the stars and the harbor. We would just lie there for hours. Or until curfew. I was overwhelmed by the smells that were heavier than air; odors thrown out onto the old cobblestone streets would stay present until washed away by the gentle tropical rains. I became aware of the inconsistency of nature. A puddle of light down below the centuries-old walls of the city – the ocean at low tide. Only the sound of the sea breaking on the reefs below would shatter the silence.

And here I was, with this woman who was making me feel as happy as any of my prior fantasies had. And she was real! I sensed a racing of my consciousness that I could not escape. There was an influx of data, a sharpened clarity, and a cold precision to my awareness. I would sit with Rosa by the old walls, looking at the clear starry sky, and I would give myself to the whole experience. A strange awareness flowed into a timeless plane where I could visualize the future: I could see myself in a life with this woman; married, having children, going to work…all my experiences of the past, all my experiences of this present moment, and this vision of the future would combine in a way that permitted me to see time become space.

There was a danger of overflowing my senses. The contrast between the old city and my new life was supplying too much data for me to comprehend. I felt a need to trap my surroundings in their present form in order to stop my mind's wanderings. For the first time I felt a crossroads within my life, a boiling of possibilities, wherein the minutest action—the wrong word, the wrong move—would move a gigantic lever within my world. I saw all my emotions towards this woman, blend and compete with all my prior emotions. The slightest change in my infatuation would create a vast shift in the pattern of my life.

The vision made me want to freeze into immortality, but this too, would carry many different consequences. Countless consequences, some of which would take a lifetime to decipher. A sill of silver pushed above the horizon to our left: the moon was rising. As it lifted into view it drew a new image: I saw Rosa's face, the pits of her beautiful blue eyes. The familiarity of that face, the features out of numberless dreams shocked me to stillness. When I finally snapped out of the trance I realized that it was time to leave.
Curfew.

That night I had my first heterosexual wet dream. We were at the swimming pool where we had our regular workouts, but only Rosa and I were there. There was no one else. At first we were in our bathing suits, but later there were no clothes between us as I was holding my beloved Rosa and, as we held each other, I got aroused. The pleasure increased and I saw myself as a little sperm – like when Woody Allen played a sperm in *"Everything you always wanted to know about sex..."*—a sperm that was about to leave my body and swim towards Rosa's body. I liked being that little sperm. I enjoyed the swimming in the pool and I could see Rosa's crotch as I was going closer to it. I swam to the right, and then to the left, yet everywhere I swam, I saw my beloved's body. It was impossible to lose track of my destination. As I approached her beautiful body, I sensed an arousal I had never felt before. Pleasure and excitement never felt before. I awoke as I came. I was, for the first time, able to wake from a wet dream and feel like I was normal!

I could not wait to tell father Eduardo. It was a great effort to make time the next day, but I was able to get an appointment.

"Forgive me father for I have sinned." I started with joy to tell my friend of my newfound normality. "It has been one week since my last confession," I continued. "I believe I have good news! I have lusted for a girl: I think I love my girlfriend Rosa."

All I could hear after that was a cacophonous laughter from father Eduardo, with Jimmy joining in from somewhere. The more I tried to convince them that I really wanted to have sex with Rosa, the louder they laughed. As tears started rolling down my cheeks, I awoke to the realization that I had not talked to anyone and that it was all a dream. I could not wait to tell my mentor about it.

My curiosity was raising my anxiety level. It was as if my sense of reality could not be trusted. All that I once held as truth would have to be contested until proven true again and again. I had gone to a fun house early as a kid and stood in front of two parallel mirrors. As I tried to find the end of the images self-projecting into infinity, I realized that the only real image was the one that was not being reflected: mine. Seeing my "self of selves" created infinite permutations. Reflections of reflections ad infinitum: all that my senses could pick, the hundreds of vision of me, were not real.

For the first time in my life, I realized that my senses play tricks on my mind and I need to be able to detect reality from reflected images. As I dealt with the concepts of fantasy— **fan·ta·sy**— (f?n?t?-s?, -z?) and reality— **re·al·i·ty** (r?-?l??-t?), I became utterly confused as to what is "that which exists objectively." Since my psyche was strong enough to form capricious, fantastic, images so real that I was unable to distinguish one from the other, how could I ever be sure of anything again?

Not just in my mind, but also in my body. I could sense

many experiences as if I had just awakened, knowing I had dreamed, but unable to recall my dreams. This dream-stuff called up knowledge that I felt I would never possess. It felt like there was *someone else* in my mind, because I could never be the one who had *those* feelings

Chapter 24

"**J**uan, why are you so excited?" Father Eduardo could tell that there was something wrong with me. I just wanted to make sure that I was not dreaming again, so I told him what had happened the night before.

Once again, I told him my dream. "I woke up as I reached orgasm. I was, for the first time, able to wake from a wet dream and feel like I was normal!"

"Then the dream shifted I saw myself telling you: 'Forgive me father for I have sinned.'

'It has been one week since my last confession,' I continued. 'I believe I am finally a normal teenager. I have lusted for a girl: I think I love my girlfriend Rosa.'

"All I could hear after that was you and Jimmy laughing. The more I tried to convince you that I really wanted to have sex with Rosa, the louder you laughed. As tears started rolling down my eyes, I woke up to realize that I had not talked to anyone and that it was all a dream. I couldn't wait to tell you about it."

"Juan, are you worried that your dream has any connotation on your sexuality? Or are you upset because you are unsure as to your feelings for Rosa?"

As I heard the good father ask me these things, a sense of relief ran through my body. I was dealing with my feelings for a girl; and not just a girl, but also, a very special girl. I suppose I should be thankful to both Jimmy, who had introduced me to dating, and to the good father who had been patient to listen to my evolution into this special relationship, but at the moment all I wanted was to get closer to Rosa. I wanted to be able to tell her all these things.

"Father, I don't think it is quite that simple. Some people never do anything. Life just happens to them. They get by with a little more than a kind of persistence, and they resist with anger and resentment anything that might lift them out of their false tranquility. I am lost here and do not comprehend where this is taking me."

"Juan, love. But guard against it. Know that love is deep within the human genetic makeup, a safety net to insure continuation of the species. Please pray that your sins may be forgiven."

"Yes, Father. Thanks for seeing me."

I was so immersed in deep thought all through the day that I was unaware that it was time for our daily workout.

As we were leaving swimming practice that afternoon, it happened. It happened so fast I had no clue it had happened at all. After a long day at school, we had convened for swimming practice as usual. As I had been doing for the last few weeks, I spent all the time trying to get close to Rosa. Even though she was a breaststroker and I was not, I had started practicing my breaststroke just so that I could be close to the girl of my dreams.

Elena had noticed the change in my practice routine and asked me why I was spending so much time with this girl Rosa. I felt honesty was at hand, and replied that Rosa was my girlfriend. I hadn't noticed until it was too late, but from the corner of my eyes, I sensed Rosa's presence.

That night we went out and I took Rosa to our corner in Plaza Rogativa. I told Rosa my feelings for her. You could say that I did not leave any details out. I told her about how she made me feel, I told her how I had dreamed about her, I told her how I could see us raising a family together...I even used the "love" word. We had a great time and we were out until her curfew. As usual, she gave me a goodnight kiss.

I went home and never gave it a second thought, but the next day Rosa was with a much older swimmer. Mickey was two years older than I, and he was holding Rosa's hand in the pool. He was a good swimmer and being older, he was taller, by about three inches. He had black hair that he combed straight back (when it was not wet) from a high narrow forehead. He had those Latin brown eyes that were commonplace in the country, and already had the shadow of a moustache that he very carefully didn't shave. To be perfectly honest, I thought he was very handsome. I was unable to get close to Rosa and I felt that she was avoiding me all throughout the workout.

Finally, after what seemed an eternity I got Rosa alone and confronted her with my questions. Confused, I asked Rosa what was going on. She chose her words as if she had been rehearsing her speech: she told me that I was a great guy, but that the age difference was going to be a problem. She felt she needed an older guy, someone with more experience, and besides, we could still be friends. Rosa told me that she had never had a better friend than me and was sure to remember me forever.

I did not know if I should feel upset or relieved. I felt that I should not think too much about the value of my fate: I would run the risk of being rejected by it. I had no idea of how to deal with the situation. I was unsure if I was hurt by Rosa's rejections, or if I felt jealous because she was getting the handsome Mickey and I was not getting my Jimmy. Was it the dream of creating offspring with her, as if it was a profound drive shared by all creatures that are faced with mortality—the drive to seek immortality through progeny? Or was it something deeper and more meaningful? Was I really in love with her, or was I just running through the motions because that was what was demanded by peer pressure? (The need to carry on my family name).

As I asked Jimmy for advice, we would walk random, empty, walks under a wasted sky, but we could not come up with any meaningful explanations. Calling up memories of my Rosa created a magical universe where my abilities were amplified beyond any of my expectations. No atoms existed in that magical universe, only waves and awesome movements all over the place. I had finally erased all of my barriers built out of belief and understanding. This universe I created was transparent. I could see through it without any interfering picture screens upon which to project its wonderful forms. My magical universe reduced me to a core of active imagination where my own image making abilities were the only picture screen upon which anything could be projected or sensed. I realized that my past with Rosa was not a complete loss, that her memory could be used to enlighten me. I felt I had my first chance to learn from experience.

Alone, without help, that first night in my room, I felt that a part of my existence was sifting though my hands. Dreams were not coming to me. The next morning, when it all finally sank in, I sensed that what I had wanted so desperately to understand was also sifting through my hands.

Chapter 25

Senior year at San Ignacio. My last year of high school. Even though I was only 16, I was so busy filling out applications for colleges that the realization I might lose Jimmy had not entered my mind. I had chosen M. I. T. as my top choice, and then settled for Tulane University and Holy Cross College as my safety nets. I had to apply to University of Pennsylvania, since my father had graduated from Wharton School of Business. Jimmy had chosen Princeton as his first choice, and was open minded to other options. Overnight I had to decide between being a doctor and going to school with my friend, or being a engineer, and alone.

Our student counselor, Father Roberts was a nice, middle-aged priest, who to this day probably is coloring his hair fiery golden red. He was average height, slim and kept himself in shape. He loved to swim in the school pool and rumor has it that he would bring all kinds of male guests to swim with him. But, since priests take a vow of celibacy, no one gave it a second thought.

As part of career day, the good father had started showing films on different careers and he brought a film of a birth. I remember clearly the sight of the birth canal opening and the woman trying to expel the baby. I was doing fine until I saw the head of the baby rip the vaginal tissues and blood poured out. At that time, I excused myself. One look at me and no questions were asked. The good father let me go out to get some air.

I weighed my options and came to the only reasonable conclusion: I decided that I was going to be a doctor like Jimmy, and changed my first choice to Princeton. In as much as the sight of blood was nauseating to me, the absence of my Jimmy would have caused me much more pain. I wanted to follow him to college at any cost. If being a doctor was what it took, I would manage somehow. I felt with Jimmy around I would be able to overcome my fear of blood: just like I had overcome my fear of girls. And besides, there were so many kinds of doctors that I never had to watch a head come out of a vagina again.

In future years, and when asked why I had chosen to become a doctor, I rarely admitted to this moment in my life and would choose the usual: "I just wanted to help my fellow man."

I talked it over with Jimmy and we both decided to apply to Princeton as our first choice. Johns Hopkins University would be our close second and we would keep Holy Cross and Tulane as our safety net. Jimmy had talked about New Orleans and that was why I had Tulane in my college list to begin with.

Since we were too busy, I with swimming, and Jimmy with dating girls, we could only talk in class. This caused some trouble. Mr. Flanagan, the English teacher, had to separate us because we were always talking and not paying attention to him. I was very upset at this development and the next time that Jimmy was scolded for talking in class, I told Mr. Flanagan that I wanted Jimmy back next to me; separating us solved nothing.

While I did not get Mr. Flanagan to move Jimmy back, I did get other students to start talking about us as if we were a couple. Unknown to me this affected Jimmy. It was one thing to know that I had an uncontrollable hormonal passion for him, but it was another to have all our classmates aware of this information.

Jimmy became withdrawn, and for the first time in our friendship, started avoiding me.

It started with his new friend Miguel. Miguel was another classmate that lived very close to Jimmy. He was our age, our height; dark features with thin black hair engulfing a round face that seemed to have no special features. He liked sailing, and his family had a sailboat.

Suddenly, he was substituting for me at the sailing races and Jimmy was too busy to hang out with me. My phone calls were not returned. To me, these actions were like moments ticking away. I could feel time flowing past me, the moments never to be recaptured. I sensed a need for a course of action, but felt powerless to move.

This thought was both reassuring and frustrating. I could feel a demanding race of consciousness within me; a terrible purpose, and I knew that no small action would go without an equal but opposite reaction. I was gathering weight and momentum for the confrontation. I could ignore everything and continue in the present path, or I could confront my friend and risk alienating him even more.

The day of the confrontation came. It happened after school, it happened at Jimmy's house. I drove to Villamar and rang his doorbell. It was a wrenching sensation within my awareness, as though trying to grasp some thing in motion and render it motionless...

"Jimmy, we need to talk." I started the flow of action and emotions.

"Juan, I don't want to hang around you anymore." And he just walked away.

For no reason I could explain, and this bothered me more than the sensation, I suddenly shuddered. I turned away to hide my confusion and was just in time to see the sunset. A violent calamity of color spilled across the cloudy Puerto Rican sky as the sun dipped beneath the horizon. It began to rain – or so I thought. The rain was coming from my eyes.

I inhaled deeply. The smell of rain! I thought about what had just transpired and the essentials of life were amplified and smoothed by the falling water. Today's rain was different. It left an unbending after-smell I could taste. I did not like it. It carried a resentful message of life. I wanted all rain stopped and locked away. There was not a message of cleansing, it no longer gentled and brought new life. It had an inescapable feeling of change.

I drove manically home trying to make sense of the day. Night was beginning to utter its shadows along the distant countryside and the beach. I relived my friendship with Jimmy in one glorious instant. Bits and pieces of my precious moments with Jimmy registered on my memory. Somehow, I felt the differences as though they were physical, and the force of that one line "Juan, I don't want to hang around you anymore," made me come through a narrow door into the present.

The variables and connotations of this one line came back to plague me. My new understanding told me that there were too many swiftly compressed decisions to be made ahead, yet there was no clear path ahead to show itself. Variable piled upon variable, it was like a gigantic rock thrown into a river, creating maelstroms in the current around it. It was as the first rock in an avalanche; once the critical force is met, there is no putting it back the way it was. All the knowledge of countless experiences hinted at the strongest currents of the future and the strings of decisions that guided them. This was both real and now. Anything could tip the future here, but the irreversible force of events had been unleashed. I was to start a new life and there was no room for Jimmy in it even if he had wanted to be.

With the new pain came an odd clarity. I found myself capable of removing my awareness of any intrusion from the outside world. It was as if that pain was happening to someone else. I had found a heaven where nothing could touch me. There was no pain, no agony. As I accepted reports about these sensations, I shifted them to another world.

That night I dreamt. I tried to open my eyelids but, in my dream, they would not obey me. Suddenly, it all came flooding in on me that Jimmy had rejected me. I could relive the episode from this afternoon, identify where it had taken place and, as if floating above, I saw both Jimmy and myself in the scene. I felt that another person was sharing my flesh, pre-empting my movements. I allowed myself to follow the workings of this new person. It could order me to blink, fart, gasp, shit, piss—anything. It could command my body as though I had no thinking part in my own behavior. I was relegated to the role of an observer.

I heard an artificial voice: "Juan, I don't want to hang around you anymore." I saw scars at the sides of the jaw. There was the look of a mechanical robot where Jimmy used to be. An almost neckless head attached to thick shoulders, arms that seemed oddly jointed at both shoulders and elbows, legs appeared to swing only from the hips. I stood motionless now, but remembered why I had gone to Villamar.

"Jimmy, we need to talk." "Jimmy, we need to talk." "Jimmy, we need to talk." "Jimmy, we need to talk." "Jimmy, we need to talk." "Jimmy, we need to talk." "Jimmy, we need to talk." "Jimmy, we need to talk."

Silence is often the best thing to say. The sounds of suffering could not be avoided in my nightmare.

Chapter 26

I finally realized that trying to control my tears was useless. I was talking to Father Eduardo and complaining about my rejection. My life without Jimmy was too hard to carry on.

It was one thing to lose Rosa, but another to live without my friend.

While Father Eduardo tried to reassure me that I had done nothing wrong and that I did not need to weigh what other students thought, I was too upset to make sense of his words. Father Eduardo tried to persevere by saying that: "God does not give you a cross any heavier than you can bear."

I would have none of it. "What good is any of this if Jimmy won't go to college with me?"

I was too hurt to understand any of it. I became withdrawn and started avoiding my friends at school. I had never felt so lonely. I suffered a paper cut at school, and then my favorite dishes started tasting like blood. As I sucked the blood clean from my fingers, I came into the realization that rice and beans or blood, it made no difference. It all tasted the same. Food or blood— blood or food, was there any difference at all?

I felt that for every laugh there was a tear. For every happy moment, sadness would land on Earth. I had the sense that at this point someone was very happy and I just happened to be at the wrong end of the continuum. Then I felt that this could not be. If there were such a law, someone would have stated it somewhere.

The fear and desolation of the moment brought the thought of suicide. But I immediately realized that there was no purpose in that. Neither Jimmy nor Rosa would care about my death, and I realized that I would be more alone in death than in life.

Besides, there was hope that I might love again.

To give meaning to my life I just had to throw myself into some enterprise, and there was college! I had all of my life ahead of me, yet I was focused on the next few days— I was going to hear any day now about the rest of my future. My parents had offered me a car if I stayed on the Island. Yet, I knew I was destined to go to the States. I had a sense that going to the States somehow involved my life's purpose: I was at the beginning of a new phase.

It was during this time that my father made a very warm gesture, the scope of which I did not understand until many years later. One day, as he returned from work, he called me into the dining room where we always had our family meetings and politely asked me if I knew what I was going to do with the rest of my life. I told him that I was going to the States to become a doctor. He then tried to persuade me into going to see a counselor to help me choose my career and I told him that there was no need for it. I was going to become a doctor; I was going to school in the States and nothing he said or did, nothing the counselor said or did, would make me change my mind.

In the end, both Jimmy and I were accepted to Tulane. When I asked Jimmy if we could be roommates there, Jimmy politely refused. I decided that I would be better off at Johns Hopkins University. I had vacillated so much that when the time came for the decision to be made, Papi offered me the help of the same professional to make sure I was doing the right thing. I knew I didn't need anyone's help to figure out what I had to do. As long as I loved my two friends, I would not allow the smallest grief, or the sweetest memory to be forgotten. Parting with friends is sadness, a place is only a place, and anyplace will do.

Noises, aromas, the sound of their voices, even the words that were never spoken between us would be carried away and remain alive. They would forever have the power to give me happiness or sadness. All my high school years would roll into one; that was why I needed to get away. I did not have the strength to carry on in the familiarity of my hometown atmosphere. Any place would do. Johns Hopkins just felt right, as right as any other.

PART FOUR

You tell me I'm different,
I try to guess how.
You tell me I'm smart,
So I figure it out.

It deals with that place,
Where love unspoken arises.
It deals with my body,
And all pubertal phases.

Sixteen candles I blew out,
Everyone sang me a song.
I get my hands on a car,
And out I go, trying to belong.

Looking for my kind,
I stumble on a place.
People like me, alive,
Enjoying a happy face.

Determined to break the fear,
Of crossing into the unknown.
I struggle with a door,
That will take me beyond.

Wooden frame threshold,
Innocently naming the bar,
But for the knowledgeable,

It's a step you can't take back.

Struggling with inhibitions,
Letting loose, setting pace.
You finally cross the threshold,
You finally become yourself.

Juan Subirá-Rexach

Chapter 27

I had a bad night last night. I would sleep for a while, or so I think because I wouldn't or couldn't dream, I would wake up and look at the clock on the wall and I knew that time had passed. You might think that slumber would be a lovely rest without visits by spirits or visions. Yet it is a dry dead thing, as if I only nap on the surface of sleep. The tyranny of my wall clock marks the passing of time. I am still aware enough to read time and make a conscious effort to grasp this concept. The principle of least action requires that reality and fantasy co-exist in harmony.

Your defenses get really low. Not being able to get out of bed, not even to go the bathroom, make coffee, even if you were just to go back to bed right away. Having your mental stimulus consists of: "in a scale from one to ten, how bad is your pain today?" Or "let me check your lungs and heart, please lean forward." Being closed to the universal language of dreams, not getting release from the fantasy world. I don't understand. I would have welcomed a nightmare, just as much as anything that could get me away from these four walls.

Drugs are supposed to ease the pain. With me, they slow down all the sense of time (is time pain?) and release me to a soft classical music (like the Mozart CD I was so fond of). My chief pain is the loss of dreams, the numbing of the memory. Images of my past (as the day I came out to my family in a letter) surround me. A swimming contentment (as the day I was ok with kissing another man) succumbs to the pain. I lie in this dark and narrow room and every time the door opens I wish for a familiar face from my past. I wish for my Bill or any of my friends—something to anchor me back to reality. You may be unworthy of their love, falsify their values, but no matter how irritable you may think they are at their worst, in this situation they can be all that matters.

"Good morning, Dr. Subirá. I am Pungi your day shift nurse. In a scale from one to ten..."

"Twelve"

No, it is not a dream. She is too noisy to be mistaken for one. I am still dreamless, without even a nightmare to my name.

She is a pleasant short Indian nurse. Her cheeks are like taffy apple under a flawless permanent tan. Very red lips, one clean canine on the right side that overlaps another tooth and left a little gap. She has a small black dot in the middle of her forehead. When her face is immobile, it takes a luminous appearance. It is somewhat of a shock when she says:

"I see. Are you awake enough to enjoy some reading materials?"

"Sure." Well this is new! Why hadn't I thought of asking for a book to read? It might help pass time.

"Here is something I feel you might enjoy" and I was handed a *Jesus will save you* pamphlet.

"Ms. Pungi, what makes you think that I need Jesus?"

"Well I thought that since you may die from AIDS you might wish to be saved."

"What makes you think that I need salvation? Just because of my diagnosis you have no right to make that assumption. I honestly believe that God judges us according to the standards we believe to be true. I am afraid you should go back to your church and your Jesus, and pray so that he may not judge you with the same standards you are judging me. I would be very afraid...your harsh judgment might send you straight to hell. Remember when Jesus saved a prostitute from being stoned? All he did was write on the sand each of the people's names and next to it he would enumerate their sins. I strongly urge you to go back to your church and beg for forgiveness. I promise to pray for you and put on a word of exoneration if I am to die before you. Now stick to your nursing and leave religion to the professionals."

I never could understand these Christian fanatics. How could a just God expect his creatures to pick the one true religion out of a multitude of false ones? By faith alone? It strikes me as a sloppy way to run an organization, whether a universal or a smaller one. All of us are prisoners of our early indoctrinations, for it is hard, nearly impossible to shake off one's earliest training. I created parallel universes to try to accept my homosexuality. Reshaped molecules to feel accepted by my God and tolerated by my heritage, all of which to no avail.

I figure if Jesus could transform bread and wine into part of our symbolic cannibalism, I might have a chance at softening the blow of my parent's rejection by creating a parallel universe where homosexuality is accepted. As a devout agnostic, as I tend to cynically feel these days, I consciously evaluated all religions. From my days at Hopkins where I was fascinated in my comparative religion studies, I am as taken by the early worship of the sun by the Egyptians or the Incas, to the most sober and intellectualized of the major western faiths. Having had this brush with death, I am forced to take them all as equal. I really want to cover my ass (I am more afraid of coming back as a housewife with bad taste than I am of hell). It does not help me that I dislike some religions more than others. The evangelical movement that this nurse practiced sets my teeth on edge.

If God exists (a belief that I have always leaned toward), and if He desires to be worshipped (something that I find improbable, but conceivably true, explaining why we have so many options to choose from), then stipulating one form of worship over another seems unlikely to be relevant. I always have thought that God omnipotent, which could shape galaxies and create or end life, would not be swayed by this stupid nurse's bigotry performed in the name of "worship."

And if there is no God, at least, not the Supreme Being that these fanatics are talking about; what if there are spirits, millions of spirits that are ambiguous, unpredictable, as slippery as quicksilver, yet more flexible than the all–or–nothing Almighty. In as much as it is nice to have Christ die for our sins, I believe I will take issue with a God that is so fond of torture that only the brutal death of his Son can persuade Him to torture us a little less.

And what if there are no spirits whatsoever, only fate? When death comes, it would be over. Would this be more like an improvisation, an invincible hand that tucks and pulls; a score that does not reveal itself until the piece is over?

Ms. Pungi and I are bound today by our exchange. We could die today, but instead will die just like we were born: one by one, on our predetermined time.

I have studied enough to be convinced the universe did not just happen. This 'just happened' theory is as probable as the night I tried to rearrange carbon molecules to create a universe full of homosexual acceptance. In as much as I do believe that evolution is a tool in our creation, I am convinced that random selection is not a sufficient explanation to our universe. For that matter I am convinced that I am created a homosexual for a specifically divine reason and my chance pairing with Bill has some sort of religious undertone. I truly believe that even gay love is just another way by which great religions are taught, each with its own answers and each claiming to be the truth.

Religion is a solace to many people. It has been called the "opiate of the masses." It is conceivable that some religion, somewhere, really is the Ultimate Truth. In most cases it is nothing more than a form of conceit and havoc. In parts of Ireland and the Middle East, it is more trouble than it is worth. Catholics vs. Protestants, Jews vs. Muslims are doing deeds in the name of their faith with which no God would want to be identified. I could never become a prophet, I would settle for the right to be a critic. It just seems to me that owning the last Cher CD, being able to recite all the words to every show tune Monday night at Sidetrack, being able to dress in style, and having disposable income to splash on yourself is more to God's liking than what these people are doing in their God's name. That is not religion—it is a madhouse.

I envy the Pungi's of the world that can convey their God in a more appealing way. I am cursed by the fact that I push all the madness into life. Instead, Ms. Pungi gathers misfortunes, violence, error, pain—all her fears (homosexuality included)—up into heaven where her God can call it and give it purpose. We are each of us full of sins, regrets, contradictions, and despair then try to dissolve them in the fire called God purging our souls without destroying our bodies. Therein lies the pretty phrase: "to be born again."

In any case, if this nurse is indeed in possession of the "divine truth"; if she, and the ones like her, are the only ones going to Heaven; and my homosexuality is condemning me to go to Hell with all my prior friends that I have lost to this disease, then, God, having granted me free will, will understand why I prefer an eternity of dinner parties, good music, great Broadway musicals, and the company of my real friends in eternal damnation. I may not be able to see the naked face of my God, but at least I had foresight enough to be in great company and would have such a good time that I would not have the time to miss him.

As I listen with my whole soul, I tell you that I have lost my Christian God, but in truth, I never had Him. I am too cold of temperament to have any God. I think of God as I think of poetry: the poetry of war, the poetry of battles without end, and of noise in Heaven.

As I dwell in the realm of my subconscious, I remember one of the jokes my father would be so fond of repeating:

> *"In life, there are two worries.*
> *You are either healthy or sick.*
> *If you are healthy,*
> *You have nothing to worry about.*
> *If you are sick,*
> *Then you have two worries.*
> *You either get better or you die.*
> *If you get better,*
> *You have nothing to worry about.*
> *If you die,*
> *Then you have two worries.*
> *You go to Heaven or you go to Hell.*
> *If you go to Heaven,*
> *You have nothing to worry about.*
> *If you go to Hell:*
> *You will be so busy enjoying the company*
> *of*
> *   your friends,*
> *That you will have no time to worry.*
> *So don't waste your precious time worry-*
> *ing*
> *   and enjoy life."*

"Juan, I am Father Rodrigo. Would you like to have communion?"

"Yes, father. I would also love for you to hear my confession." (Sorry, just in case, it never hurts to play it safe. I don't have a religion of reason and logic. Because with the passage of time reason may fail you and when it does, you may find yourself taking refuge in madness. God could be anywhere. My present emptiness is such a vast kingdom, a faraway religion as mysterious as death itself).

Life can be such a disorder of things, an injustice, and a crazy game by our Cosmos. Could it be that God is also crazy? What a terrible thing to have given men a consciousness so that we can understand chaos and terror, but not to give us anything to defeat them. In a way, madness is the only order of life. These are the only people that have figured out that there is no possibility to explain, reason, or clarify our total chaos. Since they understand that there is nothing they can do about it, they realize that the only way to achieve the ultimate truth is to join the madness. We who are sane, can only be comforted by terror...

No wonder I wished to believe in life after death. I have lived so many lives after death here on earth...

This exchange feels strangely religious, like praying to a God that might not exist. He probably exists, but as with any god or ghost, one does not know if he would respond in words, signs, or silence.

Chapter 28

Mr. José Antonio Subirá had attended Wharton School of Business at the University of Pennsylvania. He had achieved this because Grandpa John was able to pay for tuition in spite of the great American Depression. Going off to college in 1933 had its advantages, especially if you were a D- student but your family had the cash to pay your way. He had proceeded to graduate with a C average from Wharton, with a minor in women and cards. He did not understand why, I, his son, wanted to go to Johns Hopkins University, nor did he understand why I wanted to be a doctor. For that matter, neither did I. He knew one thing for certain: it was his duty to send me off to school, as only a father should.

Papi had been married before and had a child from that marriage living near Baltimore, Md. After helping me pack all my belongings in my three suitcases (the maximum allowed by the airlines without paying for excess baggage—they had no idea of the excess baggage in my head), we got on a Pan Am flight to Baltimore and my half brother, Manny, was at the airport to pick us up.

I had met Manny a long time before; but I hadn't met his wife and two kids. Bits and pieces registered in my mind to alter the present memory: we were here in Maryland. Manny had white hair in close ringlets that seemed incongruously excessive above his sullen blue eyes.

I suppose I was not ready for the reception we got from him. After exchanging some pleasantries, Manny took us to a Gentleman's club in the outskirts of Baltimore. The club was in a strip mall (how ironic) and was innocuous from the outside. Unless you knew it was there, you would have never found it.

There were no signs, no ads. As you walked inside you were met with a raised central stage with bad lighting. There was a smell of stale cigarettes that would not be politically correct these days, but in those days, it was just a matter of fact for this place. Night was beginning to spread its shadows along the Maryland countryside, but in here it seemed it was always night. I had never seen exotic women before, much less with as little clothing as these women were wearing. They seemed nice and wanted us to buy them drinks.

We were all having a good time, but I was not used to drinking that much. My head began to hurt as I tried to imagine the place without the girls gyrating on the stage and around us. My head began to hurt more as I tried to maintain my grasp on reality. The last thing I remember was my father telling Manny that it was time for me to become a man. Next thing I knew I was in a dark room with Connie, or at least I think that was her name, and she was ordering me to undress. I was too inebriated to argue, so I decided to go for the ride. And for a ride I went. It was the first time that I had seen a rubber, for that matter it was my first time with a woman (not to mention the first time with another human since I was a kid), and thanks to my state of mind, I got away with not knowing what to do. Connie, thinking I was too drunk to apply it myself, took care of the condom business. I was ordered to lie down. As much as I was sure I was in the hands of a professional, this was the last thing I remembered of the evening.

My first seduction, for which my father was responsible, had me quite unprepared for the melting ecstasy of my successive orgasms. It was mutuality and sharing as old as the old profession itself, perhaps older. And with powers capable of overwhelming reason. A look on the professional's face, a sweet kiss, a total abandonment of all my self protective reserves, unguarded by the effects of alcohol and supremely vulnerable.

To this day, I have no recollection of what went on in that room other than coming. If you were to ask me what the room looked like, I would be as ignorant as I was oblivious that evening. For that matter, if I were asked to pick Connie from a line up, I would probably have trouble even if you place her among four Japanese men. I recall a woman, perhaps the generic "Woman", with the essence of cheap perfume on her face. I recall an instant of ecstasy (well, several). For that instant, I allowed the raw expression of my sexuality, going through the motions, but avoiding any intimacy. Outside, my father and Manny were in similar rooms, probably doing similar things.

I assume something happened, but to be honest, I have no clear memory of losing my virginity. I do remember my father coming to get me and hurrying me to get dressed because we were late. Manny's wife Linda was quite upset at us because the plane had landed several hours before and Manny had not bothered to call her. They lived in Edgewater, a town about forty-five minutes from Baltimore in a very rural part of the state. Manny had a nice four-bedroom house near the water so he could enjoy his boat. You can take the boy out of Puerto Rico, but you can't take away his boat. His back yard had a small marina with his pride and joy: a 23 foot Boston Whaler. He was a truck driver and made a good living—he owned his truck.

Linda was golden haired and willowy, her perfection of figure clothed in a flowing gown of polyester—simple flattery of form without ornament. Gray green eyes stared back at us. She had an estranged-wife/serene repose about her that I found subtly disturbing. Manny and Linda had two sons, ages 7 and 9. There was an air of tension in the house, which spoke of some unresolved marital discordance. My dad, a charmer even in his moments of mischief, worked his talents and proceeded to intercede on our behalf.

He started by telling both kids that: "Every time you call me uncle José instead of Grandpa I will give you a quarter."

"*Tío José, tío José*" was the echo that broke the ice, as Papi would empty his pockets.

He then looked at Linda and said, "I'm told you are a great dancer. Will you dance with me?" And immediately the records were going on the phonograph and there was an instant party. The evening was followed by a gourmet macaroni and cheese dinner and ended in a friendly poker game where not only were all four of us involved, but also the Adamson's from next door. By bedtime, the air had turned festive and we were all ready for a well-deserved sleep.

My father was of the belief that there were two things he could help me master before going away to school. He was working on a short schedule, but he was making sure he would achieve both of his objectives. As it turns out, he had called ahead to have my brother to work out all the arrangements. This way, he was making sure that I knew enough about women and cards to survive. He tried to teach me enough so that I could handle myself with the pleasures of women and also to make sure I would not lose all my money at poker. I suppose he did not count on all of us having so much to drink. Alcohol has an amnesiac effect, among other things.

I stared around me; I saw the bedroom where I slept with my father lying next to me. The room had two single beds; Manny's two sons had been displaced to make room for us. No Puerto Rican sleeps in a hotel—and it's lowest man on the totem pole that gets the couch. Beyond the shadows under a full moon glow, I saw my father's pleasant sleep. It stretched away into the shadows, both deep and black, perhaps with a satisfied desire no longer lusting. I could sense its deepness and resisted a deep desire to share the pleasure of that sleep—I had too much to decide.

I could feel the demands of the future within me. My father had defined my terrible purpose in life. No small thing could deflect the juggernaut—it was gathering weight and momentum. Had I died at this instant, I would still be my father's son: good with women and good at cards (I had managed to win $5.75 at the poker game and hadn't gotten kicked out of the "Gentlemen's Club" for passing out or giggling inappropriately).

I remember the sound of the bedside clock: its noise marking the moments ticking away. I could feel time flowing through me, instants never to be recaptured. I sensed a need for a decision, but felt powerless to move.

Just before I finally succumbed to sleep, I felt a vital moment had passed me. I felt that I had missed an essential decision and was now caught in my own myth. I had never seen this new land before, but I felt I had experienced it in a faraway dream in Puerto Rico, with the details of the place being filled in as I started my new experience. Movement stops, even the movement of evolution. While you cause a granular universe to persist in your awareness (who you are), you become blind to movement (or change). When things change (as today), your absolute universe vanishes, no longer accessible to your self-limiting perceptions. The universe has moved beyond you.

There was nothing else for me to do but fall to a dreamless sleep.

Chapter 29

There were many half dressed men and women playing Frisbees and walking their dogs. There were some students singing with their guitars. Everyone seemed happy: everyone except my father. I suppose he had expected to see students in jackets and ties, I suppose he was startled (or uncomfortably aroused?) by the sight of so many half dressed women. Whatever it was, he left that day straight to San Juan and left me alone in my new town. I had not even met my roommate yet.

Johns Hopkins University undergraduate campus is located on 3400 N. Charles Street. It is a set of Victorian buildings surrounding grassy quadrangles. The Baltimore Museum of Art creates the southern border, and beautiful residential areas are to the North. East of campus is the student ghetto, known for its low-income housing and the home of the Baltimore Orioles. (A trip to my 15th year class reunion would reveal a gentrification of the area with University buildings now rising above the ashes of our old ghetto).

Manny had driven us to Campus. I had registered at orientation and both Manny and my father had managed to help me unpack at my dorm: 305 Sylvester House. I got the orientation schedule and was discussing it with Papi when Manny suggested a tour through campus.

"My name is Punjab Singh and I will be your guide. I am a third year pre-med student." Our guide was clearly of Indian descent, but no accent could be detected that would give his origin away. His black hair so carefully coifed, with a slight hook at the nose, thin lips, skin stretched tightly over high cheekbones and dark skin that gave him an exotic glare.

"The Dorm quadrangle is comprised of the old and the new dormitory buildings on the north and the east sides. It is completed by an administration building, Homewood House, and the Eisenhower Library on the south and the Dunning Hall (chemistry) on the west. You should read in your admission papers as to which dorm you will be assigned."

We then walked north where he said: "the Newton H. White athletic center with the lacrosse/ football, and baseball fields are located here. Some of our students have a great career in sports. Lacrosse is our school's most famous sport and Hopkins has won the NCAA Division I championships many times. Homecoming is always the lacrosse game against the University of Maryland, our perennial adversary."

As we walked south and west, he continued: "If you could follow me I will now take you to the upper quadrangle made by the Remsen Hall (chemistry) and Jenkins Hall (biology) on the north side, the Eisenhower Library on the east side, Gilman Hall (humanities, post office, bank and bookstore) on the west side and Ames Hall (psychology) and Krieger Hall (physics) on the south side. These last two buildings make the north boundary of the lower or Wyman quadrangle, thus named because it is at a lower altitude than the upper quadrangle and the large set of double stairs that lead to it."

As we descended the steps to the lower quadrangle, he kept on going: "The Shriver Auditorium is at the south end of the lower quadrangle (facing south) with Shaffer and Maryland Halls on the east side (pointing east) and Barton Hall and Latrobe Hall on the west side (pointing west). West of this is Levering Hall, the student center, with the foundations of the Glass Pavillion where the Rathskeller Student bar entertains many students until closing." (Come to think of it, maybe this tour is what made Papi leave in such a rush...)

We then walked south where he added: "these last two buildings are the main administration building or Garland Hall. With
this, our tour is concluded. Please make sure you go to Shriver
Hall auditorium to listen to our president give his welcoming
speech."

(I felt I was in a river. It flowed somewhere. I could stand
on either bank and observe its flow. A map might tell you where
the river went, but no map could tell you the more essential things.
A map would never show the inhabitants who made the river its
home, where they went, where they shopped, or where they went
for work or for fun. There had to be a better map, just like there
had to be a better tour. One attached to all our lives. You could
carry that map in your memory and take it out occasionally for a
closer look).

Papi took me to Gilman Hall where the student bank was to
help me open a checking account. I got a mailbox number so
Mami would be able to write. Then all three of us walked to the
auditorium where we were greeted by the president of the University.

The speech was short, but to the point. We were 598 students, coming from 43 states and 2 US territories. There were
also 6 foreign nations represented. We were 189 female students and 409 male students. We were all welcomed and wished
successful careers here at the University. A short reception followed at the Hopkins alumni club where we were allowed to
shake the hand of the president, Mr. Steven Muller.

I don't know at what point Papi was overwhelmed, but I do
know that he was scheduled to stay another two days to enjoy
orientation with me; instead he called the airlines and asked
Manny to drive him to the airport.

I said good-bye to my father and walked to my dorm room to find a stranger had occupied the other half of it. His name was Chris Witty and he was a native Baltimorean from the east shore of Chesapeake Bay. Chris was an impressively tall football player, as impressive in height as in width. His physique seemed to hide his inner soul: a small man, weak looking. His face was weaselish with overlarge blue eyes. His hair was receding at the temples. And his movements: he moved a hand or turned his head one way, and then he spoke another way. It was very difficult to follow. He had played football in high school and wanted to try out for the team here in college. I told him that I was a swimmer and wished him luck. He was an only child; his mother was a widow. I told him that my father had dropped me and had already left for Puerto Rico where I was from. We wished each other good luck and got back to registering for our fall courses.

I was a chemistry major; Chris was a Math major. The only class we shared was Calculus. Chris was trying out for the football team; I was trying out for the swimming team. That night, alone in a strange bed and place, I felt scared. My new life was beginning and even with all this official "orientation" that had been going on all day, I was as disoriented as the day I left home. My experiences from these pasts few days told me that I knew now less of what I wanted from life than when I was home. I was wondering if I should have taken the same flight home with Papi.

As I fell asleep on my first night away from home, I felt a sudden reluctance to be alone with this man. It came to me that I was surrounded by a way of life that I could not understand, not even after analyzing new ideas and values. I felt that my Puerto Rican world was fishing for me, trying to capture me in its ways. And I knew that if I lay in that trap, there would be a moral war, a war I felt I should avoid at all cost.

Chapter 30

"**M**y name is Ted White. I am looking for Juan Subirá" I was taken by surprise as this handsome tall stranger entered my room to greet me.

"My name is Juan and I am glad to meet you." It was the best I could come up with on such short notice.

"I am your student advisor and I will help you with your study load and anything else you have trouble with." Ted continued.

I was alone in my room and was struggling with my fate. Ted immediately delighted me, but I was unable work out a way to exploit the situation to my advantage. Ted was a junior from Alabama. He was also an only child and he lived off campus with three other juniors. He was a pre-medical student, just like me, and we immediately connected. He was three years my elder and, at 20, he stood exactly six feet. He had a big smile that played with a receding sandy blond hairline. He could light any room with his features, but he was lighting mine right now. I was overtaken by his southern friendliness and decided that I was in need of tutoring in Chemistry. Ted offered to help me that night with my homework and we agreed to meet after dinner at his place.

Ted lived on 30th Street, just east of campus in the student ghetto. It was a nice September night, just the right temperature so that minimal clothing was comfortable for the three-block walk. I grabbed my Chemistry textbook and headed for Ted's. He lived on the third floor of an old apartment complex and I was greeted by one of his roommates, Paul. Ted was inside waiting for me. He sat at his desk, catching a moment of quiet between homework. It was a pleasant room; much larger than the one I shared with Chris. The place had thick rugs on the floor, soft cushions, a low coffee table near at hand, multicolored posters on the walls, and a broken antique light fixture hanging from the ceiling. The room was permeated with an acrid funny odor that I soon associated with upperclassmen—stale beer. As much as the room tried to emanate a sense of security, I knew I was in an alien place. It was the harshness that the rugs and hangings tried to conceal. I sensed that he was as anxious to get to work as I was so I opened my book to the first chemistry problem and asked for help.

Even as Ted spoke, I leaned towards him. As though two magnets had found their point of critical attraction, we moved together. Ted pressed his cheek against my shirt, his arms around me feeling my hard muscles. I rested my chin on his desk, stale beer filling my senses.

"This is insane" I heard Ted whisper.
"Yes"
He lifted my chin and kissed me. I moved my erection towards his body.
Neither of us doubted where this would lead, as inexperienced as we both were, Ted did not resist when I lifted him off his feet and carried him over to his bed.
Clothes were never removed, yet in the post coital peace, Ted put both hands behind his head and stretched, twisting on the rumpled bed. I sat with my back to him. Looking out the window...

It must have been mutually agreeable since my tutorials became a nightly event. Because I had a roommate in my room, we were always at Ted's. We would close his bedroom door and the long sessions of Chemistry would intertwine with our chemistry. Inexperienced as we were, we learned to explore our bodies. Oral sex was soon discovered, and we slowly discovered the pleasures that our bodies had to offer. Since neither one of us knew about lubricants, penetration was never an option. (I don't remember if we ever tried it!) We enjoyed rolling over each other and pleasuring each other as best we could. The joys of innocence...

I could tell I was very special to Ted, when I got an invitation to go home with him for Thanksgiving. Ted knew that I could not afford to go home, and he surprised me with an airline ticket to Mobile, Alabama for the holidays. I was unable to resist and agreed to the trip with excitement.

We flew from Baltimore to Mobile Wednesday night and we went directly to Ted's home. There was no one there so we were able to sleep like a couple and, for the first time, we were able to wake up in each other's arms. I remember I asked Ted why he had trouble achieving orgasm, and he confided in me what would become my first sexual discovery: one can achieve pleasure without achieving orgasm. I would have lived from one orgasm to the next, but in this bed, next to me, was the only man I ever met that was just content with my company. Orgasms were a secondary benefit to the pleasure of my company.

We were to drive to Pensacola to meet his parents Thursday for the Thanksgiving feast. I met Ted's mother, Stella, and her new husband, Joel. Truly people from the south: average height in their late fifties, polite to the point of hiding any hint of anger or confusion. There was a pride about them, which seemed to undress me, as if they knew what was going on between us. They were very friendly, but I could not understand why everyone wanted to watch football all weekend, so I was bored for most of the time. I got Ted to find me a second TV so I could watch a rerun of "My Fair Lady" while the gang watched USC trounce Notre Dame at the Hoosier dome.

All said, it was the happiest time of my life and I was saddened by the fact that Sunday came and we had to return to

Baltimore.

Back in my room, whirling silence settled around me. With the expectation of class tomorrow, every fiber in my body accepted the fact that something profound had happened. I felt I was on a subconscious island, smaller than any subatomic particle in my chemistry class, yet capable of motion and of sensing my surroundings. Like an abrupt revelation, as if curtains where whipped away, I realized I had become aware of an extension of myself. It was as if I was the island, yet not the island. It was as if I was doing homosexual acts, but they were not homosexual. I had a companion and we had sex—but that doesn't mean I was "homosexual."

The room was still around me, Chris was there asleep in the bed next door, and I sensed all my surroundings. The desks, with my carefully packed books and orderly belongings on my side, and Chris' disorderly books and belongings in total disarray, on his side. But I felt that they were suspended in time. I stared at the frozen images around me, seeing a dust particle on Chris' head and I stopped there.

I waited. I waited for what I felt was like an eternity, yet at the same time it was no time at all. The answer to this instant came like an explosion in my self-consciousness: my personal time was suspended to save my life. The rules of physics were to change to accommodate my newfound sexuality. Dancing particles, I began recognizing familiar structures, atomic linkages: a carbon atom here, helical ring; and then a glucose molecule. An entire chain of molecules confronted me and I recognized the one we had just discussed in our chemistry class before the Thanksgiving break: a protein, a methyl-protein molecule.

I heard a soundless mental sigh within me as I saw the nature of these molecules. I saw myself moving them, shifting an oxygen molecule, allowing another carbon molecule to link, reattach a linkage of oxygen, then hydrogen. The charge spread, faster and faster as the catalyzed reaction achieved completion. I was changing the structure of that dust particle to accommodate my newfound reality. All would be well.

I had created a universe of magic. There would be no atoms, instead only waves and motions all around. I discarded all my prior beliefs and perceptions of morality. This new universe could not be seen, could not be heard, and could not be detected in any way by fixed perceptions of my upbringing. It had become the ultimate void where no preordained screens occur where judgments can me made. There is only one awareness here: the realm of the magical. Imagination. Here I would learn to be human. I would create a new order of beautiful shapes and systems. I would organize my chaos.

The suspension of time relaxed its hold on me and I sensed motion again. There was a fly in the room whose buzzing noise brought me back to reality. I then sensed a forced shift in my awareness. I saw another universe. The other universe darted wildly here and there, circling. It radiated pure terror. It was full of prejudices and preconceptions that went back all the way to my ancestral Spain. Terror threatened to overwhelm me. I saw my father judging me for what I had just done and I saw no salvation. There was no mercy for this sinner. I knew the experience had happened: there was a lover: virile, American, blue-eyed, but male, lover. I saw his strength and tenderness, all of him in this one moment. There was no time to think what this was doing to my self-esteem, only time to accept and record. Experiences poured into my self-conscious, important matters and unimportant. They were all converging in this single view of time.

I knew with a generalized awareness what I had become. The experience had transformed me. No one had to explain the mysteries of what had happened, I knew. The end result of all

the rearranging of my molecules was the same. I had not been
able to change the universe.

A terrible sense of loneliness crept through me with the realization of what had happened to me. I saw my own life run in
front of me. It was a pattern that combined all my past experiences; it fast-forwarded to my prior sexual experiences so that a
dancing interplay became clearer. Before I could react, I felt the
presence of all my prior memory. There was something that
needed doing…

"Juan, Juan, wake up! You are going to be late for class."
With these words Chris steered me off to class.

Chapter 31

Coach Comfort was a great swim coach; it helped that I was able to adapt my class schedule to the swimming team practice. He had sessions five times a day at the Newton H. White athletic center so we could all get in three hours of swimming a day. I was immediately assigned to the backstroke team, as that was my best stroke.

There I met Bob. He was a year ahead of me in class, but two years my senior. He was also a pre-med student. He was six foot one, sandy blond hair, blue eyed and with a chipped front tooth that was the most striking feature of his smile. I had the third fastest backstroke time and Bob had the second. Since only two team members compete per event, he was the one I needed to beat if I wanted to make the varsity team. As much as I was content with just being "part" of the team, I secretly desired not just to beat Bob; I was also extremely attracted to him. This rivalry and attraction got us close. We always hung around practice and tried to learn from each other. He was helping me improve my turns, since I was used to a pool twice the length and only half the turns.

Bob was the one who told me of the first team party of the year. He wanted to show me around since he was the older one and he was dating his high school sweetheart. He did not feel threatened by me, even though I believed he was aware of my attraction for him.

The party was held at the team captain's apartment. It was a large three-bedroom house on 31st Street in the heart of the student ghetto. Milk crates were the recurring theme of the décor. They were used for everything: to hold books, the stereo, the TV. The old Victorian architecture tried to come to the surface but with little success. There was a shadowy atrium with hard wood floors, glittering designs worked in the crystal of the windows. Beyond the atrium was a covered courtyard. Light admitted by translucent filters spread an opulence as silvery as the white light of the moon. The street door welcomed you into this, the party room.

There was much beer and little food. The beer was in the form of a keg and the food was only what would come out of a bag. It was the first time I had seen beer that way, and, once I got used to the pumping; I was able to drink it like all of my teammates. There was also a very tasty fruit punch.

There, I met John, who would some day become my brother in law. The light from the eastern windows fell directly on his face, leaving shadows on his nose and chin. He was a second year and was extremely uncomfortable with my friendliness. Even though we all got along and enjoyed each other's company, I remember John asking me if I was a homosexual. I was drunk at the time, so I thought he was just joking. We had a lot in common: we mostly wanted to go to medical school, we wanted to swim well and we wanted to have a good time. That evening, the former was the farthest from our minds. I did not notice when Melanie was leading me back to her dorm room.

She was a student of Baker House in the new dorms. She was my height, five foot ten, blue eyed and red headed, and she was not into medicine at all; a chiseled beauty with those eyes that look past and through their prey. She had a small nose with a wide and generous mouth. She had clearly passed into womanhood, beautiful with the first blazing innocence of youth. I found myself surprised that I had not noticed her before. She was quite the talker.

"Hi, I'm Melanie."

"I'm Juan, nice to meet you."

"You have a wonderful accent, where are you from?"

"Puerto Rico"

She was soon dancing with me. We continued drinking.

"Is it true what they say about Puerto Ricans?" I was later told that the punch had been spiked with grain alcohol, which may explain why I answered:

"Yes, we all have big dicks, but I'm afraid mine is cut."

The alcohol was having its usual effect on me, opening desire like a flower. I found I needed to steady myself on Melanie. The mixture of whipcord and softness I felt beneath her clothing stirred my blood. Who did what or in what order made no difference, but I am sure she was aware I had an erection as I danced with her.

As it got late we agreed to walk home together, since it was clear that I was not going to make it back by myself and we were both heading in the same direction (our dorms). We were at her room.

"Is it a custom in Puerto Rico to escort me to my room?" she was inviting me in. Melanie was a junior and, because she was an upperclassman, she had no roommate.

"I was brought up a gentleman and always abide by what my lady desires." I thought I enunciated this through my drunkenness.

The exact sequence of events is partly blurred by the alcohol, partly by the fear, but I believe that I was voluntarily raped that evening. I enjoyed myself. I just wish I had better understanding of what I was doing. At least I knew what a condom was and how to use it this time. I also knew what was expected of me, and much to my amazement, not only was it pleasurable to me, but it seemed to be pleasurable for her. When it was over, both of us knew that it was time for me to go back to my room.

By the time I stumbled back into my room, I was both satisfied and confused, but content. I held myself in what I thought was a poised attitude in the stupor of inebriation, seeing time stretch out in its weird dimension, delicately balancing yet whirling, narrow yet spread like a net gathering in homoerotic and hetero-erotic worlds and forces. It felt that there was a tight wire that I needed to walk, yet all I had was a teeter-totter to achieve balance. Alcohol had me again in thought and I felt anew the hyper-illumination with high-relief imagery of time, sensed the future becoming nothing but memories – the tender indignities of physical love just shared as a communion of selves with softness and violence.

I never saw Melanie again. I never even bothered to look her up. I can still tell you that it was at Baker 205 where it happened, I can describe the *"Virginia is for Lovers"* poster above her bed, but I never bothered to go back there.

The guys from the team had suspected something since they were quick to ask the next day. I pretended for a second to be a gentleman, but the more I tried to deny it the easier it was for them to confirm the truth. By the time it was all out, I was just bragging about it with them.

Whatever sense of normality and belonging that could be achieved from my college experience, I was nowhere near it, but at least heading in the right direction. I had swimming, friends, my family and then Ted. All of my experiences from the past four months were culminating in one night of both extreme pleasure and sense of belonging. The universe opposed me at every step. It eluded my grasp, conceiving countless disguises to delude me. That universe would never agree with any shape I gave it.

My task at hand became Organic Chemistry lab. According to the Hopkins pre-med saga, this lab would either make or break you. If you were able to get at least a B, you would not be eradicated from going to medical school. A "C" would make your chances for admission almost impossible.

On my part, I always felt like Vladimir in Becket's *Waiting for Godot*. I went to the lab because I needed the course to get into Medical School (my Godot). I merely went through the motions.

I remember that I used to go to class completely unprepared. I had not read anything prior to the start of the experiment. Lucky for me, Bob had his station right in front of me. We had agreed to take the lab together.

Just as I always swam with him at practice, I simply watched his every move. If he took a petri dish out, or a beaker, or the Bunsen burner, I immediately followed suit. When he went over to get his substrate from our proctor, I was right behind him in line. When he cooked, I cooked; when he distilled, I distilled. As he separated and formulated his yield, I did the same. My only mistake was that one day he was not able to show up for lab and in my fury of dealing with the unknown (today's experiment) I turned to my left where Lisa had her station.

Lisa was your typical Jewish American Princess, straight from Brooklyn, who achieved a perfect score on her SAT's and would have no qualms about letting everyone know that she would be her family's first physician. I tended to avoid her, not so much because she was not pretty, but because she always made me feel like her inferior.

"Stop staring at me! You are ruining my concentration!"

I had completely forgotten how competitive medical school is supposed to be and had to make do with my own reading. I spent the next ten minutes reading what I should have read the night before. This turned out to be my worst experiment! (That was the day I learned that the less I prepared for class, the better I would do!)

Funny how life sometimes works in mysterious ways: in spite of just going through the motions and feeling like an observer, I ended up with very good results for all my experiments, thus getting an "A" in the course. Both Bob and Lisa took home a "C."

Chapter 32

I cannot tell you how or why I stopped seeing Ted. I still cannot tell you if it was related to my teammates or my experience with Melanie. But I can remember having him come to my room after I had not been to his apartment for two weeks. He wanted to know what he had done and why I had gone from worshipping him to trying to avoid him. There were tears in his eyes. I was completely numb. I did not feel anything.

Just as he had attracted me when I first met him, I was now simply not attracted. There was no other explanation. I thought it to be the most logical thing at the time. I never knew that being on this side of the rejecting could be so easy. I never knew that there was no rationale behind it. One thing age has taught me is that as much as I do not care if I ever see or meet Jimmy or Rosa again (the ones who rejected me), I have tried several times to locate Ted to apologize. I only wish that I knew then what I know now: I would have never let him go. (But isn't that what we all say. If I had only known…). Details impressed themselves on those days and as much as I want to rationalize them, I cannot.

Ted was the most loyal and true friend I ever had. He was not only attracted to me; he cared for me. If there was ever in my life a moment where I was loved, I believe Ted was the one who was responsible for the loving. When I was in medical school, he had called my mother to find out how I was doing and to wish me well.

We managed to take one psychology class together and we were always studying together. As we became closer, it was evident to my roommate, my teammates, and Ted's roommates the true relationship between us. For the first time in my life, I had a name for it and I could not handle it. Instead of trying to rationalize it as true love between two men, it became "the love not spoken." I was ashamed of it: I understood that it was wrong. And, I panicked! I did to Ted exactly what had been done to me just a couple of years ago.

I started avoiding Ted and, instead, started hanging out with Bob and the guys from the swimming team. I started dating a Puerto Rican girl from our sister school, Goucher College, and tried to erase my past with Ted. Then there was Annie Fernandez, another Puerto Rican girl, who went to Notre Dame College in Baltimore. I tried to erase my feelings toward men by immersing myself in the world of heterosexuality. It became the talk of our swimming team when Annie had sneaked me into Notre Dames girls' dorm for a visit.

Annie was a sturdy figure with a direct gaze that focused intently from beneath the black cap of her long straight hair. Her skin was darkly tanned, but a slight movement of her body revealed her naked pale shoulder: the tan was fading from too much winter. Annie was dark skinned, of medium height who concealed her figure in robes whose rich fabrics and simple cut spoke of wealth. Her black hair was usually held in a narrow band that matched her robes. Everything about her would be in character, including her dress: a last piece of finery saved for the moment. I suppose I was happy. I, at least, kept the girls happy. It was easy going through the motions: I was a gentleman with the girls (funny how "I'm a gentleman" is so easily accepted by women when they don't want to know the truth) and if need be I could make them achieve orgasm when they wanted sex. I suppose it was all the same, but with a different person. I was resigned to my place in society and was finishing my first year in college with good grades and a healthy social life.

In those days, we would sit together at Rathskeller Bar to

drink and sing songs from Puerto Rico. Singing "En mi Viejo San Juan" I was trying to capture the culture my surroundings were making me lose. Was it homesickness or just trying to fit in? All I can remember is singing for hours and hours until closing.

I became a man with mixed emotions and was able to bend them to fit my needs. Deep in the human unconscious is a pervasive need for a logical universe that makes sense. The real universe is always one step beyond logic. I had the feeling that I might still avoid the fate I could see so clearly in my path. As I look back at those days, I experience the dizzy feeling that I had lost my way, lost control over my life.

I could not escape the fear that I had somehow overrun myself, lost my position in time, so that past, present and future mingled without distinction. It was as if both my homosexual and heterosexual feelings would coincide in the same plane of reality. Yet, by choosing the easier path I would avoid an emotional fatigue. I knew this came from holding the present as a kind of memory that was intrinsically my past. There is, in all things, a pattern that is part of the universe. It has symmetry, elegance, and grace—the qualities that you try to capture. You may find it in the turning of the seasons. As Baltimore was heading into spring, I was experiencing a change in my psyche. The way a branch clusters its leaves and then sheds them away, just to grow them back. The way sand trails along a ridge, we try to copy these patterns in our lives and our society seeking the rhythms, the dances, and the relationships that give us comfort.

It is possible to see peril in finding the ultimate perfection. I wish I could believe that the present is a distraction: the future is a dream; that only memories can unlock the meaning of life. It is clear that the ultimate pattern contains its own fix, in such perfection, all things move toward death. It will be on that day that I will be held accountable to Ted.

But, the shoddy way in which I handled leaving Ted; I have come to believe that memory unlocks no meanings, just pain. Without anguish of the spirit, which is a wordless experience, there is no meaning anywhere. Perhaps this will be my absolution. To dwell on the past is to cease to exist in the present. By dwelling on the past, we hope to correct our mistakes. That doesn't work; it just ruins our future because we're too preoccupied to see it coming our way. The only way to avoid memories that haunt us into the future is to not create them in the first place. If I had only known then what I know now....

Chapter 33

I had been to the drugstore on Charles Street many times. I had bought books, presents and even my daily Coke there. (I was still drinking regular Coke; I didn't have to worry about the calories). I was there on one of my countless errands. There was nothing special about the trip except that it was Friday night and He was not a student. I also noticed that He was in the section where the sex magazines were and He noticed me. I looked at Him and He made no effort to move his gaze away from me. He was tall, with black hair parted in the middle and swept back like the wings of an insect, flat and slick against His head. He had jutting predatory features that accentuated His dark blue eyes that were drawn into an intense frown. He was very attractive in ways that went beyond His chiseled physique... it was as if He had the beauty that was learned from a quiet acceptance of oneself.

I had bought the pens I needed to finish my term paper, and was walking out with my Coke when I sensed a strong presence behind me. As I turned, there was His gaze: His dark eyes were penetrating my soul and discovering the truth I had been hiding from myself.

I wish I could say that He "recruited me"; I wish I could say that He "seduced" me. But the truth is that no words were spoken. All the laws created to suppress what I was feeling at the moment, were just strengthening what was prohibited. There was a magical connection between us. Somehow we managed to exchange names: I suddenly became "José."

He asked me: "José, are you Mexican?"

I responded: "No, Puerto Rican. Where I come from that could be interpreted as an insult."

He lived downtown, in an apartment by Himself and He offered me a ride. His place was on a small street off Charles Street near the Hippopotamus.

He told me, "That is the gay bar."

"A happy bar?" I thought he meant "happy" (just naïve about the English language or was I practicing "avoidance therapy"?)

He had to explain the term to me. "Gay is the term we like to use for our kind." He told me "when you discover that you are not alone you will be going there to meet people like US."

That made no sense to me: why would you need to go to a bar to meet people when we were everywhere.

He lived on the third floor of a three-story brick building (come to think of it, everyone seemed to live on the third floor). He was the only one with a balcony and He was proud of that. Rugs and cushions covered the floor. Woven hangings everywhere with a large tapestry hiding a hole in one wall. A low field desk at one side was strewn with papers from some male porno magazine, which was clearly opened to what seemed to be His favorite picture. He worked at the hair salon on the corner and had all His necessities within walking distance: work, grocery store, entertainment, and bar. He had to drive to the bookstore—the one exception.

"Would you like something to drink?" He asked

"I would like a coke." Yes, I still had one in my bag from the store, but I'm not one to pass up a free Coke.

I followed Him into the kitchen and patiently waited for Him to serve me the Coke then I followed him into His bedroom like a stray puppy.

Windows were covered with heavy burgundy draperies. It was dark. I lay on the bed; there was no place to sit. He stood against the wall. A single globe above the room illuminated both of our faces. He changed into a black robe. It covered His beautifully carved chest, leaving masculine arms unclothed. His exposed skin looked waxen, rigid. There was no movement or words.

My awareness flowed through and around me and into darkness. I glimpsed the place as He dimmed the lights and before my mind blanked away from the terror I was feeling. Without knowing why, my whole being trembled at what I was about to do. A small breeze started some sparks on my skin as I felt His hand guide me towards Him. Rings of light expanded and contracted, where rows of tumescent white shapes flowed over and around the shades of light, driven by the darkness and the breeze out of nowhere.

Parts of a veil began to lift from me. Absorbed in the bliss of the vision of His body, I had forgotten that each vision belongs to all those that are still on the way, still to become. In the vision I passed through darkness, unable to distinguish reality from insubstantial accident. One hungered for absolutes that should never be.

Presently I opened my eyes, saw Him staring at me. He still held my hand; but the terrible fear was gone. I quieted my trembling and as He released my hand, it felt like a crutch had been removed, so I staggered back and would have fallen had He not grabbed me in His arms.

Why I told Him I loved Him makes no sense now, but it did at the time. I kissed Him and He kissed me back.

After a while He told me: "I think I could learn to love you, you are beautiful."

Too embarrassed to answer, I asked, "How do two men make love to each other?"

He showed me. We went over the procedure and he introduced me to lube (what a wonderful invention).

I did it with a man for the first time! I reached orgasm very quickly and I felt very ashamed. I pulled out of Him before He achieved orgasm and wanted out of the apartment. There was no reasoning about it. I got dressed, I got my things and I left and ran all four miles back to my room. I realized that there was a full glass of coke that I left untouched. It was the last image I have of the place. I do not know what He must have thought of me, and I never found out. I never saw Him again.

It was a time of ancient formulae intertwined, tangled together as they were fitted to the needs of my new conquest and the heraldic symbols it conveyed. It was a time of struggle between my beast demon on the one side and the old prayers and invocations on the other. There was never a clear decision.

There was a feeling in me that my body had become the manifestation of some power I could no longer control. I had become a non-being, a stillness that moved itself. At the core of the non-being, there I existed, allowing myself to be led through the streets of Baltimore, following a track so familiar to my visions that it froze my heart with grief.

Coke would never taste the same again, and I avoided the drugstore for the rest of the semester.

Chapter 34

As much as I tried to eliminate the Hippopotamus from my mind, I could not. I was in complete denial of my experience with Him; but there is a place where people like Him gather. The curiosity of the place was too intriguing for me. He had said that "*gay*" people hang out there. How does one word have so much power? It felt so right and so wrong at the same time.

Clearly, I could not be a homosexual. There was no way! I had no problem performing with women. Yet, no woman I had met until now was able fill the void left by Ted's disappearance from my life. I knew the key was in that place.

Saturday night, I told my roommate Chris that I had a date and would probably not come home. I dressed in my best jeans and my Hopkins swimming T-shirt and took the bus down Charles Street. I knew the general direction of the place, so I figured I would get off a few blocks before and walk.

I saw the discreet Hippopotamus sign just where He had said the bar was. My knees faltered. I started walking back home to the dorms. There was no way I was going to go there. I was terrified someone inside would recognize me! (Why is it that ten minutes after we admit to being gay, we think everywhere we go there will be people we know who will "tell on us?") I found the first bus heading back north and jumped on it. As soon as I settled on the bus, I realized that my attraction for the place was bigger than the fear of recognition and I hit the stop button and got off. I was upset that I was so scared of just going in. I walked right back to the bar and started to get in line. There was a line! What if someone saw me in line? I ran away and went to the corner drugstore. I walked inside and managed to get near the window where I was able to monitor the line. I waited until the crowd outside had thinned out and when I was sure I would not have to wait, I got back in line.

The doorman asked me for my identification. I panicked! I told him I had left it home and ran out the door. Once again, I started heading back home to the dorms. This time I thought it was for sure. There was no way I was going to reveal who I was to those people.

This time I never made it inside another bus. The draw of the place made me go right back. Even though there was someone else in line, I stood there. I waited for the guy in front of me to show his identification and luckily, there was another doorman. I showed my identification and was ordered to pay a cover charge.

I have to pay to get in? Why would anyone want to do that?

I paid and walked straight in. It was so dark that I realized no one could possibly see me, much less recognize me. (What is it about newbies in a bar that attracts all the attention?) I walked in and followed the hall around to the right and into a central bar that lead to an area where men were holding their drinks. If I had turned left instead, I would have walked to a dance floor. It had a disco ball in the center and there were lights changing to the tune of loud monotonous music. There were men dancing with other men! Not a woman in sight. I must have made a mistake; after all, it is dark, I can't see well. I explored the entire place and proceeded to the bar behind the dance floor where a man with no shirt asked me what I wanted to drink. He had chosen a bland round-faced appearance for his words, jolly features and uninspiring full lips, however, the body of a chiseled Adonis. It occurred to me, as I studied his intent, that he had made an ideal choice for his prey—out of instinct perhaps. He alone in this bar could manipulate a wide spectrum of bodily shapes and features. He was a human chameleon, and the face he wore now invited me to judge him lightly.

He asked me: "Is this your first time at the Hippo? I've never seen your face before."

"I am new in town." I told him.

I knew it was time to go home when he asked me if I was from Cuba. I had been inside for less than ten minutes!

I was able to take the bus back to the dorm without hesitation this time. It was the best night's sleep ever! As the cool shadows of the night enveloped me, I felt my muscles relaxing like worms. My firm bed where I lay was insubstantial. Only space was permanent. Nothing else had substance. The bed flowed with the many bodies I had seen at the Hippopotamus, yet they were all my own. Time became a multiple sensation, overloaded. It presented no single reaction for me to analyze. It was Time. It moved. The whole universe slipped backwards, forward, sideways. I was finally at peace. It would be several months before I would go to another gay bar, but my curiosity had been satisfied. There were other men like me. I was not a freak! I just needed to sort things out. (I also decided that night that next time I went to a gay bar I would wear a shirt that said: "I am from Puerto Rico.")

My attention shifted to my little sister. She was now in her final year of high school and, even though not a very good student, I felt that she would be trapped in Puerto Rico unless I could convince my father that I would be able to *"chaperone"* her here at Hopkins.

Dean Suskind
Director of Admissions
The Johns Hopkins University

3400 N. Charles Street
Baltimore, MD 21218

Dear Dean Suskind:

I write to you because my sister, Elena Subirá, is currently applying for admissions at Johns Hopkins University.

Elena is a bright young girl, who has spent most of her free time in competitive swimming. Inasmuch as her grades may not reflect it, I know my sister and, after being here at Hopkins for two years, I can honestly say that she would be a perfect match for our school.

I wish to attract your attention to a special custom in Puerto Rican culture: the chaperone. Unless Elena can come here where I can acceptably chaperone her, my father will never allow her to leave the Island. I feel that one of the biggest parts of the secondary education is the transition to independence. I fear that unless you make special provisions for her, she may be doomed to live life at home and never experience the growth attained by the Hopkins experience.

I strongly urge you to accept my sister to the class of 1979.

Sincerely,

Juan A Subirá
305 E. 30ᵗʰ Street
Baltimore, MD 21218

Chapter 35

Juan A Subirá
305 E. 30ᵗʰ Street
Baltimore, MD 21218

Dear Mr. Subirá:

Congratulations!
After careful review of your application and upon recommendation of our Admissions Committee, you have been accepted to begin enrollment for the Fall semester as a first year medical student.

You are given three weeks to either accept or decline, in writing, your place in the Tulane medical student body. If you accept your place, you must send a deposit check of $500, made out to the Tulane Educational Fund, no later than May 15. This deposit, which is credited against your student tuition, is not refundable and, therefore, applicants are advised to send their deposit only after they have made a final decision about attending medical school.

A letter of withdrawal is required if a student wishes to relinquish a reserved place in the class.

Accepted students are asked to be considerate to others in the applicant pool awaiting an acceptance. Tulane strongly encourages students to not hold more than one seat at a time, but recognizes that a final decision often cannot be made until all information, including financial aid information, has been provided. In cases where a multi-successful applicant is awaiting additional information before deciding upon which school to attend, we encourage the applicant to narrow the choice to two, or three schools at most, and relinquish any additional places being held.

We are sending you an admissions package that we hope you will find informative of our program. Hoping to see you here in the fall, I am,

Sincerely

Ian Logan Taylor, M.D.
Dean Office of Admissions
Tulane Health Sciences Center

Where had time gone? What was I headed for? After three years of college and experiences with both men and women, I still did not know what I wanted or what I was.

Elena was a proud member of the John's Hopkins family. She was happy and had started dating John. She had broken every school record in the butterfly and individual medley events and was keeping her grades up.

At our last swimming meet, dean Suskind took me aside to tell me that he had been coming to every one of our meets to see Elena swim. He told me point blank that my letter had made the difference in her admissions process, but that he was extremely pleased with the school's decision.

On my part, I was going to medical school because my friend Jimmy was going to be a doctor. I was still afraid of blood. I was still confused about women and there was no one to help me with either of my problems. I was forced to put down a deep sense of loneliness. It startled me. Melancholy is as mind clouding as affection... or even love. I felt compelled to accept the fact that one day I would be no more than a set of memories in someone else's mind.

This period of my life was quite celibate. I became extremely drawn to windows because I was lonely. I did not wait in front of them to actually see people inside, although the thought of it was thrilling. I felt drawn to windows because having spent all day studying by myself, I was curious as to what other people's rooms looked like. There was something enticing about other people going about their business. Students getting ready for an exam with an unselfconscious concentration—students playing their guitars trying to relax, athletes lifting their weights, hunky guys working on their bikes on the balcony.

It became my only form of intimacy. I developed a game of guessing the students' major by reading the titles of their books. Their bookshelves became alive and would talk to me. Organic Chemistry textbooks told me that there was a pre medical student inside the quarters. Shakespeare's plays spoke of literature majors or maybe pre-law.

I was hoping to find in a window the insane hope that one of these students would be accessible in a way he could not foresee. It is like waiting to buy a house that has no "*for sale*" sign out front. I assumed they were not homosexual if they were men and I could not sleep with them. I assumed I would not know what to do with the girls if they wanted me. I avoided sex because I was afraid of it.

It was not very bad. Watching other people is more entertaining than it sounds. When people think they are alone, they become very uninhibited and interesting to observe. They scratch in various "inappropriate" places and they often have conversations with themselves (a habit I carry myself to this day, as Bill will attest). People go under the velvet ropes designed to keep them out of certain sections and, since dioramas were not covered by glass then, (something that has changed with the times) some people actually throw coins at them as if they were a wishing well. It was fun to watch people absently picking their noses, (something I usually do when I get in the car alone to go anywhere – like people can't see me through the impenetrable, clear windows) or removing stale gum from their mouths and innocently hiding it under a piece of furniture. Even the way they conveyed food to their mouths said something. Where did their eyes go as their fork brought the food to their mouth? Was there a quick stab and a rapid chew before a convulsive swallow? I loved to watch. Then there was a delightful one who looked at each mouthful wondering if there was any poison; a creative mind behind my boredom.

Many things we do naturally become difficult only when we try to make them intellectual subjects. It is possible to know so much about a subject that you become totally ignorant.

I was delighted with the move south to New Orleans. Baltimore winters, although mild in comparison with the rest of the country thanks to the warm breezes of the Chesapeake Bay, were still much colder than I was accustomed to from my childhood. Growing unaware of the change in seasons your senses react quite wonderfully to fall. The change of color in the leaves could not be interpreted as anything other than the aging process, the first full-blown snowstorm – nothing but a mantle of death. My first winter in Baltimore I wrote:

Winter

Everything is leveled to the same height by the snow.
White everywhere – the gentle blanket of death.
Lifeless trees trying to carry the burden,
As if sleeping to escape the death that surrounds them.
Peace – the peace created by the absence of noise.

Melting drops of snow feeding into the gentle streams.
Reflections of sunlight amplified by the white.
As if to make up for the lack of heat,
As if to bring us back another rainbow.

Just like there was an end to the great flood,
The rainbow reminds us of the coming spring.
Nature will be coming back to life – renewal
The start of another cycle and another chance.
The cycle of life and a borrowed time

There is nothing more peaceful than the first ray of light as it passes over the white blanket of powdery stuff early in the morning. The cold air: it felt like the chill of another world, empty and giving starlight free access to the forest around our campus. The thin light reflected cleanly off the snow covered ground and the white dust of concrete buildings. Dark lines of pine trees and the leafless branches of deciduous trees displayed only their whitely diffused edges. The quietness of the woods as it tries to rid itself from the previous night's snowfall as witnessed by the gentle dripping sound of the melting snow.

Yet, somehow, I felt I just wanted to get away from it all. New Orleans, whatever it might bring, had to be a lot closer to what I could call home. Once, just once, I had bridged Time to a place where my voice would pass. The web of Time passed through me like rays of light passed through a lens. I stood at the focal point and I knew it.

PART FIVE

When I was a little boy,
Growing up in a parental unit,
I gained my strength from my father,
I gained my wisdom from my mother.

Twenty candles and a song,
Sent me to far away lands.
To learn a new language,
To learn a new life.

My new body awakened,
Hiding in a locker room.
Fighting to be discovered
By my gym buddies.

The swimming team brought my first love
The first revelation, my first rejection.
But the worst situation,
Was that I was not safe at home.

To learn to cope with my image;
I created new situations.
I hid behind a mask,
I grew far from all relations.

But I was not alone,
Soon discovering
God creates them;
And they find each other.

Wiser and older,
Relationships blossomed.

Outing was a reality,
Life became tolerable.

My pride and joy became,
To predict acceptance
From family, and friends.
I earned a new Image.

I am now a Proud Boy,
Living in a gay community.
I gain strength from my friends.
I gain wisdom from my lovers.

Juan Subirá-Rexach

Chapter 36

"**H**i Honey. How are you today"

Bill's face brings me back to reality. I tell him of my brush with Ms. Pungi and I can sense how infuriating the tale makes him. I am more of the quiet type. For ages I stayed in the closet, both at work and with my family. Bill is more the activist. He brought me to the local human rights organization (Equality Illinois) and always seemed ready to carry the burden of correcting all of humanity's injustices. Always ready to pick a fight. I tell him that I had held my own, and that I had done the best to send her back into the "right path."

"I assure you, she went straight from work to her church to pray for forgiveness."

He intends to file an incident report and tells me that he wishes they fire her. I remind him that we need to be tolerant of other people's beliefs.

"Are we not as much of a bigot if we want her fired for her beliefs?"

"She should stick to nursing and leave the preaching for her church."

"She is a good nurse, just let her be. Besides, with this high, nothing hurts, nothing bothers me." Besides, people will forgive you almost anything once you are old and harmless, even if God or his nurses do not.

Bill asks me how do I feel. I try to tell him. Language has words for almost any concept. Lord knows I can communicate in three. I feel the need to create new words and definitions to communicate my high: my perception of time and awareness. A nervous system that is able to verbalize can't avoid verbalizing; it is automatic. I suddenly find myself struggling in three different languages to communicate my sense of reality.

I, who brag of bribing myself out of Morocco in my crude French, was lost for words. I, who love to speak my piece, discover that my speech is failing me. I, who like to define both reality and fantasy; I, who love using the phonetic expressions to help me accentuate the words, I am struggling with a mental picture to tell Bill where I am.

The phone rings. Saved by the bell!

Bill answers: "no, this is Bill, (pause) he is right here." To me, "it's your mother" as he hands me the phone.

"Mami?"

"How are you, what is going on?"

"I have pancreatitis"

"You remember Mr. Rodriguez? He was the president of the Puerto Rican delegation when you went to Miami. He died of pancreatitis three weeks ago. This is very serious. But he was known to have alcohol binges. Have you been drinking too much? Are you doing drugs?"

"*Mami*, you must know that alcohol and drugs are not the cause of all pancreatitis. Although I will not be able to have a drink for the next six months, I know for a fact that I have not done anything to cause this illness."

We talk some more nonsense. It is a crisis of the soul. We exchange news about my sister Elena and her latest pregnancy. She has just found out. I tell my mother that I diagnosed her over the phone. She was being scheduled for a hysterectomy for a rapidly growing uterine fibroid, but I had questioned her about her last menstrual period and form of birth control. When she mentioned to me that she was a few weeks late, and remembering that she had gotten married with a three-month baby in her womb, I advised her to have a pregnancy test before the surgery. My mother and sister are adjusting to the fact that Elena was about to have a baby, even though her oldest daughter is in college, and her youngest is ten.

"Are you ever going to tell her about your HIV status?" I thought I heard Bill ask as he puts the phone receiver back.

"You know that she will never be able to cope with that reality. She is too old, too Catholic, and, thank God, too far away (all the way in Puerto Rico) to be of any help. If we have agreed we will not call her to take care of either one of us, why bother her with that piece of information? With luck, she will go before me."

"What if this kills you before her. What do you want me to tell her? She probably thinks that we are snorting cocaine and drinking heavily every night and that is why you are here right now and I'm sure she'll blame it all on me. Why not tell her the truth?"

"Zulema is too prudish. She is a person that thinks her own rules of propriety are natural laws. We are almost entirely free of this prevalent evil. We have adjusted, at least with passable urbanity, to many things that do not fit Zulema's code of propriety. She will never be able to handle this dose of reality. Lies are the oils that keep the machine of the world running smoothly. Hypocrisy is a virtue when there are other people to consider. It is best to perpetuate her fantasy world."

I do not expect reasonable conduct from my mother. I live lies because I can't endure the weakness of her anger, and I can't admit the irrationality of my love for her. I consider most people like her fit candidates for protective restraint and wet packs. As high as I am this very minute, I simply wished heartily to be left alone. I wish to have the entire world vanish except for Bill; but he could shut up and just be with me for a while. I am truly convinced, that left to these wonderful drugs and ourselves, we would achieve Nirvana. We would just float inside our own bodies and become invisible to the world. Why couldn't the world just leave us alone? Why would a person with a dot on her forehead want me to find Jesus? Would I have felt any better if she had given me a small Buddha? Bill would have!

"Remind me if I ever survive this lovely hospital visit to write a book about religion. The theme will be that most neuroses and some psychoses can be traced to the unnecessary and unhealthy habit of the daily wallowing in the troubles and sins of a few billion strangers. I might title it *'Religion Unlimited'*— hell no, make that *'Reality Gone Wild'*"

"You know damn well that you are surviving this 'visit', so remind yourself!"

"The worst that can possibly happen to me is death before I have time to say my piece. I know we all have to die someday. We are all going there, if not this trip to the ward, perhaps at another time. But, perhaps because I am rolling in this beautiful high, I feel a capacity of enjoying even the inevitability of death. This wonderful drug that is now flowing inside my bloodstream, has convinced me that I have the guts to actually go meet my creator. It's not the 'Freudian death wish' cliché; I think I am sure of that. It has nothing to do with life being unbearable because I have this dreadful disease. It is more like 'thank you God for morphine' and 'lay me down with a will.' (The PCA bell interrupts my speech) Honey, I just medicated myself. Would you be kind enough to let me get some sleep?"

My melancholy cures my nausea; the pain shifts from belly to heart. It is a relief to be sicker in the body than in the soul. I want to puke my troubles and fears. Yet somehow I feel that even if I vomit my guts I would not be able to purge my guilt. "God, why did you make me Catholic?"

Chapter 37

Magazine Street is the center of urban renewal in New Orleans. The best shopping is the thirteen blocks between Louisiana and Napoleon. Among all the antique shops I found a decrepit apartment building that would rent a one-bedroom apartment for $225/month. It almost had a view of the street and it was furnished. I had sent my books and some of my belongings ahead from San Juan, one week before classes were to start.

What was even more amazing is that in the excitement of starting Medical School, I had forgotten all my troubles. I had forgotten about Ted, about swimming, about dating and about sex.

Things went just as I anticipated. Immersed in my books; I had no time for a social life.

Mardi Gras eased up on us before I had a chance to realize it. The natives in a huge drinking binge celebrate Fat Tuesday. As tired as I was from an all night studying session for an exam, I could not help but notice that by five in the morning, people were on their porches with coolers and cold beer. The bus from school to my apartment would normally take twenty minutes, but by six in the morning, there was a traffic jam going into town.

Brought up Catholic, I knew about carnival. The last chance to party before the sacrifices of Lent, Fat Tuesday has made Rio de Janeiro and New Orleans famous. Nothing could have made me ready for this though.

I took my exam and by ten in the morning I was home sleeping. By the time I woke up at four in the afternoon, the party was in full swing.

Bourbon Street in the French Quarter was wall-to-wall people. I was immediately attracted to what were obvious men dressed in women's clothes. They were going up to a stage near the end of the Street. There was a bar, the Bourbon Pub, which was the center of the party. People were going in and out, drinking and having a good time. People on the balconies were encouraging any man within range to show his dick, and in exchange, they would throw beads. After a few beers, I lost my inhibitions and was able to amass my own sizeable collection of beads.

My classmate, Luis Pérez, approached me by chance. He was at the corner of Café Lafitte on Bourbon Street. A tall Latin beauty, he wore a splendid robe of blue whale fur and matching hat, most likely dyed for the festivities. Gold earrings glittered at his ears. He carried himself with aristocrat hauteur, but something in the smoothness of his features betrayed his intentions. He was also a first-year, and also Puerto Rican, and he was happy to see me. Luis, of course, had figured me out. He instantly became an ambassador to an alien world. It helped that he was an outsider himself, that he was largely a mixture of childlike need and grownup kindness. The two of us filled in the blanks for each other, meeting in this corner of the world, a place not of our invention, which existed to enjoy something common for the male species. He told me that all the action was going on at Lafitte.

I was drawn there without a moment's thought. It was as if some younger, more reckless version of me had taken over, emboldened by my solitude and the raw anonymity of the situation. As I headed into the bar, then up the steps into the poolroom, I saw a room full of semi-naked men engaging in all varieties of sexual activity. For all their big warped bravado, they seemed less threatening to me than dating a woman in college. The air was thick with a feeling of ritual—and something else—

an emotion I could not quite identify yet it spoke of abrupt understanding.

"Café Lafitte en Exile" —the oldest gay bar in New Orleans—has not closed its doors since the fifties, and runs on a twenty-four hour schedule. There on the second–floor pool tables was the biggest orgy I would ever witness to this day. Had I known then, what I know now, I would have never let the alcohol take possession of my judgment.

Although I was <u>not</u> gay (at least I was telling myself over and over), and I was sure I would some day marry, I ended up coming four times that day. It was all right, since I had not kissed a man on the lips.

Actually, I think it was easy for me to have a good time because I was not committing to anything. I could even feel a little noble in the process; if things got too scary, I would just go get the next guy. I was telling myself that I would someday settle down and marry a good woman. Almost like a chant in the back of my mind. But for now, I see myself back at the bars, chasing my dick around one more time before it got too late to do it. All the while, I was imagining the girl I would meet some day, who would embrace my past as part of a growing experience and we would get it right, finally. I thought about a future as a married man, in a three-bedroom house with twenty-three kids and a dog, but just kept going to the bars. When I met the next great looking guy, I put this future away for just another little while, until I was ready.

I can't explain how I dealt with these thoughts at the time. All I can remember is that they came to me and rather than feel guilty I reshaped my reality. Reality was like a dream. I was aware of many things, of stagecraft and profound consequences in my decisions. Yet I felt this knowledge and subtlety as a thin veneer covering an iron core of simpler, more deterministic awareness. And the older core called out to me, pleaded with me to return to cleaner traditional values.

"What am I?" Dangerous question. Asking it would put me in a universe where I would confront my social upbringing. Nothing matched the undefined thing I sought. All around these clowns and carnival costumes, I was reacting as if pulled by hidden strings. I was sensing these strings were jerking me into movement. People make mistakes, and those mistakes moved invariably toward great disasters. I was sure that tomorrow's hangover would not let me forget about tonight.

Chapter 38

My first summer back in San Juan and I was very happy to be home. I had just completed my first year of medical school and was looking forward to my coaching job. It would help me pay for most of my tuition (back when postgraduate education was affordable).

Without the burden of school, I was left to roam the streets at night. I had figured out the spots where I could find people like me. I would do the Condado circuit, this would be the route of Magdalena Avenue to Ashford Avenue and back to Magdalena Avenue, and so on, until I spotted someone in a car that was responsive to my glances. Helped by the fact that most straight people do not look around when they drive, I was able to find more sex than I knew what to do with.

There was a wonderful exhilaration from spending a lot of time on the preliminaries: circling in my car over the same route, spotting someone that would pay attention, feeling bulges in loose khaki shorts. I understood the essence of that youthful longing, the exquisite ache of anticipation and denial. This, I must admit, still excites me to this day. After all these years of experience, this is what I cherish with the fondest memories.

The perennial problem was what to do with the ones I found. After enjoying the liberties of my own apartment in New Orleans, I was having trouble dealing with the Latin tradition of not leaving your parents' home until you are married; there was never a place to go. This applied to both straight and gay couples. (Of course, no one had sex until married; we were all good Catholics). The beaches, the park, the car, an abandoned building, all were sites of close encounters and innumerable orgasms. Creativity was the key. One of the little games I played with myself was to see what my limits were on space—how small a space in which I could accomplish the act. Or how many different locations I could find so that I never had to use the same spot twice, or how many I could get in one night or how long I could make him wait before letting him come.

There was this empty house near the beach; it was on Atlantic Street in Ocean Park. Just a few feet from the beach, it had the unmistakable smell of fresh semen. As you entered, there was usually evidence of recent action somewhere in the house: a discarded condom package (probably straight people, it was before the age of condoms), old containers of Vaseline, tanning lotion, butter packages from the restaurant around the corner (anything would do in those days), empty bottles of poppers.... I would start walking on the beach until I spotted my prey or he spotted me.

"Hi, how are you?" I was having trouble understanding why the locals would address me in English.

"*Yo hablo español.*"

Then the man (I had my limits on age—anywhere between 18 and 25 was my prime market) would come and stand next to me, we would exchange glances that would express a level of interest, discuss that I was now living in the US, no I do not have a place since I am here on a visit, and, if we were in agreement, I would invite him to join me in the empty house. There I would manage as best as I could with whatever our pleasure would be. Once we walked in on two guys really going at it. I briefly toyed with the idea of joining them, but I prefer to keep my men to myself. So, pretending not to notice the obvious, we found another spot, wondering if we had spoiled their game. There were only a few giggles followed by a brief shuffling sound before we heard them going at it again—sounding a good deal like the soundtrack to a bad porno flick. The darkness (lack of electricity) made it possible to avoid the straight couples that would sometimes come here also.

I have not done anything similar since that just-came-out period of my life, but even then, I didn't do it for the danger, the threat of exposure that some men find so thrilling. For me, the thrill was—other than that great sex that only a kid in his 20's can have—the tacit implication of brotherhood, the stripped-down humanity of connecting with a stranger and betting every-thing on his decency as he did the same with me. Deep within our collective awareness, we carried a language that could say things to each other. The cruising ritual spoke of it. We all learned it. It was composed of glances, tone of voice, subtle movements usually invisible to everyone but the intended tar-get, and our male hormones circulating in the air. It had evolved out of a complex, subtle combination just like any other lan-guage had evolved— out of necessity.

It is hell to lust for people that can condemn me, to know that my deepest needs can only betray me, only expel me from society. So, as I grew up, I searched for a society of my own, with guys just like me, to keep from feeling condemned ever again. Every now and then, there is an old pain that comes out of nowhere to remind me that I would never be strong enough, young enough, or good enough to be a man among these men. I was sure I would never have the courage to accept my sexuality as they already had.

These people introduced me to the gay bar in San Juan: *Bachelors*. Once I was told where to go, it became easier to just do it. It simply became a way to save gas (this was the 70's after all). I would take the new Expressway to Ponce de Leon Avenue, then North on De Diego Avenue just before the exit for the air-port, turn left and look for parking. Amazingly, my grandmother's only living sister, Donna, had an apartment in the neighborhood and she didn't own a car, so I would park in her building and walk to the bar.

It was this summer that my life changed forever. I arrived at Bachelors at midnight and just before the drag show, I noticed that my father's brother, Enrico, was at the bar. I panicked at first, since I thought that it would get back to my family. But my friends around me told me that he would not tell on me because he was "one of us." (I suppose passing horrific clouds of gas is not the only genetic trait I had inherited).

Enrico lived in exile in New York City and was never acknowledged at our family gatherings. There was a mystery about his life that had always fascinated and attracted me, but that I was unable to understand. When grandma Maria died, Enrico, her son was in attendance. Mami told me that he was a homosexual; we all needed to pray for him to be saved from his sinful ways and hide this from everyone else. Finally, things were making some sense.

Armed with this, I decided to go up and say hello. He was a tall man; over six feet tall, in his early fifties; bleached blond hair and the number of plastic surgeries was visible in his facial expressions. He was enjoying himself with three other men when I approached.

"Hola tío Enrico," I interrupted.

"Who are you?" was all he could answer.

Hurt, but undaunted, "I am your nephew, Juan."

"José Antonio's boy? I could have sworn you were an American tourist." Pause. "I knew you were gay! It's about time you figured it out. This is Peter, my lover of ten years. Peter, this is Juan, the one I've told you about. The swimmer."

Peter was about twenty years younger than Enrico. About the same height, he had thick black hair with Italian features. He had a thick Manhattan accent and seemed very nice. They had an apartment at 174 West 74th Street, in the West end of New York City and I was welcome there any time to be acquainted with the gay life there.

I told them that I was supposed to get electives starting next year and that if they would house me I could do them in New York. We agreed to stay in touch and I left with a feeling that I had finally found my true family.

Chapter 39

I arranged to have two electives at New York Medical School for the spring semester. I was to stay two months in New York City and live with my uncle to save money on room and board. Mami called me to warn me of Enrico's evil ways. I basically told her that unless she wanted to pay several thousand dollars in rent for an apartment in New York City, I had no choice. More interestingly, Elena called me to warn me that I could be "recruited" by my uncle. If only "recruiting" actually worked! I know a few men I'd like to draft.

Manhattan in 1979 was the center of the gay world. The sexual revolution that had started in the Sixties had come to the gay world with the riots of Stonewall in 1969, thus achieving a sexual freedom never seen before the end of the Seventies.

My uncle and his lover were the perfect introduction to this world. Twelve West, Studio 54, Crisco, The Village. Peter knew it all and knew how to get the best of it. We never even stood in line to get inside Studio 54, Peter knew the owner. I found myself in their basement with the likes of Andy and Richard (both surrounded by very glamorous women—the gerbil rumors hadn't started yet).

The men were many and incredibly beautiful. I finally broke both of my taboos; I kissed a man, and I danced with a man in public. How could I not, Enrico and Peter would host dinner parties with ten to twelve of the best looking men I had ever seen, and invariably I would end up in bed with the pick of the litter. I discovered I hadn't even dreamed of most of the things two men can do together.

One day, after having a dinner party, Peter asked me what I had done with Johnny, the trick from last night. I just told him I had fucked him. He asked me directly if it had involved *beso negro* (licking his ass). It turns out Johnny had a case of Giardia, the parasite transmitted by the fecal oral route. As I said before, I discovered new things, but rimming would have to wait until much later, so I was safe. (Wasn't it great when this was all we needed to worry about?)

The funniest part was the night that I found myself at Twelve West and I recognized Father Eduardo next to me with three other Jesuits all having a blast on the dance floor without their collars, robes, hoods or rosary beads (beads yes, but not rosary). Finally, I was able to put together all the questioning from my high school days. I also realized that it must not be too bad to be gay, since even priests were members of our fraternity.

Then in the midst of loud, thumping music and gyrating sweaty men, Father Eduardo dispensed with some long-missed wisdom. Come to think of it, I've had some of my most insightful conversations on dance floors around the world.

"Religion always leads to allegorical authoritarianism; the Jesuits are the best at it. It leads to self-fulfilling prophecy and justifications for all manner of obscenities. It shields evil behind walls of self-righteousness, which are proof against all arguments against evil. It feeds on deliberately twisted meanings to discredit opposition. We Jesuits call that 'securing your power base'. It leads directly to hypocrisy, which is always betrayed, by the gap between actions and explanations; they never agree. Ultimately we rule by guilt because hypocrisy brings on the witch-hunt and we need scapegoats."

"What are you trying to say?"

"Live your life to your fullest capacity and don't let anyone tell you how to live. Do you understand? Messengers from a militant religion can share the illusion of the 'proud past', but few understand the ultimate peril to humankind – that false sense of freedom from responsibility for your own actions. Homosexuals have been among the best Christians in our history. They were among the best priests and nuns. Celibacy was no accident in religions. Don't pray for a miracle, or to be accepted. God does not respond to prayer. He looks on prayer as attempted coercion, a form of violence against Him. As if the miracle would be dependent on his existence."

I felt the silent unity, a force that sought to enter me and take me over. I opened my mouth wide and took a deep breath. I fought against something that I sensed as a physical invasion. My mind searched for something to which I could cling, something to shield me.

Finally, I did understand. I was able to rid myself of guilt. While talking to him, I felt an ecstasy run through my body like I had just come. (I suppose that is why glory holes are similar to confessionals). I realized that I had found my true religion, my "cause." No further need for hypocrisy—to pretend. Every time I would walk into a backroom, bar, disco, or alley, I was on a mission —looking for Him: the wonderful one. Truth was that every time I walked into a backroom, bar, disco, or alley I would find a new Him. It would only last until I would go out again, then it would start all over. What could compare with the immense joy of waking next to someone you had never seen before and would probably never see again. I finally understood what Freud had meant by the "object." The object ceases to be the object once it is attained.

I never thought of myself as "off the market", so I never was. The issue of my looks was never a deterrent (I had "Goldie Locks" looks—not too gorgeous, not too ugly, just right), and it worked in my favor with people who took the admiration of others for granted. The more handsome the object, the easier it would turn out to be to go home with him. It seemed that most beautiful men were just bored with their own beauty.

The best part about it was my new found family, Peter and Enrico, and the sense that I was not going to have to deal with this all by myself. There was now someone who could help me sort out my new life.

Peter and Enrico had told me about "cruising." They said that I should prepare a survey for people that reject me, so that I would know why. I was to hand them a brief set of questions:

1. *Am I too*:
   - a.   Young
   - b.   Old
   - c.   Innocent looking
   - d.   Not innocent enough?

2. *Do you like men with*:
   - a.   Visual impairment:
     - i.   Glasses
     - ii.   Contact lenses
     - iii.   Neither?
   - b.   Eye color:
     - i.   Brown
     - ii.   Blue
     - iii.   Green
     - iv.   Grey
     - v.   Black?

3. *Do you prefer*:
   - a.   White
   - b.   Black (it was the 70's still)
   - c.   Latin
   - d.   Oriental (it's still the 70's)
   - e.   Any mixture of the above?

4. *Preferred Hair*:
   - a.   Color
     - i.   Blonde
     - ii.   Red
     - iii.   Brunette
     - iv.   Black
   - b.   Length

              i.   Short

              ii.   Long

              iii.   Bald

                  1.   With hat

                  2.   Without hat

     c.   Style

              i.   Neat

              ii.   Messy

              iii.   Whatever as long as there is hair?

5.   *Was my opening line*:

     a.   A turnoff

     b.   Should I have pretended not to notice you at all?

6.   *Was my voice*:

     a.   Too high

     b.   Too low

     c.   Too feminine

     d.   Too butch?

7.   *Were my shoes*:

     a.   Wrong size

     b.   Wrong color

     c.   Just wrong?

8.   *Do you prefer (footwear)*:

     a.   Boots

     b.   Loafers

     c.   Sneakers?

9.   *Do you prefer (pants)*:

     a.   Jeans

     b.   Leather

     c.   Cut offs

     d.   Khakis

  e. Corduroy pants?

10. Do you prefer the crotch/ass/pecs:

  a. Visually enhanced

  b. Natural?

11. Was I:

  a. Too aggressive

  b. Not aggressive enough?

12. Did I:

  a. Wait too long to make my move

  b. Not long enough?

13. Do you prefer:

  a. Top

  b. Bottom

  c. Versatile

  d. None of the above

14.

Preferred Penis:

  a. Size

    i. Normal

    ii. Microscopic

    iii. Huge

    iv. Anything that has a pulse

  b. Shape

    i. Straight

    ii. Hooked

    iii. Up

    iv. Down

    v. Sideways

    vi. Thick

    vii. Thin?

15. Body type:

  a. Size

             i.   Thin
             ii.   Thick
             iii.   Tall
             iv.   Short

b.   Shape
    i.   Bean pole
    ii.   Pear
    iii. Muscular
    iv. Triangular
    v.   Bear

c.   Follicular quality
    i.   Smooth
    ii.   Like a rug
    iii. Just on the chest and nibblie

bits?

16. Are you
a.   Listed in the book
b.   Do you have caller ID?

17. Are you into:
a.   Vanilla sex
b.   S&M
c.   B&D
d.   Role Playing / Uniforms
e.   Tit torture
f.   Water Sports
g.   Other?

18. Are you currently looking for:
a.   Fuck buddy
b.   Relationship
c.   Play date
d.   Sugar Daddy

        e.   Anonymous sex
        f.   A Quickie
        g.   Blow Job
        h.   Hand Job
        i.   A good rimming
        j.   Whatever comes your way except me?

19. Preferred employment of said sex partner:

        a.   Professional
        b.   Professional student
        c.   White collar
        d.   Blue collar
        e.   Anything in an uniform
        f.   Independently wealthy
        g.   Waiter
        h.   Flight attendant
        i.   Florist
        j.   Artist
        k.   Anything in a uniform?

"You see," Peter would say, "the trouble with being rejected in a bar is that you never know why. How can you learn from your mistakes if you do not know why you are rejected? How can you learn to improve your odds?"

He always advised me to be evil. "Nice people do not do well in bars, because people are not looking for nice guys when they go out. They are looking for sex—not cuddling. Be in a bad mood, act suicidal and you will score. A friendly, open face interests no one."

Enrico would say, "Going to the bars is like going to the grocery store to buy meat. You stand there looking at hundreds of cuts of meat and then leave with just one. And sometimes you grab the cheapest one because you're on a budget just to get home to find out it tastes great. The saddest part is that you will always think that the cut you left at the store was the best one, not the one you brought home."

That is why I ended up going to the bars and just going to the most handsome man I found and would tell him: "happiness is a bottle of poppers and my face up your ass." Wasting time, the posing, all the games, I eliminated. I had found out that most men in the bars were waiting to be picked up but they were afraid of rejection. As long as I was willing to be the rejected one, I had the upper hand. "Just do it" was the best advice I ever got from my adoptive parents.

My electives at school were very easy, thank God, because I suddenly didn't have time for school. There was no call schedule, no homework. My daytime existence became inconsequential. When dusk fell, I would walk home and get ready for the evening. At seven, I would swim at the school's pool. At eight, I would wash the chlorine off my body. I was undisturbed by the beauty of the other swimmers because I had discovered the bars: in a moment, the world began to change into something sensual. After dinner with my adoptive parents at the newest hot restaurant in Manhattan, I would spend at least an hour trying on various combinations of shirts and pants – oh, the many permutations will give a girl a headache. It was not enough to have the right pants; they needed to be just out of the wash, not worn or stretched—showing off my crotch just so. (And Peter had just taught me the importance of accessories: handkerchiefs, scarves, bracelet, rings, matching your stones…). When I was satisfied I had the right outfit, I would set out like a shark in search of its prey.

Seductive eyes! In all the faces attached to the bodies I had conquered, I had yet to find them. Few people pay much attention to the importance of eyes when it comes to seduction. Big chest, or a large bulge in the crotch, especially if it's balanced with a tightly callipygian* ass, these were utterly important. But without the eyes, the rest of it would go for nothing. Eyes were essential, just like music to a good opera, or the image captured in a painting, I could drown in the right kind of eyes, sink right into them and be unaware of what is being done to me until my cock started responding, (and then, who cares?).

Here in New York I went to my first opera. Peter and Enrico took me to The Met's production of Vicenzo Bellini's "*Capuleti.*"

I Capuleti e I Montechi is the history of the feud between two families and the love between Romeo Montechi and Giuletta Capuleti.

The opera premiered in 1832, at the dawn of the Romantic age when women in travesti were beginning to take over the roles previously assigned to the castrati. (Why is it that parents think it's ok to cut things off their young boys?) My only vision of the life as castrati is from Anne Rice's "Cry to Heaven," but I found it ironically illuminating that Bellini reversed the castrati Giuletta role for the innovative travesti Romeo and assigned Giuletta to a soprano. Romeo being a "beardless youth" lent himself readily to the purpose. The first composer to make a success of this was Bellini's teacher, Nicolo Zingarelli, whose Giuletta e Romeo of 1796, furnished with a happy ending (like a good Disneyfied story), was still in circulation during the composing of Bellini's piece.

A speechless audience endured a warm kiss on the lips between the two women in the lead role in the middle of Scene Two, Act One.

Ulisse Santicchi designed the most dramatic set, which was met with awe by both Enrico and Peter, especially in the Third

Scene of Act One when he portrays the wedding scene in a large hall of the Capuletti's palace with amazing use of staircase, columns, and mirrors.

"The subliminal message of the loss of life between two youths for the sole purpose of loving each other is not lost on most of the gay couples you could see throughout the audience." As Peter would later explain to me, "Here the message is doubly stated by the fact that you have two young women killing themselves because of a tyrannical father who will not allow his daughter to marry her heart's desire."

"If you assign the role of the feud to the role of societal prejudices, you will end up with a great summation of our lives, all with beautiful music. That is why you need to learn to appreciate a good opera," Enrico added as we were leaving. Even though I had slept through the first act, I just thought this to be a sign from the arts to go ahead with my new life.

It was also here in New York that I discovered Van Gogh. On a run at the Metropolitan Museum of Art I was first introduced to his *Starry Night*. Dating from a time so ancient (remember I was twenty-one) that I was perplexed how such a painting had survived the ravages of time. His name was there on the left corner of the frame: Vincent Van Gogh. Immediately, I was engulfed in the true genius of the artist—his feeling—and imagined him as he had stroked each of the thick brush strokes. For the first time in my life, I had felt totally human, aware of cottages as places where people dwelled, aware in some complete way of the living chain that had paused here in the person of the demented Van Gogh.

It was through art that I was able to balance my sexuality. Both music and paintings were defining my humanity in a way that my sexuality was not. The best art imitates life in a compelling way. If it imitates a dream, it must be a dream of life. Oth-

erwise, there is no place where we can connect. Neither heterosexual, nor homosexual sex had led me to the feeling I was still
yearning for love.

The last night of my elective rotation in New York, Peter
took me dancing at Studio 54 and there, on the dance floor, dancing to the beat of the music with a very handsome man, as I
looked at him through the flashing lights, I knew I had made up
my mind. I knew I would never go back to live in Puerto Rico,
I knew I would never be able to give up this new life. I knew
who and what I was. I felt relieved, free.... I would spend the
rest of my days looking for the right kind of eyes, a man's eyes....

Some actions have an end but no beginning; some begin but
do not end. It all depends on where the observer is standing.
The bass relief of imagery began. There was no true separation.
I knew I had to flow with this thing, but the flowing terrified me.
How could I return to my native Puerto Rico? Yet, I felt myself
being forced to cease every effort of resistance. I could not grasp
my new universe in motionless, labeled bits, as I wanted to do
so badly. No bit would stand still. Things could not be forever
ordered and formulated. I had to find the rhythm of change and
see between the changes to the new me. Without knowing where
it began, I found myself moving in a gigantic pleasurable moment, able to see the past in the future, present in past, the new
reality in both past and future. It was as if there was an accumu-
lation of centuries experienced between one heartbeat and the
next.

My awareness began to float free. No objective psyche to
compensate for consciousness, no barriers. Homosexuality/het-
erosexuality remained lightly in my memory, but it shared awareness with all my possible futures. And in this shattering awareness, all of my past, every inner life I claimed for my possession. With the help of my greatest strength in me, I came to my
conclusion.

I thought about something I had once read: "when you have
achieved this much happiness, only from a distance can you see

its driving principles." I had achieved the happiness and now I needed the distance to fulfill my own life. The past in Puerto Rico and its memories were my burden, my joy, and my necessity. But here in New York I had added another dimension and my new family now stood guard within me. I saw my life, both back at home and in Gotham. I saw through the distances clearly – past and present. The clear distances of this new city provided a new philosophy, new dimensions and possibilities. Whichever life I now chose, I would have to cherish my individuality and live it out in an autonomous sphere within the mass experience, a trail of lives so convoluted that no single lifetime could count the generations it involved. Arousal between men – homosexuality – held the power to develop my individuality. It could make itself felt between an individual, a nation, a society, and an entire civilization. That was why I had to escape Puerto Rico both physically and mentally; that way of life could not be allowed to destroy this freedom within me. No one could keep me from fulfilling my goal.

I believe I slept with everyone available in New York during my stay but I never found my eyes. When I finished looking, I went back to New Orleans; all the notches had worn my bedposts down to nubs.

callipygian (k?l??-p?j??-?n) Having beautifully proportioned buttocks. From Greek kallipugos: kalli-, beautiful (from kallos, beauty) + pug?, buttocks

Chapter 40

I met Bill (In case you are all wondering, this Bill is not my current boyfriend. "Bill" is the quintessential white-boy name just like "Juan" is for Latinos) at the Anatomy lab. He was the first thing I saw when I came back from my fainting spell. We had all been warned about the effects of a cadaver; but nothing they say can get you ready for the strong smell of formaldehyde. At first, I enjoyed meeting Elsie, as we affectionately christened her. Bill and I were two of the four students assigned to her. We had started with the prescribed "Y" incision. It was only then that the smell became unbearable and I passed out.

I woke up at the Emergency Room at Charity Hospital with Bill holding my hand as I came back to my senses. I don't know if it was the fact that he was the first thing I saw, or that he confided that he was about to faint and was brought over with me to the E. R., either way I thought it was sweet. I fell for him immediately.

Bill was a third year medical student like me. He had light brown hair, small blue eyes which were perfect for his small preppy-boy face. He had roving eyes, which showed intelligent alertness and humor. At six feet, he had the perfect chiseled body I had dreamt of all my life. He wore short hair in an "all-American boy from the 50's" kind of way. His hair was thick enough to stand straight up without any cream or gel. He had thick legs, big hands, broad chest and beautiful ruby lips. There was a sense of virile strength in the broad chest and neatly tapering body, which no clothing could conceal. He gave the impression of being amiably aloof. He liked wearing blue sweaters that match his eyes. Here was what would become the prototype of my desire: your basic Midwestern, corn-fed all American boy. We were paired at anatomy lab out of luck, my last name being Subirá, his being Smith. We were both "S" and thus paired by chance.

Since we both had to overcome the smell of formaldehyde, we decided to study together with a jar of the stench nearby and talk it through. He had an apartment near mine on Magazine Street, which made getting together easy. We decided to eat at the corner deli, and then catch up on our Anatomy. I wanted to catch up on Bill's anatomy, but we had to study.

It was going well, and we had already covered most of our lesson: the abdominal muscles. Unexpectedly I felt I was about to faint. I told him so and walked into his bathroom thinking I was about to get rid of dinner. There, under the sink, I found that magazine with pictures of naked men. To this day I cannot recall its name, but strange thing, my nausea went away and Bill walked into the bathroom to find me both sexually aroused and with the magazine at hand. Had Bill been less handsome, there would have been a different outcome; however, that was definitely not the case. In truth, words were never spoken: a stream of passion ensued and ended an hour later in the bedroom.

For most men, sex and love is like the yolk and white of the egg. They can exist together, but they can also be separated, and most men are ironically skilled at separating the two. That had been the case with my prior sexual escapades. With Bill, my eggs were scrambled.

In my mind, sexual desire is like diabetes: manageable. If ignored and left untreated it will create havoc. It will overwhelm you, body and soul, making you physically and mentally unable to function. Treated, with insulin or a good blowjob, life will go on in harmony. From that day on, Bill and I were inseparable. We were each other's treatment for both our sexual fantasies and career ambitions.

With this, I let go of myself and became myself, my own person welcoming my past. It was not a victory, not defeat but a new thing to be shared with this man that I chose. I savored its newness, letting it possess every one of the cells in my body, every nerve, giving up what was presented to me and recovering a new totality at the same instant.

I lost track of time. ("Could this be love?" I felt no different when we had sex. There were just the subtleties, small details that made me wonder. When Bill brought me a steaming cup of coffee in the morning, it tasted better coming from his hands). I was already in that place where just the heat of someone's body across mine seemed to eclipse anything that had come before. I was struck by the sense of relief I felt, the feeling of coming home again to my body. Sleeping alone all my life, I would have never guessed how deeply I would be moved by the sound of another heartbeat so near me. A warm, entangling, animal reassurance that was not a disembodied voice on the phone or a distant building winking in the fog. This was the real thing. Everything seemed possible again – or at least redeemable. (I've become so dependent on the feeling of someone's heartbeat that I now have two dogs that occasionally have to fill in for a missing body when my boyfriend is traveling).

Elena called. "I am pregnant"

I could not contain my surprise. "What happened?" I should know what happened by now, or my education wasn't going too well.

She proceeded to tell me how she and John had been going steady and had decided to have sex. Since they were good Catholics, they could not prevent children, but at the same time they were bad enough Catholics that they wanted to become intimate.

Next phone call was from Mami—"How could your sister give herself to that man? She was supposed to wait until marriage like a good Christian!" Why she was asking me I had no idea and didn't really care. However I, being the eldest, I guess it was supposed to be my business and I was the one who had gotten her out of San Juan with the promise of chaperoning her.

John and Elena were getting married and were hoping the old saying of *"mayo, más mayo, más el mes que nos casamos..."* (May, plus May, plus the month we got married—a common Puerto Rican refrain used to explain premature babies that were full term, as if people could not do the math) would hide their "premature" baby.

The sad part about it was that it did not go well with my new in-laws. John's grandmother refused to meet Elena because she was one of "those Puerto Ricans." His family, to this date, still thinks that Elena entrapped her husband.

Chapter 41

I had never been so excited in my life. Bill was going to
Puerto Rico to meet my family and for my sister's wedding. It
was spring break and Bill had no place to go, so I invited him.
He accepted.

I had told my parents I was bringing my classmate home
because he had no other place to go for Easter, and he had never
been to the Island: all of which was true. I chose to leave out the
fact that we had been sleeping together for over six months now,
and we were in love as much as two men can be. Bill was afraid
to take me home to his parents, for not only was I a homosexual,
something we could hide, but I was also one of "those Puerto
Ricans," something his parents would never approve of. Whereas
we were able to hide the first, the color of my skin or my accent
would give me away in a second.

Bill and I had a great flight down. Elena was already home
for the holidays and busy with the wedding preparations. We all
had to share Mami's car. At one point, I was so frustrated with
Elena's car hogging that I lashed out at her for making my guest
(and me) wait for the car because she was late from an appointment.

As my family was busy with the wedding preparations, I
had the perfect excuse to wonder around: I showed Bill the
Island. We spent a day in Old San Juan: the city is over 450
years old, but it started on Old San Juan Island, joined to the
mainland off Condado by two bridges. The inner city still preserves its walls and has a series of fortresses: San Felipe del
Morro (or simply el Morro) at the entrance of San Juan Bay, La
Fortaleza (presently the Governor's Mansion), San Cristóbal on
the East end of Old San Juan Island and San Geronimo in front

of the Caribe Hilton. The old architecture of the city is greatly preserved and you will find multiple plazas: Plaza Colón, Plaza De la Rogativa, and Plaza del Morro. The two main drags for shopping are calle Fortaleza and calle del Cristo; but most shops are tourist traps. I showed him all of them, and like tourists, we shopped. There are multiple galleries in Old San Juan: Galeria Botello in *calle del Cristo*, which specializes in Botello and "*Santos*" (old Catholic saints, some several hundred years old). We bought a painting together by the Puerto Rican artist, Arnaldo Roche: a self-portrait, oil on canvas—with a big, gaudy frame that we could change when we got home.

Since we were making a day of it, we stopped at Amadeus for lunch and stayed almost until dinner. Ralphie and Juan José joined us. They're a couple who have been together since Muñoz-Marín's second term. They're a Puerto Rican version of Laurel and Hardy. Ralphie is a charming version of a bear and very proud. He wears a thick beard that he likes to stroke as he charms you with his words—which will be on any topic you can conceive. Juan José is a Puerto Rican Beauty who is manicured to the last detail—matching stones, matching patterns, matching shoes—who keeps from spending money on a face lift by using only the best skin care line. He's pale in complexion but has tightly curled hair.

In the middle of an otherwise pleasant conversation, Bill suddenly decided to practice his Spanish.

"*¿Juan José, eres mulato?*" (Are you mulatto?) Conversation stopped. Waves suddenly sounded loud as they could be heard clearly in the far distance breaking against the walls. And I wanted the volcanoes that had formed this island to resume their violence and take me with them. Three rounds of drinks later it was forgiven. Not forgotten.

We went to the rain forest and hiked to the top of *El Yunque* and we made out there. *El Yunque* Mountain and Rain Forest is on Highway 2 about forty miles east of San Juan. Hikes up the mountain are about three to five miles long, depending on how high you want to go. We went all the way up and right at the top of the world, there, we made love and promised to love each other for an eternity as only kids in love can do. After we came down we continued East on Highway 2 to Luquillo Beach, one of the most beautiful beaches in the Caribbean. We went to the private side, not the public *balneario*. We body surfed on the waves and we made out. There is no better way to tell someone you love him than by having a group of trees hiding your love nest which is nothing more than a towel over the sand.

We went to the gay bars; there were all of three. Krash was the big disco at the time and Bill seemed to enjoy even the drag shows (although they no longer had any attraction to me), even though they were in Spanish. The drag queen by the name of Pantojas picked on us because we looked so American and asked Bill where he was from. Bill was so cute when he told her that he was here with his boyfriend (that would be me).

We went to Ponce. Mami's family is from "*la Perla del sur*" (the southern pearl). Located seventy-five miles southwest of San Juan on the coast, and easily accessible via Route 52, Ponce preserves its colonial style and architecture. We stopped at the Plaza and saw the ubiquitous cathedral and old Fire House. Also we took a tour of the Castillo Serralles (*El Vigía* mountain, next to the big cross); the old Serralles family castle which combines the history of Rum, sugar cane fields, and aristocracy Puerto Rican style (I was doing my best to impress my boyfriend).

I had my uncle take us on his yacht to Coffin Island, a small island about two miles southeast of Ponce. It is only accessible by water and at the time, only people with boats could get there. My uncle owned a fifty-three-foot Hatteras motorboat and Bill was quite impressed, much to my pleasure. While I was busy impressing Bill, the real reason for the trip was to impress Elena's new in-laws. But in my mind I kept thinking I would have to deal with the same problem sooner or later. My aunt and uncle took to John and Bill and wanted to show them around. They felt important dealing with the American doctors visiting from the states. John was graduating from Georgetown Medical School next spring.

It is a very private island and we actually swam around the Island for about two hours and made out on the beach at the opposite side. As we were heading back to the boat, my cousin had to come get us on the dingy because it was getting late and they were getting ready to leave for the shore. Nobody asked us what had taken so long.

We were in love: we were inseparable. We had fun! After all, it was my unofficial wedding, too.

Mami's mother, "mamita" was living with my parents during these days (it seemed only logical after the two of us had gone away for college and her spinster sister had died of renal failure) and I believe she was the only one who noticed our relationship. When I was dating a *mulata* she had warned me to stay away from her because she would get herself pregnant so I would have to marry her. Zulema had taken me aside and warned me that our lineage had never had any black blood as far back as we could trace it. (How ironic that Elena had gone through the same discrimination from John's parents). Yet, they were all smiles with Bill and John, the *americano*. Even mamita wanted to know if Bill came from a good family and when were we to meet them. The day we were heading back to New Orleans, she hugged him very tightly and told him to please take good care of me. I suppose I was "enhancing the Race," just like my sister was. (Racism, in all its forms and subtleties, is pervasive. Everyone always wants to "whiten-up" the race. They may say "better the race"—*mejorar la raza*—but they mean whiter).

Elena's wedding was a very small affair. In view of the circumstances, there was no time for any major preparations.

Only the immediate family was present. John's parents and two of his four brothers were in attendance. My aunt and uncle and Bill were the only ones on our side. Then there were their close friends.

There was a short church ceremony at our parish followed by a reception at the house for fifty people. Zulema hired one of the best bands in town and all I remember was that I ended up with the same bottle of champagne all night (or so I thought). I danced with my new mother in law, and Bill danced with his new mother in law.

I learned to lose track of time. It was easier to pretend tomorrow would not come rather than face reality. I was struck by the sense of relief I felt, the feeling of having come home again to love. But. "How on earth had I gotten here? How could I get away with it knowing I would have to face these people, my family, someday?" Nothing had ever met my expectations, since nothing could compete with my interfering imagination, my pathetic compulsion to make the world a better place and more mysterious than it actually was.

Some time before I met Bill I had tried phone sex. I was lured by a magazine add that showed great looking men "hard, and waiting for you to call." After several busy signals, I managed to connect. There was a very faint voice: "Hello?" and I answered the same. After getting myself aurally aroused, I insisted upon meeting him and found myself—that very same night—sipping rum and coke at the Bourbon Pub waiting for my dream man to show up. The guy was not ugly by any means, and he had not mis-advertised himself (other than a false name, but then, I had been José), but he was not anything like I had pictured him. I just could not connect; I could not make the voice on the phone receiver match the reality sitting in front of me. It was like an artsy movie in a foreign language where the dubbing was so bad that it would not work for you unless you

could actually speak the foreign language in question. (Or a Godzilla movie). Neither one of us did, so we ended up trying to beat the other one to an excuse to leave the place. After that, I never again met anyone on the phone. I did not, however, give up phone sex! For a person living in his own fantasy world anyway, phone sex is heaven. No need to shower or go through that endless clothing permutations mess just to find someone to strip with and get dirty. And no uncomfortable post-coital moments—"when is he going to leave???"

Now, I was finally hooked to a real person, a person that matched my aural and visual expectations and I considered myself very lucky. To have to start all over again, to build a relationship from the ground up, would be a catastrophe. I knew I had to come to terms with my family; they needed to be told so my partner would never feel like an embarrassment.

I wanted to tell them, yet I left the island without doing so— in reality, so that I wouldn't have to tell them. (Avoidance therapy works wonders in the Latin world). I wanted them to see the whole truth of my life, at least the effects of my truth: my charming boyfriend, my presentable friends, and my blazingly evident happiness. I wanted to share with them as I could share with Peter and Enrico. I wanted them to feel what I had been feeling in the hope that it might transform them, force them to see the rightness—the staggering bliss—of this thing that I had fought so foolishly for most of my life.

I felt as if there was nothing I would not tell the truth about; "I am gay," hear me say it. If my true family would not have me, I would build a family of my friends and lovers and to hell with anyone that could not cope. And though I meant every word of it, my zeal served as a convenient distraction, a shield against the unthinkable that lay ahead.

Chapter 42

May 1, 1980

Dear everyone:

This letter goes to all of you. It is long overdue; however, my last trip home has made it a necessity.

Some of my friends will be critical of this letter, but they do not know all the people concerned. A family that respects and loves me will take this letter as an act of love—a way to finally share my life with you all.

Last time I was in San Juan, my friend Bill came with me. He behaved impeccably (except for that one incident) and we hid all our feelings for each other, even though, in a way, it was our honeymoon. We have been in a relationship for fifteen months now. We love each other and we are proud of our accomplishments together. We will both be graduating from Medical School soon and wish to start a life together.

I beg your forgiveness not because of what we are—I can imagine how you are feeling at this moment—but because I have hidden something this important from you all these years. I know how you are feeling, because that is the way I have felt most of my life. Repulsed, ashamed, unable to accept reality: I rejected myself for something I knew, for as long as I could remember to be an integral part of my nature—as integral as the color of my skin.

No one recruited me. No older homosexual was my "mentor." I was very lucky to have uncle Enrico and his lover to counsel me: to tell me everything is all right, that I am OK. That I can grow to become a doctor as anyone else in my class. That I am not crazy, nor mentally unbalanced. That I can be successful: be happy and achieve peace with my friends and family. Who I share my bed with is not important because I can

love and be loved. I do not have to hate myself because I am sexually attracted to men.

No one guided me. I had to fight and discover these things by myself. With the help of this great city of New Orleans, which has adopted me, and the help of this man, who has shared my bed and my life for the last fifteen months, and Enrico and Peter, my adopted family I have finally achieved my spiritual happiness.

It may surprise you all that in many cities in the world there are people both straight and gay (even some priests) who do not feel sexuality should be the way to measure a human being. They are not radicals, nor strange men or women: they are everyday people. Everyone at school knows of our relationship. Bill's parents have complained more about the fact that I am Puerto Rican than the fact that I am gay. Yet, they have received me as their "other son."

It bothers me that my relationship with Bill is not recognized and given the same respect and love it deserves, especially because I have tried to keep it a secret. I truly believe it should be given as much respect as Elena and John's relationship.

I'm sure I don't have all the answers to your questions, but I will tell you that I have always been proud of all of you and I could not have been any luckier to be part of our family.

I must tell you that being gay has taught me tolerance, kindness and modesty. Being gay has brought people to me whose compassion, sensibility, and goodness have provided a sense of strength, tolerance, and compassion.

Bill and I are not planning an announcement in the social register. We are not planning a big wedding (we already celebrated in Puerto Rico). We both feel that our sexuality is a very personal thing. At the same time we both refuse to hide our relationship from the people we most love.

I am not expecting a response but I want to keep the lines of communication open. My love for you has not changed. I have not changed. Our home in New Orleans is open to all of you. I feel that as soon as you accept our situation it will be easier for all of you to come visit and share with us.

Bill sends his love.

Juan

This letter went out with the change of address to everyone on my mailing list. Bill and I bought an apartment in the French Quarter together. We were both accepted to do our residencies in New Orleans, Bill at Tulane's Internal Medicine Department; myself at LSU Obstetrical and Gynecological Department.

Zulema did not talk to me for four months. I heard that she aged fast. She stopped dying her hair and the gray that came to life was probably in mourning for her "lost" son. I was soon to find that there was another reason for her depression – Papi was also aging fast for reasons totally unrelated to me.

Then there was Elena, "You need to give up sex since Christ died for your sins."

I reminded her, "You got married with a three-month gestation in your belly, so you look awfully silly trying to tell me about right and wrong and you should know what it is to be attracted to another man like I am."

"I have long repented for my mistakes and you should do the same. It would be all right to be gay as long as you don't practice."

"I was done practicing a long time ago and I am really good at it." but she did not seem to get the humor.

I stood my ground as never before. At twenty-four, I was sick of pretending, tired of playing the old games of placation and retreat. This was about becoming my own version of Juan Subirá, though I had no idea of what that might be. I was beginning to feel that the only way out of this mess was to change my name and abandon my family since they wouldn't let me be who I really was. On my father's side there may have been something else at play, something to do with being diagnosed with a lethal disease (I was still unaware of this). Maybe it had struck him—out there in the warmth of that sunlit Puerto Rico— that he might have to face his mortality soon and had no time to deal with my homosexuality.

So, I ended up with my uncle Enrico and Peter, and it would be three Christmases and the death of my father before I would share a holiday with my biological family.

I was quite upset when Zulema sent me a copy of the Catholic Medical Association's views on Homosexuality. The little booklet had the official position from the Catholic Church on both Abortion and Homosexuality. It called them both preventable sins made by choice. I was enraged! It came with not even a note from my mother!

For the first time in my life, I recognized the precise moment of crossing a dividing line. This was a line that until this day I thought was not real. As I crossed it, I realized that I had always known that it was there: a place I could enter the void and float free. I was no longer vulnerable. I could not be hurt, I could not be defeated. Political and personal activism is, for most people, a private thing. But there comes a point, usually unseen and always unexpected, when private activism becomes very public. All of my existence depended on my standing up for my rights and respect from my family.

I had to reply to this new affront. I felt a freedom to respond in my own way within my new universe. Where had I gotten the strength? Was it from my letter? For years I had been afraid of my family rejecting me because I am gay. Now that I've told them and I have been rejected, I have nothing left to fear. Conflict is easier to deal with now that I don't feel held back by secrets. I came to a decision to never again follow another guidance but my own. This inner stability upon which I now stationed myself was not pure morality, not bravado, those were never enough.

January 2, 1981

Zulema Rexach de Benítez
Calle Geranio # 40
Urb. Santa María
Río Piedras, PR 00927

Mami:

Thanks again for your concern and interest. I wonder if you are sincerely interested in understanding something that you have to deal with (a homosexual son) or if you simply have a passion for arguing the unarguable. Or are you still mad because you weren't born a man so you could be a priest?

Your views on choice are as far apart from mine as your booklet is on homosexuality.

On the first issue, I firmly believe that it is nobody's business other that the woman in question and her private physician to decide what is best for the case; and each case is different from the other. I truly believe that there is no scientific agreement as to the origins of life (from the Catholic "Every sperm is sacred" to the people who claim that only when the fetus {parasite if you want to go that far} is viable outside the mother is it a different individual). You and I can argue until our tongues fall out and I will probably not be able to change your mind. There will be no scientific proof that you will be willing to accept because you are firmly rooted in your religious belief. In as much as I will always respect and admire you for them (I have never wanted a family as big as yours) I must object to your wish on imposing your moral views on others. If you are against abortion: do not have one. Personally I believe that Planned Parenthood has done more to prevent abortions than the far right, since they have attacked the root of the problem better than anyone: unwanted pregnancies. (E.g. provide adequate birth control – which is, of course, another problem with the Catholic Church). I am utterly offended by the misogynistic views of the Catholic Church where it is ok for men to have sex for pleasure, but the woman is the one that is stuck carrying the consequences.

As you know, grandmother Maria Subirá was a nurse midwife in the early 1950's in Puerto Rico known for performing abortions and you constantly fought over her work. She had a wise response to anyone that criticized her: "If men got pregnant, there would be an abortion clinic on every corner instead of a bar. As long as my girls are going to get one anyway, I will make sure that they get a clean and safe one so that they'll live to have a child when they want one."

On your second topic: that pamphlet you sent me is so scientifically inaccurate that I would be ashamed to be associated with it. I would have let it go, were we still in 1950 when homosexuality was still considered a psychiatric illness. I feel it would be immoral for me not to respond to your pamphlet, since it has probably already added fuel to the fire of bigotry. Not to mention the hypocrisy of some of the priests that write it who are closeted gays themselves.

I must also point out to you that in as much as women do have a choice to end a pregnancy, we gays do not have a choice. I have as much power to change my sexual attraction as you do to change yours. If this is going to be a futile exchange of ideas, please tell me so. I do not need your approval to go on with my life. But the number one way to eradicate prejudice is education, and I have fully committed my life to that endeavor, now that I refuse to be afraid of what I am.

Sincerely,

Juan

PART SIX

I dream of an ideal place.
It has no race, it has no sex.
There is only one religion,
Countries are not formed yet.
People commute in unison,
No one starves, everyone is well.
Love is of no importance,
Everyone is on an equal plate.
Faces blurred in mankind,
Trying to determine where
You last remember you were alive.
You last remember pain.

For the Paradise Lost
Those masses have searched
Runs contrary to our Creator,
Who loves to be entertained.
With the spices of individuality:
Pain, Suffering, Starvation, Death

Juan Subirá-Rexach

Chapter 43

When I get back to the reality of these four walls, there is a hunky male nurse in my room.

In life Mr. Jones has a nametag. Tall, black hair, clear green eyes, he would blend in any Chicago gay bar as one of the Midwesterners: corn fed farm boy. For our purposes, and in my dream world he is eternally youthful, a charged field of particles, a polyphony of voices. While nothing he ever does for me is anything more than what a professional nurse would do, in my reality he is a pure product of my desires; he generates body heat, creates an impression of nervousness and effeminacy (here I know I am projecting), that he is unaware of. Someone without a gaydar would have never been able to pick up on any of it (even though in reality neither one of us would have passed as straight).

"Dr Subirá, I am Mr. Jones. You can call me Joseph. I just started at three and I am your nurse. I am here to give you a bath. Unfortunately I have to rearrange you in bed. On a scale from…"

"Twelve. Perhaps it will be easier if I help you." As I try to bend my knees to push my body up higher in the mechanical bed, I feel a set of strong hands raise me and move me upwards. He pauses to allow me some more of that wonderful PCA juice. He very gently undresses me and with the care of an angel, uses a sponge to get the sweat and dirt off my body. He listens to my lungs and heart and upon looking at my IV site informs me:

"You are going to need to have your IV rotated again." It is hospital policy to rotate the IV site every few days to prevent infection from the catheter in the skin. I suppose I am due for another stick.

"How long have I been here? What day is it?"

"You were admitted Friday morning and today is Wednesday. It's very easy to get disoriented in time and space in the hospital. I will get you a calendar and each day we will tell you what day it is. You should also look at the clock and keep track of time. It will help you stay focused on reality."

"Thanks" and I go back to sleep.

Chapter 44

I can still remember his voice. "I got it!" my uncle Enrico had decided to tell me that he had the gay plague. A tragedy condemned to repeat itself time and again. It did not even have a name at the time. I felt an instant of pain, perhaps something dead, which seems to be alive; an emotion suspended in time, like a blurred photograph or an insect trapped in amber—he was going to die from it.

Bill and I had settled on a nice townhouse on Esplanade, in the French Quarter. We were both doing well in our respective careers. Yet, all of a sudden, our worlds were faced with this new and imminent reality. Questions were our enemies. For each question there was an answer that leapt up like a frightened flock. Not one answer suffices, for each answer left many more questions in its place. We both tried to find as much as we could about it; there was no information available. With no name it was hard to search for it.

Government is a shared myth. When the myth dies, so does the government. We were to find out later that the Republican administration of President Reagan had wanted to spread the gay plague and did nothing to prevent it. At first, we thought it was because we were fags, but later on, we realized that it was all a political ploy. Everyone knows that 79% of all homosexuals belong to the Democratic Party. By allowing the gay plague to proliferate, Mr. Reagan was just allowing the opposition to die. Rulers are notoriously cynical where religion is concerned. Religion, too, becomes a weapon. What manner of weapon religion is when it becomes the government is all too obvious when our government dealt with the gay plague.

Leaders make mistakes. These mistakes, amplified by the

people who follow without questioning, move inevitably to great disasters. In the months that ensued, both Bill and I watched my uncle drop from 200 pounds to 80. We saw purple lesions slowly eat him alive. As much as my uncle was being rejected by the conventional straight world, it was nice to see him so loved by Peter. You can accuse us gays of being obsessed with beauty, youth and money even though, in the end, most of us would have none of the three. However, when it came to the plague, we took care of our own; of course it started with the lesbian community rallying their endless energies to come to our aid. I made three trips to see him; my father joined me on the last one. By then, Peter was doing everything for uncle Enrico. Peter would bathe him, clean him after he would both defecate and urinate on himself. It was the first time that I had seen my father since my "letter" and we were civil but nothing more. José Antonio was impressed when he saw Peter caring for this man who used to look like his brother.

What memories flash when I remember this period of my life? I feel like a chip of shattered flint enclosed in a box. The box gyrates and quakes. I am tossed about in a storm of mysteries of which I have no possibility of understanding. When the box opens, I return to a presence of death like a stranger in a primitive land.

At dinner that night, my father confided that he had both good news and bad news for me. The good news is that he did not need any surgery, but the bad news was that he was dying of metastatic prostratic cancer. He was pleased to see Peter take such good care of Enrico, and he only hoped my mother would be as good. Even though Elena had given me the news a week before, it was the closest I ever was to my father.

I had him flown to New Orleans where Mami joined us. A sense of mortality began to grow in me like a cancer itself. I found this an interesting emotion, one I began to fear. I took him to Charity Hospital and held his hand as he was placed under anesthesia. A friend of mine, Dr. Anarek, a Urologist, diagnosed him. He had poorly differentiated carcinoma of the prostate. He was given options of castration or estrogen therapy. Either way he would loose his sexual function. It was a big surprise to find out that my parents had long stopped being sexual. He eventually decided to have hormonal castration with estrogen therapy.

For the pain, he was irradiated and sent home. I remember how he started joking that he had gone to the United States to get treatment for his cancer and had grown three bra sizes. In the end, all we have is our sense of humor; thank god he had a good one.

Enrico died in November of 1981. The disease had yet to have a name and he was dead. If my family's fear of homosexuality is the nature of our universe, this tragedy was the most profound irony. It is in the ways we deal with tragedy that we reshape our reality. Peter took him to Puerto Rico to bury him. For the first time we all sat as a family. The Puerto Rican saying that our families come together only for weddings and funerals would hold again. His sexuality was completely hidden and his cause of death was listed as cancer (Kaposi's Sarcoma). Peter was introduced as a friend of the family.

But everyone in the family showed up to pay their respects, as if he was the long lost son of Puerto Rico that had never left. In as much as I mourned him as if he was my father, I was still going to face another such gathering.

Next time we would all be together, we would be burying my father, two years later.

The funny thing about this trip was that the empty house on Atlantic Street was leveled off and a new condominium building was going up in its place. For the first time I was denied a safe haven for sexual escapades in my hometown. Bachelor's disco had closed and as the progress in Puerto Rico bloomed, I was starting to feel like a stranger in my own country.

Chapter 45

Charity Hospital is one of the few dinosaurs left in this country. With 18,000 deliveries a year, it was only second to L. A. County in number of deliveries/year. It was a great place to train if you were interested in a practicing career, not academics. They got their residents from anywhere they could, including Tulane, LSU and anyone else who cared to work hard for low wages. While in an academic institution you would be taught the feel for a D & C: at Charity, you would see one, do one, and then teach it to the next guy coming along.

It is the medical society's dream that residencies make doctors. They worship at the shrine of residency programs, which are both fascinating and fearful. Fear has no experience like your first night on call alone; it takes pure guts and the establishment knows it. It unleashes arrogance and ego and never again can the genie be stuffed back into the bottle. This will breed anarchy; it distributes your adrenaline at random. The ability to make life saving decisions in the flicker of an instant falls inevitably into smaller and smaller groups until at last the group is a single individual —YOU.

It was fun to come home to Bill and compare stories of our respective specialties. Women are profoundly different from men in their pain tolerance. They find it easier to mature and have a compelling physical way to move from adolescence into maturity. The cradle of genesis ultimately predisposes them to it: carry a baby for ninth months and that changes you. Funny how ten minutes before birth they are in intense pain and yelling to have their babies ripped from their bodies if necessary; yet, two minutes after delivery they do not remember any pain. Sex is a way to subdue the aggressive male. In their own way they continue the species. But, if it were up to men to get pregnant and carry a baby around for nine months, either morphine would be a legal, over the counter drug, or the species would be extinct.

The female sense of sharing originated as a familial experience—care of the young, the preparation of food, sharing joys, love and sorrows. Women were the first medical researchers and practitioners. I suppose that it was no coincidence that my grandmother was one of the best nurse-midwifes in Puerto Rico. (I suppose I had also inherited this love for Obstetrics from my grandmother).

As a resident, the first rule of survival is to listen to your nurse. The first night I was on call, I was awakened at 3 in the morning to examine a patient in labor.

"Doctor Subirá you have a patient. You better come and examine her. Now."

She was huffing and puffing, but was not dilated at all.

I asked her "how far do you live from the hospital?" and offered her the option to go home or walk around. My nurse looked at me as if I had no idea of what I was doing. I came to know that look, half condescending half pity, very well.

Between huffs and puffs she said: "I don't mind going home if you say I have not dilated, I will come back later. Sorry to have disturbed you at this time of the night."

The nurse was right, within 25 minutes she was back with the baby between her legs. From that day on, I would always look at the nurses' faces before sending a patient home. If they made funny faces, I would keep the patient.

I also discovered how much power these people have. Be nice to the nurse, you sleep. Be nasty and they will call you all night. In my inexperience, I instructed a nurse, "Take the patients vitals every fifteen minutes until she is stable and let me know if there is a change." She thought that was too often but instead of arguing with me, which would not be proper, she followed my directions to the letter and called me every fifteen minutes with a report. It was a miserable night! I got no sleep! I learned to consult and trust my nurses and be extremely careful about how I worded my instructions. This was, of course, a teaching hospital. How better to teach young, would-be doctors than by making them suffer the consequences of their own actions?

I also learned to respect their judgment. At Charity, we manned a gynecological Emergency Room. One of the many emergencies occurred late at night; I was awakened at three in the morning because this little old lady had lost twenty dollars.

"Dr. Subirá you have a patient. She has lost her money and needs your help."

I was furious that I had been roused to help some old woman find her missing money—what does this have to do with me? Upon further questioning, I realized, she had lost her money inside her vagina. It turned out that she lived in a bad section of town, and that was the only safe place to store her money. Had she been a young woman that might have been a different story all together....

Another time, I got a referral to evaluate a 15-year-old girl with a "liver tumor." Before I could send her to the medical ward, the nurse turned to me and said: "Doctor just do a pelvic!" As if that was the most obvious thing in the world and why hadn't I thought of it.

The patient was completely dilated and about to deliver! I sent her to labor and delivery instead and called the referring doctor with the good news.

"Dr. Ramírez, this is Dr. Subirá from Charity Hospital. You just referred María García to us for a workup of a liver tumor. I just sent her to the delivery room. Her liver tumor turned out to be a healthy six-pound baby girl. Just wanted to let you know."

It turns out, the girl was having abdominal pain and the doctor had never asked about her sexual activity. For that matter, she claimed to have had her periods all through her pregnancy! She didn't even look pregnant! The nurses took just one look at her and triaged her straight to the right place.

Then there was the sixteen-year-old girl that walked into the Emergency Room in hysterics screaming she was hemorrhaging to death. It turns out she had never had a period because she had always been pregnant. She got her first pregnancy at twelve, then one after the other until that day when someone had wised up and placed her on birth control pills and she saw her first period ever. She could handle pregnancies, but not this curse!

Then the thirteen-year-old girl who we took to the ultrasound room so she could see her baby. Even as we showed her this, she continued to swear to her mamma that she had never had sex.

"I swear to you mamma, on the Holy Bible, I never had no sex with no man."

I basically told her: "Two thousand years ago the same thing happened and we got Jesus Christ. Perhaps you are the second Virgin. Unfortunately, the odds are against you." Needless to say, her mother was less than happy with me. The "virgin" was speechless.

Then there was the one who even after we delivered her continued to insist that the baby had not come out of her.

"Take that thing away from me! I am not pregnant and don't

want someone else's baby…" We obviously called social services to help her adjust; the law required it of us, for the baby's sake.

Even more interesting were those very religious women that we would see protesting at our abortion clinic. But when their twelve year old babies got pregnant, they immediately wanted referral to the very same clinic.

"Dr. Subirá do you know how I can make this problem go away?" I would hand them the phone number for Planned Parenthood. Abortion was wrong until it was her own daughter that needed one…

Some patients were abused by the system. If you did not want to deal with a person, you would refer the patient out. The idea was that when you sent the patient away for referral, you might talk someone into keeping the patient in their service. That way, you would have a lower patient load.

Thus, I got a "pregnant" diabetic for management that ended up with no pregnancy. She was evaluated and referred back to Internal Medicine. But every now and then, you just felt for these patients. I remember the time I was consulted by Pediatrics on a thirteen-year-old girl for abdominal pain.

As usual, my first question was, "When was your last period?" Followed by "when was your last sexual activity and did you use any birth control?"

By the look on her face, I knew she was saying the truth when she said almost in tears: "I have never had sex, don't even have a boyfriend."

This meant that if she was sexually inactive I had successfully ruled out most of the gynecological pathology and could just send her back. Her pelvic exam was normal.

The problem was that she looked very sick. If I sent her back to pediatrics, they would not help her. So, I kept her on my service and ordered a few simple tests. It turned out she was in a diabetic ketoacidosis (her blood sugar was so high that she had a Ph imbalance with a tilt toward acidic blood and hyperventilation to counteract it) and we ended up transferring her to pediatrics with the diagnoses made for treatment.

Slowly, but surely, I had lost my fear of blood and this place was making a doctor out of me.

It was around this time that I hooked up with another gay resident at Charity, Luis Pérez. After our encounter in my first year of medical school (as in the orgy at Café Lafitte), we had grown apart. I had moved in with Bill and my social circle became his "white" friends, Luis had stayed with the ex-pats. (Yes, he had managed to find a group of Puerto Rican ex-pats)

A native of Mayagüez, PR, Luis was an only child who was the pride and joy of his parents. He had his daddy's gold American Express, a card he was allowed to take to unprecedented limits of expenditures. Now in an Obstetrical residence at Charity (but on the Tulane side), we were sharing rotations. It was impossible for us not to socialize.

Amazingly, Bill was also hanging out with his friends (mostly American), so it became very easy to hang out with the Latinos. I realized that there might me a problem when, for Christmas, Bill was at the home of one of the socialites (third generation Louisianan) having a sit down dinner for twelve and enjoying Christmas caroling, while I was at Luis' fabulous apartment in the Garden district with fifteen crazy gay Latinos having an *asopao de pollo*. Of course we danced to the rhythms of *salsa* and *merengue* after the host had graciously removed all the furniture, rolled the expensive oriental rugs and stored them away, and pulled all the shades so we could dance with each other uninterrupted until the early hours of the morning. Typical Puerto Rican party!

Chapter 46

"I don't love you anymore" I heard Bill pronounce as I got home from work.

"What?" my world was about to change again. "Jesus, Bill, how can you say that? All I ever wanted was to spend the rest of my days with you!"

Bill and I had grown apart for the last year. Our sexual lives had become like our parents': non-existent. I always assumed it was because of work; we were both residents and hardly had any free time. But in reality Bill had started seeing another medical student from Tulane (one of those very boys he was hanging out with). They had been having an affair now for three months and Bill wanted to come clean.

"I have been seeing a man from Baton Rouge, a student at Tulane." Baton Rouge is a small town two hours west of New Orleans. It is as pretty as its setting: grungy little grids of auto repair shops, video stores and pizza parlors with their windows steamed gray against the cold. The houses that crowd its outskirts are small and shabby; their drafty walls plastered with asphalt shingles that are meant to look like bricks but never do. Everywhere there are satellite dishes aimed hungrily at heaven, each house competing to see which is the largest, unconcerned of aesthetics, like broken-down cars on blocks or a bedspring left to rust in the woods. There was a "high car to person ratio", most of them on blocks in the front yard. This picture didn't match what I knew of Bill. As much as this image of the town and my adversary sprung in my mind, I tried to reason.

"Bill, I take care of you, in every way, I love you. I have shared my income with you."

Bill gave me a pointed look that made me feel I had hit a nerve.

"Your income?"

"All right, ours, whatever." At that point, all I could see was the great sex that Bill would have in that shabby town with his new beau. "Well I am sorry, it's not my fault that OB's end up with a bigger income than Internists."

"That is such crap, and you know it. Is that what you think this is all about? I am trying to come clean; I have nothing but good intentions. You are blindsided because you choose to be. You can hardly deal with what you are; you live in your own fantasy world. You have been so busy with your crowd of Latino friends that you act like the tough stuff will just go away if you do not acknowledge it. For crying out loud, we have not had sex in almost a year. I have dropped hints about it and you refuse to pick up on them. Where were you last Christmas? We were not together. Don't you find that abnormal?"

I tried to reason with him. I told him to go ahead and have the affair. Let it run its course and then when it wore out, I would still be here and he could decide whether to come back with me or stay with his new friend. But he wanted to be honest with himself. He wanted to be fair to everyone involved. He was full of good intentions.

So, he would have none of it. He was moving out and moving in with Armand. And there it was: the new name that had become my nemesis. Armand was a blue blooded Frenchman (although as big as his pedigree was, they had no money). He was what Luis would call "old money run dry."

There were lots of things that I needed to figure out by myself. I had just heard from my best friend from school who was a chief resident at Cook County Hospital in Chicago. There was an opening for my year there and he had called to offer me the position. I was going to turn it down because I did not want to move away from Bill, but with this news, I called him back and asked him if I could go and check it out.

I don't remember how the conversation ended, only that Bill wanted out as soon as possible. I do remember that Bill wrote me a check for my half of the apartment. It was clearly agonizing for both of us. We had vowed in the past to always be honest with each other, but this was clearly overwhelming to all our synapses. That check was the monster that loomed over me that afternoon, because I started to believe that Bill was as desperate as I was, but in a different way. While he had clearly envisioned the end of our relationship and was moving on, I was hanging on to it.

I dreamed about a man: a weaponless man in black armor. He was rushing at me with a hoarse, mindless shouting of a mob, waving hands wet with red blood, and as the mob swarmed over me, his mouth opened to display terrible fangs! In that moment, I awoke in a sweat.

The morning light did little to dispel the effects of the nightmare. I had some vacation time saved and I was able to jump on an American Airlines flight to Chicago the following Friday. I don't know how most people deal with stress, but in my case, it seems that I have always dealt with it through a change of scenery.

Chicago: the Windy City. You captured me from the start. Friday I arrived in Chicago and stayed with my friend Freddie. I knew him from my old neighborhood in San Juan. His parents lived across from mine and our mothers were good friends from way back. He had agreed to host me at his house for the week I would be chasing a new residence and a new life. Freddie was also gay, so he not only helped me with my career change; he also introduced me to gay life in Chicago. He had a one-bedroom apartment on Barry Street, just south of Belmont Avenue near the Lake. He was very sympathetic about my situation and picked me up at the airport. He was a Radiology resident at Cook County Hospital and had made the arrangements for my interview with the Obstetrical Department at the hospital.

Freddie was wearing a navy suit with enormously large lapels and flared legs. To go with it, he had chosen a burgundy silk shirt and a patterned silk ascot with a matching pocket square. He was six feet, tall for a Puerto Rican, with short, neat hair styled in silky waves. He loved his Ray Ban sunglasses, which he always wore since invariably he had been out late the night before.

I went directly from the airport to interview with the head of the department at Cook County and they immediately offered me a job. There was an opening in my year, and because I spoke Spanish, I would be very useful here. Hispanics accounted for 40% of Cook County's patients. I agreed on the terms of the contract and signed it.

On my tour of the hospital I met John, a third year resident, alone in the resident's call room. He had cropped blonde hair with a square block of a jaw. The jaw moved with silent words as his thick fingers carefully worked a *Mont Blanc* on his desk. He was furiously trying to catch up with paperwork with a determination that started as routine but had progressed to desperation. I immediately read his sexual preference and when he showed me his call room, I planted a big kiss on his lips.

"Hi, I'm Juan Subirá. I just accepted a third year position to County starting July 1st." He fought the surprise for a few seconds, but then, immediately embraced me and we became instant friends.

After we chatted enough to get to know each other a little, "I'm John Stroggs and will be a fourth year when you come in. Glad to meet you. Here is my phone number (as he handed me his card). Call me when you get into town and I will help you move." I gave him my number and we parted ways.

I spent the rest of the week looking for housing. After lots of math and my new reality that I was only going to have one income, I decided to rent a studio apartment on 1100 N. Dearborn Street. It was perfect! The two rooms showed a meticulous attention to comfort. Soft cushions, appliances concealed behind panels of brown polished wood. There was a beaded curtain dividing the kitchen from the rest of the apartment creating the illusion of a bedroom. The bath was a spacious ornate display of pastel blue tiles with a combination bath and shower in which at least six people could bathe at the same time (a plus!). The whole place was a low budget self-indulgence. These were the quarters where one could let one's senses luxuriate in remembered pleasures. A short walk to the subway and quite near the gay life, my new little house would sustain me for a while.

That Friday I got together with Freddie to celebrate. We went to a bar near his house: the Bushes. It was a relatively new bar on North Halsted Street, what would soon become the gay Mecca of Chicago. Then it was considered to be an adventure to go north of North Avenue. It was a small place with a few stools at the bar and a few tables. The walls were all mirrored, to give the very long, but narrow bar a sense of grandness. Despite all the mirrors, it was a dark place. The upholstery and the carpeting, both a shade of dark purple, did not help. Nor did the smoke, to which as soon as I had a drink in my hands and a chance, I took great pleasure in contributing. They had Friday happy hour with twenty-five cent drinks. I ordered my traditional rum and coke or "Cuba Libre" and Freddie ordered a gin and tonic. Freddie and I started drinking and I was feeling my newfound freedom and the alcohol getting to my head. My drink tasted great, even though it was Bacardí rum, not my usual Don Q Cristal, and I was trying to enjoy my cigarette and my new life here in Chicago. I was feeling strange, like I did not want to get drunk, like I needed to stay sober in case something would happen. Suddenly I felt some handsome man give me the eye, that way you feel someone staring at you through the back of your head.

"Freddie, I'm being cruised." I said.

He asked: "Who is doing the cruising?" and when I pointed in the direction of the cruiser, he added, "He's married."

After my recent divorce I felt that it should not be a problem, so I asked: "Who's the husband?"

Freddie told me: "that other cute man next to him. I advise you not to waste your time with them." That only added fuel to my fire, I always loved a challenge. It seems that Freddie had tried once; he failed.

I went over to the one that was paying attention to me.

"Hi, I'm Juan. I just moved here from New Orleans." I introduced myself.

It was obvious that we were attracted to each other when he replied: "I knew you were fresh meat, I would have remembered your face. I'm Vinnie"

He then introduced me to his other half: "This is Tony, my lover. Tony, meet Juan!"

"Hi Juan, nice to meet you. You are surely a cute addition to our neighborhood." It took me another five minutes to seduce them.

Tony was the complete opposite of Vinnie. Tony's grave movements and the calmness of his stride were equally remarkable in their difference from his boyfriend. He had dark skin, an oval face with regular features. Calm blue eyes stared back at me. Where Vinnie had black hair, Tony was a luminous brown. They both radiated an inner peace, which seemed to emanate from a happy relationship.

I had been primarily attracted to Tony, but I sensed an attraction growing (in my pants) towards Vinnie as we chatted. There was a classical balance about him, something not accidental. Ten minutes, and one round of drinks later, I was telling a very envious and surprised Freddie that I was going home with them. They lived on Surf, just a few blocks south of him. That was my first three-way and my introduction to Chicago. It ended up being more that a good omen. You've heard the saying: "If a tree falls in the woods and no one hears, did it really happen?" In this case, I will paraphrase my friend Freddie: "if you get lucky at a bar and no one notices, for all intents and purposes nothing happened. You might as well have stayed home alone and watched the Tonight Show." I learned to disagree with this statement. I always felt that it was better to be discreet. However, there is nothing wrong with a "bad" reputation. My friend Freddie made sure that night would never be forgotten.

There are some guys who, unless the opportunity clubs them over the head and drags them to a cave, wouldn't recognize it. That would not be me. I saw opportunity here, and I took it.

I learned to play the bar game: the game of numbers. If someone says no, just go to the next one. Sooner or later someone will say yes. I had never been happier or had more fun out in the bars. I was ready for a change. "Chicago, I'm ready for you!"

That night I had a dream. I dreamed there was an elevator in the middle of my living room surrounded by smoke and a white glow. When it opened, beautiful men would come out of it one at a time and they all wanted to have sex with me. Afterwards, each man would just go back into the elevator and there would be no trace of him or my actions with him. I kept imagining new and different men, and as I imagined each one, the elevator would bring him to me. Finally, as I am to achieve orgasm with the last man I had received from the elevator, he tells me that he has to go back. As I see him get on the elevator, I notice that Bill was stepping into the elevator and was about to disappear...

Chapter 47

The influence of geography on our history is mostly unrecognized. Humans tend to look more at the influence of history on geography. An analysis of my life would show that I believe that a fresh start in a new location would be the remedy for all of my problems.

With all my belongings inside a rented U–Haul truck that Bill had helped me pack, I was to drive Interstate 55 from New Orleans to St. Louis where I would spend the night with my mother's cousin, Puchi. I left New Orleans at 9:00 AM and drove the truck for fourteen hours straight arriving in St. Louis at 11:00 PM. I used Sudafed (mainly for its ephedrine properties) as a stimulant, taking two pills every three hours. I would stop to use the restroom and buy something to eat or drink and just kept going. The U-Haul truck was not able to drive faster than 55 miles/hour and I found out that the radio did not work. So, it turned out to be a long 14 hours.

Once I arrived in St. Louis, I called Puchi from a payphone and asked for directions to his house. They were expecting me. Puchi was not as I had remembered him in my wet dreams as a child. He was average in height and tending towards being overweight. His face remained round; the large blue eyes hard and cold as if to remind me that he was straight. I met his wife Stella and Daughter Marissa. Stella had a tall and slender body, which seemed perfectly fitted for a suburbanite housewife in her forties. Long black hair streamed back from her aquiline features. She and her daughter each wore a boring black dress of tightly knit cotton. Stella's revealed the workings of her hips and stringy thighs, curiously tailored to the steady rhythm of her conversation. Marissa, 17 years old, had long black hair that was braided tightly down her back, as if to keep it from whipping in the wind as she walked. Her features copied those of her mother: gently oval and with a generous mouth, eyes of alert awareness above a small nose. Her body had developed lanky, probably from years of exercise, but it would send strong sexual signals to her peers.

Puchi had a nice house in suburban St. Louis. He was a dentist, and a successful one. He had a two-acre lot and an indoor swimming pool. Marissa raised ponies and she currently had three of them.

I was offered a nice home-cooked meal, which I gladly accepted, and then I worked the last Sudafed out of my system by swimming for an hour. I slept like a baby that night!

Next morning we caught up with family matters. My father had turned for the worse and my mother had given instructions for me to call home. I used Puchi's office phone where I could speak with my family privately. My father's cancer was not responding to hormonal manipulation and it was spreading quickly again. The urologist was again recommending castration because the pain was back. I told them I would ask around when I got back to Chicago for other opinions.

With that in mind, I got back on I–55 and drove the remaining six hours to Chicago. Freddie and John were there to help me unpack my belongings. Within a day, I was moved in. I really long for the days when I could pack all my belongings in one U-Haul! After many successful years in medicine and time to collect art and furniture, it takes a fully loaded moving van and several burly men to take me anywhere.

That was Friday, and Monday I was beginning my new position at Cook County Hospital. I was as ready as I would ever be. I thought I was rid of my excess baggage.

On the first day of my new life, I was waiting at the Washington subway station where I had to change from the Red to the Blue line to get to Cook County. That was when I noticed him. He was wearing a white doctor's jacket from County and he was looking at me. I, not being shy, asked him the obvious: "Are you on your way to County?"

"I am. I'm starting today" was his reply. "First year resident in OB."

"Really? I'm starting today as a third year OB resident. Why don't we ride together?"

His name was Mark and he had moved to Chicago from Louisville, KY. Mark's presence actually irritated people—he was too cute to be true. It was hard not to imagine anyone not wanting to sleep with him. He had been a bodybuilder for most of his adult life, and had a body to prove it. He dressed in the regulation jeans and tight, white t-shirt and had the doctor's white jacket over it. He had smooth skin, and what could be construed as a broken nose. Gray-blue eyes, lead gray thinning hair that was lustrous and combed forward over the top of a shiny forehead. Because he had such a big body, it gave the impression that his head was too small. He wore a sparse mustache that was the same color as his hair. He was nervous at the start of the residency, but I reassured him that was normal. I felt so comfortable with him I told him of my recent break up. He told me he was also gay.

We arrived at County Hospital and signed in. We both got pagers and assignments. We hadn't left each other's sight when we took the "L" to work together the next morning after a quick stop at my place for a shower and a change of clothes. (What can I say; I was feeling confident in this new setting).

It turned out we were to rotate together the first month in

Labor and Delivery. Cook County hospital had a famous Labor and Delivery suite. In its glory days they were delivering 22,000 babies a year, but now they had reduced the load to 6,000 with a concurrent reduction in staff. They would put laboring patients in line, according to which one was closest to delivery, so the suite was nicknamed the "Line", a name it holds to this day.

Patients used to be screened in the Emergency Room by an Obstetrical resident, and when a woman was very close to delivery she was coded "Red Tag." The high-pitched sound made by a Filipino nurse screaming "red tag, red tag" would raise our adrenaline levels immediately. We would mobilize and assess the patient within seconds, sometimes simply trying to make sure that the baby would not drop to the floor. Amazingly, Mother Nature takes care of 90% of all deliveries and our jobs are just that: to prevent the baby from hitting the floor. We are only there for the other 10%, the ones that get complications, some of which, so life-threatening that even with the full obstetrical team in house, a woman could bleed to death in seconds.

The uterine artery can output all of a woman's blood supply in 30 seconds. So, if there is any major arterial bleeding at delivery that may be all the time you get to save the patient. It was at those times that we had to remember the two cardinal rules of Obstetrics:

For any major catastrophe

- First, check your pulse.
- Second, remember the patient is the one with the problem.

Mark and I were on twelve-hour rotations: twelve on and twelve off. We liked to take the night shifts for two reasons: first, at night there were no elective inductions of labor, so the load was lighter. Finally, we were our own bosses: everyone else went to sleep and we were in charge of the Line by ourselves. Most attending physicians would go to bed and we would only dare wake them up for major emergencies. As we got more confident, we found ourselves letting the attending sleep and discussing our major cases with them next morning. It was a great learning experience! Keep in mind that this is the hospital that the NBC show "ER" is based on. The only difference I've noticed between the show and reality is that all OB patients were shipped immediately to Labor & Delivery. That episode where there was an emergency C/section in the ER would have never happened. ER staff would get rid of pregnant patients immediately because if the baby was born in the ER there would be paperwork for two admissions instead of one – and everyone knows that residents and nurses hate paperwork.

One of the first things we figured out was that if we did not deliver a woman by the morning, there was a chance she would be there the following night. So, Mark and I developed a system where we would admit the patient and if we felt she should deliver, we made everything possible for the delivery to happen. We were using Oxytocin to augment labor at a higher frequency than normal, but we had deduced that had we not done so, they ran a big chance of getting an infection. One of the first things you learn at any hospital is that it is a place where there are lots of germs. So getting patients out of there is in their best interest. If a patient was not in labor and she was before her due date, the best thing was to send them home with the instructions to return at the appropriate time.

With this method in place, we would arrive at 8:00 PM and evaluate the Line and target patients for delivery. By sending home the mothers who weren't in labor and starting Pitocin on the ones that stayed, we would have most of the babies delivered by three in the morning. We gave the easiest deliveries to the medical students and nurse midwives and rotated around for the hardest ones. Around four in the morning, there would be a lull, we would lie down and catch an hour or two of sleep. Wake up at six, or six thirty and start the process again for the day shift. That way we tried to have them gone before we came back at night.

Around this time, Mark and I learned to point with our lips. It grows from the fact that when both of your hands are occupied by your delivery duties (those newborns are very slippery and you have to really hold on!) and you need something, you will twist your lips to the direction of whatever you need. It is part of the ritual of the delivery suite that your nurse becomes the extension of your hands. With time, they are able to guess what your next move will be. Less language is needed which in turn makes the delivery faster, safer and more efficient. So it is safe to assume that since both of your hands are busy, you start communicating with any appendage available – an appendage with directional control that is. Mark and I would tease each other about it and would invariably point with our mouths to ease the stress of the delivery suite. (My boyfriend is to this day bemused by this habit. In my travels through Latin cultures, I have noticed that this is a very "Latin" thing).

We quickly learned about our attending physicians' routines. On my second Tuesday on call, I called the surgical OB unit for an emergency C/section for fetal distress. I was in more distress than the baby because the attending was nowhere to be found. The response from the other end of the line, "Is this your first night? He's already asleep and won't wake up until the morning when he has surgery. Just send her to the OR and we'll take care of her." He was notorious. Being the head of the Oncology department, he had major surgeries every Wednesday morning and took call every Tuesday night. We all learned that he would not answer his pager after midnight. So, whatever emergency happened, we had to take care of it ourselves.

Mark and I got close that first month. What had started as a sexual fling had developed into a great professional and personal friendship. The first of many I would develop in Chicago.

Chapter 48

I was working on the surgical ward when my mother's call came. "Your father is dying. He is pulling all his intravenous feeding lines out and wants to go home." She was hysterical. Hysterical, by the way, comes from the Latin word for uterus, implying that women are crazy—and she was (Hysterectomies were thought to be the cure for hysteria).

"Take him home! I'll be on the first flight," and I hung up.

I called around and my friend John was the first to call back. He offered to take my calls for the next rotation—with that, I would be able to squeeze four days off. I was on the first flight to San Juan the next morning; unfortunately, my dad was dead by the time I got home. I suppose I would have liked to spend more time with him. Tell him that my life was fine and that I was happy. I would have liked to tell him that my failed first relationship was similar to his first failed marriage. God only knows if it would have made a difference.

He was dead when I arrived. My mother embraced me as her favorite lost son. Elena was tearful and carrying her second pregnancy. As customary at a Puerto Rican wake, my sexual preference was hidden from the mourners and my family was courteous enough not to mention it until my last day home. Elena was almost tolerant, again reminding me to be celibate: "the only way to achieve grace."

But José Antonio Subirá was at peace. He died at home like he wanted to. The castration surgery had relieved his pain and he was mobile and showered on his own until the day before he died. He had told Zulema, that he was leaving her the night before he got ill. Next morning he could not get out of bed. They had taken him to the hospital where he became agitated and refused any intravenous help. Zulema had followed my advice by asking our family doctor how keeping my dad in intensive care would improve the quality of what life he had remaining. Unable to provide any real extension of my dad's quality or quantity of life at the hospital, she had taken him home, hired a nurse to help her with this new burden, and called all of us. He died peacefully that night at home with his wife.

We had started our healing process way before his death. In a way, it was a relief for my mother. Rooted in her Latin heritage, she had cared for my father with devotion until his last day. If he wanted anything, she would provide it with enthusiasm. We were afraid that had he lived much longer, he might have taken her along.

Not all people inhabit the same time. The past is always changing, but few realize it. This funeral distressed me. I know that *Tío* Enrico's death not too long ago is what made me vulnerable to the pain I felt with my father's death. That is how I managed to finally mourn my father. And I had lost my last connection to my homeland.

That may be why that night, when I went to the new gay bar in San Juan (Eros—Krash with a new name), I was unable to connect with anyone. For the first time in my life, I felt like a stranger in my country; for that matter I felt like a stranger in any country.

We buried my father, and the next morning I was on a plane back to work. Work can be a chore. It can also be a form of protection.

Mark had been dating Carl all winter and now that summer was at hand, we went to the Belmont Rocks beach. Carl was an interior designer, a carbon copy of the chiseled muscle body that Mark possessed. When they were together, Chicago's hectic traffic stood still.

It was on one of these outings that I met Roger. He was
reading the Sunday Chicago Tribune, minding his own business,
lovingly smoking a cigarette. He was cruising both Mark and
Carl, but since I was in the middle, I was the one who noticed it.
(I pointed to him—with my lips of course—and both Mark and
I were hysterical).

I went over and asked for a cigarette. He, later on, confided
that when he heard my accent, his first thought was "Oh my
God, not another busboy." I suppose my accent is a little better
now, but I still have one.

Roger and I hit it off well and started dating. He was twenty-
three and tall, dark hair, blue eyed, and a chain smoker. He was
wearing the Speedo uniform of the times, his blocky, muscular,
and tanned body was like that of many sunbathing at the beach.
But his face was like no other in my memory—almost square
with a mouth so wide it seemed to extend around to his ears, an
illusion caused by the deep creases at the corners. His eyes were
pale blue, the closely cropped hair bleached in the sun until it
was like old ivory. His forehead added to the square effect, almost flat with pale eyebrows, which often went unnoticed because of the compelling eyes. The nose was a straight shallow
line, which terminated close to the thin-lipped mouth. Out of
my recollection of memories, I sensed my idealized man, kind
and self-sacrificing, all sincerity. It was my most basic nature,
the place where I wanted to live. Roger found it easiest to be
truthful and open, capable of shading this only to prevent pain
in others. He remained outgoing, sensitive and naturally sweet.
I found little sense of manipulation in him. Roger was responsive and wholesome, excellent at listening. There was nothing
openly seductive about him, yet this very fact made him profoundly attractive to me.

I was, and still am, a true social smoker: I can only smoke when I drink (Something that amazes most of my smoking friends). And with our busy residency schedules, that was not often. I also enjoyed a smoke at work. When things had been hectic and, all of a sudden there was a lull, we would get a few smokers together and fly to the surgical stairs and do all of our gossiping for the day. That was how I knew that the head of our department had been sued for divorce before anyone else in my department knew (What queen doesn't love gossip).

Roger and I became quite serious quite fast and he got scared. After six months of dating, we broke up. I was twenty-eight and had already had a relationship; he was new at this. We would part our ways. The problem with sex is that you can never know what this intimate act—a rather subtle and confusing form of communication—has actually said to the other person. Sometimes the message is received and welcomed, sometimes it is not. And depending on where you are in your life a relationship may flourish or you may scare the hell out of the other guy.

At the same time, we were hearing about AIDS. The French at the Pasteur Institute and Dr. Gallo in the US had simultaneously isolated the HIV virus that caused AIDS. The horrible disease that had killed my uncle Enrico was finally honored with a name. Within a year, there was a test to determine if you were positive for the virus. We started talking about "safe sex" and would get into terrible arguments as to what was, and what was not, safe. The disease would be linked to recreational drugs (I can't have sex without poppers!) and soon the intravenous mode of transmission was established. It was also discovered that the virus was transmitted sexually. The Hepatitis B model was developed and hospitals were soon testing all their blood supplies for both infections.

With this scare going on, the hospital decided to vaccinate all the residents against Hepatitis B. A vaccine was developed the year before and Cook County Hospital was a test ground for it. I had tested negative for Hepatitis B on my admission test the year before, so I was called for the trial study. Being at risk in my job, and now that they knew you could not get HIV from the vaccine I agreed to the study. I was surprised to find that I had converted positive to Hepatitis B, especially surprised since I had not been sick a day of my residency. I was also relieved to know that I was not infected with HIV. Since I did not need the vaccine for Hepatitis, and in view that I was doubly at risk for sexually transmitted diseases, I applied and got big life insurance policies and disability insurance, both of which I would continue to increase and pay as my salary allowed it.

I had also started "moonlighting" at work. As most people know, residents earn very little, so we tend to supplement our salary with outside work. That meant that I would be on call Monday, then I would go to work Tuesday at another hospital at $40/hour and pray that they would stay quiet so that I could sleep the night.

This made our social lives almost non-existent, but I was happy with my friends: Mark and Carl, Freddie, and John.

Mark and Carl had moved in together and were constantly inviting me over for dinner. I was very happy about that since I hated to cook: even more, do dishes. Freddie had graduated and was an attending at Grant Hospital's Radiology Department and had tons of money which he did not mind sharing with his friends; i.e. me. John had finished his residency and was at Oak Park Hospital and doing well. It was time for me to move on: take my boards and find a job. I felt ready for the boards, but had no clue about work.

The Obstetrical Boards are taken in two phases. First, you take a written exam when you finish your residency. For that, they train you with yearly multiple question exams: the "in trainings." I had done very well on them, so I felt confident. The second part of the boards is an oral presentation of your work after you graduate and the soonest you can take it is two years after you finish. You defend all the cases you handled in front of three of your peers. For that you need a job.

Chapter 49

OBSTETRICS AND GYNECOLOGY – BE/BC OBGYN needed for booming practice near the Chicago area. Guaranteed income and benefits. Please call 630-492-9500 for information or send CV to The Naperville Clinic, 450 Main Street, Naperville, IL 60563.

The ad attracted my attention. It was published in the Green Journal (the Journal of the American College of OB-GYNE). I faxed my CV and spoke with Dr. Green, who was very interested in me. He had also trained at Cook County. I was to go to the western suburbs on Friday after Clinic.

I left Cook County Hospital at 4:00 PM on Friday and encountered the heavy rush hour traffic characteristic of the Eisenhower Expressway. After two hours on the road, I realized I had missed my exit – Roosevelt Road – and had gone to Route 53, forty miles north of where I should have been.

Having grown up in a place where directions were given as: "go to Burger King and turn left, then count three traffic lights and turn right," I was completely unprepared to follow direction as the North Americans did: "go west on the Eisenhower Expressway and then north on Route 53." I found a phone and apologized profusely. I rescheduled for the following Friday. Apparently, I had made Dr. Green miss the opera that evening.

I went back to my job interview next Friday, this time having located my route on a map. It went somewhat well, I felt that all but one of the four partners liked me. I also felt that Dr. Green knew about my sexual preference (of course, he likes opera) and that made me at ease from the beginning. (To this day, he calls me a "crazy Puerto Rican" and threatens me with revoking my "green card," even though he knows I don't need one).

They asked me back for a second interview where they asked me to start working a clinic Saturdays and afternoons. With clinic hours I could start building my practice and I would have plenty of patients by the time I joined the group. They would pay more than I was making at my other moonlighting jobs and it would help me in the future, so I slowly started shifting work at Grant Hospital for work in Naperville. I learned to find the back ways and avoid the heavy traffic.

Chapter 50

"**R**oger, would you get me a glass of water?"

Yes, I started dating Roger again. Now that he is three years older and has gotten the bug out of his system, he has decided to settle down with me in downtown Naperville, Illinois. We live the idyllic life. We stay out of people's faces, and they stay out of ours.

We started dating as soon as I moved to the western suburbs. Roger got into trouble with his landlord and I told him there was plenty of room in my house, so long as he did not mind the commute to work. He agreed to try it, for three months. Three months turned into six and then a year.

We started out each having our own separate lives, but soon, we found that what had attracted us initially was still there, and it is very convenient to sleep with a roommate. If we deny the need for thought, we lose the powers of reflection; we cannot define what our senses report. If we deny the flesh, we un-wheel the vehicle that bears us. But, if we deny emotion, we lose all touch with our internal universe. It was Roger's love that I missed the most while we were apart. I was only aware of my external universe and didn't even know it until I acknowledged my emotions again.

Work is going great. My practice is booming and somehow no one seems to care that I live with my "roommate."

Roger's finances have stabilized and he now contributes to rent and our trips. We are going to Europe to celebrate our one-year anniversary. We've lived together for one year so, it's our anniversary. I've always been fascinated by what gay men choose to mark as their "anniversary." For some it's when they first met—or their first trick—or their first sleep over. Some actually mark a date with a ceremony. Since, of course, we can't get married, it makes the decision of an anniversary quite a challenge.

Zulema came to visit and she gets along with Roger. She actually told me that I did a lot better than when I was with Bill. I suppose that is the best compliment I will ever get out of her.

Bill has a new friend in New Orleans. His name is Albert and he is from France. We speak regularly on the phone and he helps me keep up with my French. He has become one of my best friends.

Freddie has found true love in a radiology technician and they come regularly to visit. John is still single, but I see him around in all the Gynecological meetings. Mark and Carl's dog had a litter. They are grandparents and proud of it! Dr. Green and I have season opera tickets together.

I am a net in a sea of time, free to sweep the future and the past. I am a moving membrane from whom no possibility can escape. Whether a thought is spoken or not it is a real thing and has powers of reality. Mysticism is not a difficult thing when you survive each second by overcoming open hostility. When suffering is accepted, perhaps as unconscious punishment, it builds your character. It is good to note that acceptance of my homosexuality gives almost complete freedom from guilt. This is not because I eliminate religion from my life, but because everyday existence requires brutal judgments, which in the real world would burden me with unbearable guilt. So, we opt for knowing we are just as real, we love just as much and we have as much right to exist as every living organism created. We fit the greater plan in the scheme of the universe: we are the deep paradox. Who knows, maybe we are the control factor in God's experiment. By putting all the creativity in a species that can't reproduce, he has limited the evolution of the human race just enough to make it a little more interesting. Struggle is a good thing when you are on the outside watching those who do the struggling.

In the struggle between beast demons on one side and old

prayers on the other, we are but symptoms of the times, profoundly revealing. We betray the psychological tone, the deep uncertainties... and, striving to better ourselves we realize that nothing comes from fear. We owe it to ourselves to do better.

A lot of people ask me when I first knew I was gay. The truth is that I can't remember. I would not be able to pinpoint any moment or any fact that led me to it. The only thing I can recall is when I first knew it was OK; it is right this very minute.

What is the most profound difference between us, you, and me? It is where we come from and the forces that our cultures create. As a Puerto Rican-American, I live in two different worlds, yet am accepted in neither. When I'm "home," I am always assumed to be a tourist. In PR, everyone speaks to me in English assuming I am from the north. In the States, I am a Spic, somewhere below the level of polite society, never able to reach the A-Gay list (not that I necessarily want to be—but the invitation would be nice). No matter where I am, I am gay—and that, of course, makes a difference to just about everyone.

Some call it instinct or fate. The memories apply their leverages to each of us—on what we think, what we do, and what we are. If you think you are immune to such influences, I am here to tell you... That which moves can exert its force in ways no mortal power ever before dare suppress. I am here in this world to dare this.

Part of me dwells forever without thought. That part reacts; it does things without care for knowledge or logic. I am forced to stand back and watch such things, nothing more. There is no such thing as choice in such an event! You accept it. One never understands it or learns it too well. You just move on, go on living.

People will try to understand me and to frame me in their words. They will seek "truth," whatever that is. Unfortunately, truth always carries the ambiguity of the words used to express it.

Here is my story. Words; I have written them. They are gone. If no one reads them, they, for all intents and purposes, do not exist. If they no longer exist, perhaps they can be made to exist again, perhaps by you. That is the beginning of literature – the discovery of something we do not understand, the discovery of a forgotten story.

I was happy. I was finishing my residency; I had a job nearby next year and good friends. I thought I had all I could ever ask of life.

PART SEVEN

I love my mother,
I love my father,
I love my sister,
I love my brother.
But, for all the loving,
There is still a story,
Hiding in a mask,
That spills with fury.
Relationships require,
Honesty and a true story.
I love my mother,
I love my father,
I love my sister,
I love my brother.
With all this loving,
There is still my story.
Spilling out of my mask,
With homosexual fury.
Love requires honesty
 My true story.
Do you still love me?

Juan Subirá-Rexach

Chapter 51

What happened later I do not remember. But knowing the source of the tale, it must have been true. I know I called my ex-nurse Jane, I know I talked to her for a while. I thought I was answering her page.

As a doctor in the blue-white collar western suburb of Naperville, IL. where I was an attending physician, I would walk, eat, drink and sleep with one of those pagers that make doctor's lives miserable. I was never upset to get a page; as a matter of fact, as much as my patients paid for my services, I considered it a privilege and very lucky to be bothered. That was a lot better than to be poor and not bothered at all. Every time I would be paged, I would dial the clinic's phone number and Jane would pick up. Jane was a smart middle-aged woman, with sandy blond hair, tall blue eyes. They were tall because she was 5'10. Unlike my 5'10, hers was for real, even when she was wearing no shoes. With shoes she would be almost six feet. She had one of those generic female voices. Having spent half my career talking to her, I considered myself very lucky to have her. She had started in our practice after she had divorced her high school sweetheart after a twenty-five-year marriage that had given her two children. Inevitably a conservative suburbanite, she had cried the first time I had told her one of our young patients needed the Planned Parenthood number for an abortion counseling session. After five years with me, she was now doing the counseling herself for these "good Catholics" who were too good to use any form of birth control, but not Catholic enough to have the baby. So I was not surprised when I hear her voice telling me:

"Naperville clinic, this is Jane."

"Hi Jane, how can I help you?"

"Dr. Subirá, that this you? Why are you calling me?"

"I'm just answering your page. How can I help you?"

"Where are you?"

"I am at St. Joseph's ICU. I am sick. I think you are going to have to come get me and take care of me."

"What is wrong?"

"I have pancreatitis from my antiretroviral meds." I had told her when I abandoned the practice the real reason for my leaving the clinic. We had had a good cry together.

"Where is Bill? Let me talk to him?" And I just go back to sleep.

"Juan, what is wrong with you?" I wake up to Bill's worried face. I just got a call from Jane. She wants to know if you and I are still together and why you need to go to her house to recover."

"Oh, I remember talking with her, I just don't remember what I said to her."

Dr. Ross walks in the room: "Hi Juan!" Then noticing my husband, "Hey Bill!"

"Hey Dr. Ross. It seems Juan has been up to no good. He was asking his old nurse for room and board."

"Bill, Juan has been on a morphine drip for six days. It is a common side effect for the narcotics to give patients a temporary psychosis. It should resolve on its own as soon as we get him off the meds. Juan, I have bad news, your lab reveals you may be getting lactic acidosis... "

The phone rings and Bill picks it up.

"Hello. No, this is Bill. (Pause) Juan, it's your sister."

"Elena, how nice of you to call. How's your tummy?"

"Baby is progressing well. How are you doing? Do you want me to come over and help take care of you? I can come over if you want."

I must confess that I am truly touched by this gesture, but all I answer is: "Bill is off from work. He will be able to take care of me. Thanks anyway."

She asks to speak with Bill and he gives her the latest update on my condition. Saying goodbye, he informs me that both she and my mother had called on a daily basis. I truly believe him, but I just do not remember.

You see; Bill is my only anchor to reality. If you tell me that I have said or done something in the past few days since I have been here, I would have to check with Bill to make sure it has actually happened. It could be something as obvious as the walls in the room are white. I would look at the white walls, them I would look at Bill and ask him: "What color are the walls?" If he corroborates that they are white, then I would believe my eyes. The funny thing is that an hour later, I would have to ask again, because I would not remember either looking at them or having asked.

I feel like the first man to discover fire: fire is there all along, once Bill shows me how to use it then my mind understands how to use it and not get burned. Otherwise I am afraid to play with matches for fear of being burned.

I longed for a cigarette.
Everyone knows that there is a rare bird called the "social smoker." That would be me.

I can go days, weeks without a cigarette, then, out of the blue, my lungs would love to feel expanded by my Dunhill's, knowing that there would soon be a nicotine high. If for some reason, it is forbidden (as in most cases in the USA) I become a militant. I see no reason for alcohol or a good meal unless I can smoke. I have started boycotting anything that comes out of California because they have completely banned smoking.

Then as the nicotine would flow through my brain, my mind would slowly clear, my anger and desire for a smoke disappear until it would be re-ignited again for some other reason.

I am unable to deal with the idea that any man is able to differentiate the truth. That reality exists in its pure form. Anyone but me, right now, right here…

It is as if in my desperation I am trying to find pretty names with which I would be able to fool my desperation, my needs (do I really need a cigarette?). I suppose that is life for me right now. Being aware that we are unable to beat death, I may be able to get away with deceiving myself by structuring my new existence and I may be able to create a brand new form that would manipulate the time that we are conscious before returning to the emptiness, the nothingness. (Please give me a cigarette…).

Whereas religion might work if you are able to use it to harmonize your existence, you are still left with around seventy-seven years (our life expectancy) in which matter achieves the privilege of being consciously alive. Truth is only relevant to the masters of the universe. I have just realized that I am as far away from the truth as it is humanly possible. I am only interested in truth when it is in relation to others (my love for Bill), or history (my recent hospital admission, my need for a damn cigarette). When it requires a position in regards to Time, yet nothing outside of it (I want it now!).

Are we heroes?

I know about lactic acidosis. I know that my health is severely compromised, yet I have learned to live with this terror: HIV in my case, I have incorporated it into my life. We are just people. We are cold and we cover ourselves with blankets. We refuse to go out in the cold without proper insulation. We will smoke only when it is socially acceptable (Why couldn't I have gotten this attack in Paris?).

As I dim my consciousness into a fresh sleep, I feel the rare satisfaction of expressing my position on cigarette smoking. Was it for real? Perhaps not entirely. I feel a tremendous melancholic sadness; as if by accepting the fact that I am not in Paris, I have limited my smoking opportunities.

I whistle in the darkness.

No matter how long we live, we have our memories—points in time which time itself cannot erase. Sometimes, memory is a curse. Yet, memory could be the greatest gift. If you lose your memories, you lose everything. Narcotics may distort your backward glances, but even in a morphine high, some memories yield nothing of their beauty or their splendor. Rather they remain as hard as gems.

Someone said that we would some day understand time: Albert Einstein and his theories would do away with it. I love time. It keeps everything sorted out: like an opera that has three acts. Without time it would just be a cataclysmic single note or bang. Time separates you from things you love. Time protects you from experiences that are too painful to hold close.

I met Bill in the spring of 1993 on a trip to Kansas City. I met him at the gay bar Cabaret. I was in my worst mood. Had just broken up with my boyfriend Roger and was feeling quite the loser to have to spend New Year's Eve with old friends and no date. It had been one of my worst Christmases in recent history and a trip to Kansas City, away from Chicago, was what the doctor ordered.

I was in the bar and trying to mind my own business, when all of a sudden I felt this presence next to me. Sure enough, there he was using what I would later realize was his tried and true technique to meet men. I tried everything; I looked up, down, and to the right. Any direction but the left, where he was, so that he didn't feel encouraged to talk to me. It was to no avail. In an unexpected pivot-turn, Bill placed his face right in front of me and said:

"Hi, I'm Bill, what's your name?"

I tried to give him short and evasive answers: "Juan"

"Are you here alone?"

"No, I am waiting for my friends." This was true, I had agreed to meet my friends from Chicago later in the evening and I was just trying to finish my beer. Bill would not leave me alone.

"Mind if I wait here with you?"

"I suppose that you will whether I want you to or not."

"It's a small city and an even smaller bar."

The truth is that he was just too charming for his own good. I was unable to shed him in spite of my horrible performance. (I have always believed that you will only score in a bar when you are in your worst mood. Nobody likes a nice guy). We went back together to The Ritz, that little hotel on the Plaza (that is no longer a Ritz) where I was staying, and had a wonderful evening.

One of us turned out the lights; perhaps it was me. As he lowered me to the bed, hungrily slipping his hands under my clothes, we both learned that we could love with our hands as well as our hearts. We could, and we did. As we impatiently touched strange new continents of skin and hair, I learned the true feelings we harbored. I became not just his habit, his heaven, his friend. We loved each other, body and soul, heart and limb, sacred and profane.

Next morning over breakfast, a natural friendship blossomed and something about Bill stayed with me. We agreed to exchange addresses and surprisingly, since he was a hairdresser from Chicago, we stayed in touch. Back in Chicago, we developed a friendship where I would be the recipient of all of Bill's attentions, which for my low self-esteem was a big boost. Our relationship progressed to where we are today. And right now, as I look at his worried face, I thank the world for the time we have spent together.

One of the biggest drawbacks of us both being HIV positive is the fact that we might be faced with today. But truth be told, these past few years of immense happiness are worth the risk of the loss. Even if I am faced with the reverse: even if he were the one lying on this bed of mine, it still would be very worth our while. As I am starting to recover and the good times start to erase the tragedy of the past week and a half, I could not help but recount our experiences together.

Bill's voice brings me back towards the real time. "How are you today?"

And I slip into a coma...

Part Eight

Whose dreams these are, I think I know.
His love is in my mind, so
He would not see me standing there
To watch my dreams fill up with love.
My little love must think it queer
To lust without a body dear.
Between the dancers and the cake,
The darkest evening of the year.
He holds his harness by mistake
And with pleasure just as sweet,
Dreaming forever the wedding cake.
His body is lovely, dark and deep.
My promises are hard to keep,
So I pray I never rise from my sleep.

Juan Subirá-Rexach

Chapter 52

Finally, I dream! They are dreams, but I understand them quite well. I escape the hospital walls. I have lived a great life. I see my life in pictures, even now I can still dream in pictures.

I picture my dead friend Ricardo. Ricardo was a sweet Italian who had a great apartment on Columbus Circle near Central Park in New York. He was probably associated with the mafia, always flashing jewelry, owner of several restaurants and clubs in the city. He had a big head, bristling with dark wavy black hair that easily matched his rich black moustache. His shoulders were broad, his chest heavy as a worker's might be, yet his hands were carefully manicured to perfection, clearly his body was the payoff of a good workout routine. His waist was a slender, stylish column, which only emphasized his wide hipbones, so he always wore his shirt outside his pants to cover this anatomical trait. He was at least six foot two, and when we met he was in his early twenties. He advertised nine inches in his pants, as you would always see a large bulge no matter what pants he wore.

He had a predilection for anything and everything Latin, thus his affinity for me and his Colombian lover. He always got what he wanted; money was never an impediment to show his affection. He could get us to Studio 54 without ever having to make the rigorous line. There was a private entrance for the Ricardo's of the world and he had made me feel special that way.

I dream this evening about him: afflicted early in the epidemic, he had wasted away to eighty pounds in less than six months. He was diagnosed with a rare form of throat cancer, some sort of sarcoma, and it ate him alive. I was seated in his

Columbus Circle Penthouse overlooking Central Park and was carrying on with the same conversation we had had the last time I saw him. He was scared of dying and was complaining that not even all the money he had was going to save him from a premature death. I was but a face on his towel: his cum towel since he had a hustler leave just before I came to visit.

The dream next turns to that eighty-pound Ricardo, as he tells me:

"I don't want to meet new people, I prefer the company of my dead."

Once friendship has demagnetized someone, he may never again become attractive. But the physical strain of his physique is too much of a burden for me. I will never forget his last words.

I then see my dead uncle Enrico, also wasted down to ninety pounds from HIV, who starts telling me that:

"God is troubled and eternal as my own consciousness." (He had died in 1982, an early victim of AIDS).

I feel just like the night I buried my adolescence—not an easy moment for a person to remember. I feel that no one cares about the exact degree of treachery in my soul, the exact shade of deceit in my heart. I am scared! It feels like these two souls were showing me where my life is headed. They are also holding me accountable.

I have seen too many people die from the plague. It got to the point where after Ricardo died I needed to avoid New York because it only brought back bad memories. I would go for a weekend of theater all the way to London, just so I could avoid the painful memory of all my dead friends.

"I don't want to meet new people, I prefer the company of my dead." Is this the reason I never went back to New York?

It is as if by avoiding the city, HIV could not touch me, or the ones I love.

This dream has challenged all my beliefs. I suppose that good intentions are just not enough. A hard cold wisdom is required for absolution of your sins. It feels that these two ghosts are challenging everything that I know. Even with the advent of this new retro-viral therapy, my fate is sealed. Am I to join these two friends of mine?

I have no conscious memory of my room, or what I have seen. I am naked. Being out of those hospital clothes, I feel a tinge of a new and potent emotion. It is a vague and diffuse sense of envy, of dissatisfaction with my prior life. I have no idea of its cause, much less of its cure, but the discontent that is filling my mind is making me realize that perhaps, and here lies the key, perhaps I belong somewhere else. It feels as if I had just taken a step into my true humanity.

This hospital stay is the last thing I truly remember. My life is as surreal as the room I find myself in. It feels I have passed beyond despair and beyond hope. It is as if I am feeling the pain of all the souls I had ever seen die before me: my friends and family.

Then it hit me: AIDS is something I have dreamt about. This new feeling gives me a rare sense of exaltation – and a feeling of power. Not only is AIDS a figment of my imagination, but there is something different about the human race. My next action is about to determine its whole future. In all the history, there had never been a situation like this.

The snake bites its tail, thus closing the circle of life. My story ends at the beginning, but the meaning has changed. I will be born again, again, and again.

I'm doing nothing more than borrowing time…

EPILOGUE

Everything is leveled to the same height by the snow. White everywhere—the gentle blanket of death. Lifeless trees trying to carry the burden, as if sleeping to escape the death that surrounds them.

Peace—the peace created by the absence of noise. Melting drops of snow feeding into the gentle streams. Reflections of sunlight amplified by the white, as if to make up for the lack of heat, as if to bring us back another rainbow.

Just like there was an end to the great flood, the rainbow reminds us of the coming spring. Nature will be coming back to life – renewal – the start of another cycle and another chance: the cycle of life and borrowed time.

The End

Printed in the United States
27340LVS00002B/35

9 780915 745548